#  It's Haunted, She Said

## *A Collection of Paranormal Stories*

Lexi Wolfe

Copyright © 2020 Lexi Wolfe

All rights reserved.

ISBN: 9798696788326

## DEDICATION

This book is dedicated to my cousins Amelia and Olivia, who went to sleep listening to my first recorded stories when we were all small children, many years ago. While I can't promise these will put you to sleep - at all(!) - I do hope you enjoy them.

# Table of Contents

DEDICATION

ACKNOWLEDGMENTS

| | |
|---|---|
| Soul-Mates | 1 |
| The Rope At The Dock | 21 |
| The Mysterious Mr. Norton | 29 |
| The Audience Member | 58 |
| The Horse, After Midnight | 67 |
| The Forgotten Boy | 89 |
| Bittersweet Keepsakes | 111 |
| The Problem With Ghosts | 136 |
| The Silent Girl | 153 |
| The Phonograph | 166 |
| ABOUT THE AUTHOR | 185 |

# ACKNOWLEDGMENTS

At the time of writing, with many of us in the creative sector being told directly and indirectly to fix our efforts and focus on 'more important' matters and careers, there have been few things so necessary and important to the human spirit as art, expression and stories: serious and silly, big and small, wild and predictable. As such, there is little an artist and creator can be more grateful for, than those who champion and support their work. Thank you so, so much.

My first message of thanks must go to my business partner and best friend, Andrew Slade. Your patience, encouragement, friendship, willingness to put up with me, and your amazing cooking have saved me from a life half-lived. Thank you for making space for me to write silly, arguably unimportant things as much as I wanted to write things of note.
Thank you, Paul Goodhead, for your patronage, encouragement and seemingly ceaseless belief.
Thank you to Joshua C. Fisher, whose long-term, long-distance friendship has been supportive and a breath of fresh air. I hope to visit one of those oxymoronic Texan Medieval Fayres with you as my guide someday.
Thank you, Carl Noble, for your continuous support and dedication over the years.
Thank you also to my aunt Angela Williams, for starting me on a long-needed road to recovery I feared I'd never find.
Thank you to my Second Chance Parents, Paul and Rachel Good, for healing more than I can put into words; to my Granddad Milton Graham, and Gillian Graham whose love and consistency has been the best anchor; to Mark, for being the best boy ever; and thanks due in abundance to all of my Patreons, theatre-goers, friends near-and-far, readers and supporters, without whom my work would be completely impossible.

And thank you even to those who provided inspiration for villains and evil entities of these pieces. You know who you are.

## Soul-Mates

"Now then," the specialist said, seating herself opposite me. "I hear we might've had a few issues this week. Have we?"

It has always annoyed me when people say 'we' when they mean 'you'. It's like an inversion of the Royal We, and twice as patronising to whoever you're talking to. I had only recently met this new specialist and she was already grating on me. For some reason, though she cut a very attractive figure on the whole, she seemed, to me, Too Much somehow. Her hair was perfectly blonde, curling and styled – too perfect. Her face, too symmetrical, and her red lipstick, too much a near match with her skirt suit. Even her voice seemed a little too silky and sympathetic to me: the near-bedraggled, post-teen brain-case in the plastic chair facing her.

*I wish I liked her*, I caught myself thinking. I didn't know why I didn't. Then again, perhaps it was purely association. She did remind me a little too uncomfortably of Helen.

Edding, his arms folded, sat next to me for moral support, as he usually did during these sessions, his eyes rolling towards the ceiling with the specialist's question. His expression, unseen by the specialist, let me know that his thoughts and mine ran in parallel.

At one end of the slightly rectangular consulting room, less clinical than I was used to, was a wall-width mirror. I was trying not to look at it. I knew that the mirror worked only as such for anyone in here. Someone on the other side of the wall, my Dad for instance, and probably a member of staff with him, were looking in while the ins and outs of the specialist's work were explained, both able to look in without being observed. I didn't feel my privacy as violated as I thought I might, because I was fairly certain that while they could see us, they couldn't hear us. By this time in my treatment, Dad wouldn't need to listen anyway. Dad knew. I knew. Edding knew. The specialist definitely knew.

"The medication I'm on doesn't work," I came right out and told her.

"Oh really?" The rhythm of her voice was too fast for me to think she believed me.

"Yes. It doesn't... do anything," I answered. I had danced this round before.

The specialist started talking. I'm sure that everything she and other specialists say is very important and appropriate for other cases, but not mine. Never mine. Edding met my gaze again. For the brief moment the specialist wasn't looking, if we'd rolled our eyes further, we'd have been able to describe the backs of our skulls.

She droned on. This medication vs. That medication. Anti-psychotics. Percentages. Timing: important. Structure, diet, exercise. The usual. I had long given up trying to make them see that I did not have what they thought I had. Or, to my knowledge, any other 'psychotic' impediment.

"I don't think there is a pill for me," I said eventually, in a quiet, deflated sort of way. "Or...for what I have."

She smiled in a sickly-sweet fashion. The kind of smile you give someone as a cover, when you are convinced they are wrong. But I wasn't. I didn't know what else I could tell these people that I hadn't told them already and they hadn't already dismissed. She started talking again – I'd tuned her out by this point. It took a minute or two for her to bring me back, saying suddenly and unexpectedly: "Why do you think your father keeps bringing you to these sessions?"

That was different. I paused, analysing this unexpected question. "I...don't know," I answered honestly.

"There must be a reason," she said, annoyingly placid. "Your father obviously cares for you very much." I felt more on the spot than when any of them had asked me questions about symptoms before. 'When did you first start seeing/hearing things that weren't there?' was a party favourite that I had answered, grown bored of, and come up with many a wisecrack since I was first asked. But to ask about my dad was different. "Can you think of a reason your father would bring you here, if he didn't want to make you better?"

Again, I glanced at the mirror. I felt as if I could see Dad, huffing away on the other side, thumbs hooked into his pockets in frustration. "I've always been this way. I'm coping. The only person who isn't..." and I stared at my own reflection, meaning the gaze for the person beyond it.

"But – you do know there's... an issue," she caught me in invisible gauze.

I sunk back into my chair. "Yeah," I relented. "I know that I'm not like everyone else."

"So," she said, as if we were suddenly making progress. "I want to hear it from you. You experience it. What do you think is going on?"

Again, this was a somewhat different approach. While I'd been asked repetitive generics and to talk about my 'feelings' an awful lot, I had been told, for years and years, what it was that was wrong with me. When I was very little, it was nothing to worry about. I had an overactive imagination. Then, there was the day we went to the beach. Dad took me to several different doctors over the next couple of months, and I didn't think much of it at the time. It wasn't until one expressed some concern, that pills started. Every morning of my life since then, a pill of some form or another had been shoved into my face, my father holding a glass of water ready for me to take it with. At age eleven, the counselling started. That was a waste of time. They always wanted me to talk about my mother. *How did I feel, when asked about my mother?* I had no idea – it was my normal, I tried to explain to them, to know that at one point, in the very, very beginning, I had had a mother. But I didn't now, and I couldn't remember the one I had. *Did I feel different from other people and children my own age?* I didn't know. I guess, a bit. But then, no one really fits in properly, right? Normal doesn't exist – I knew this, aged fourteen. *And so, was my brain protecting me from my reality?*...Doesn't everybody's?

Dad took me place after place, chasing diagnoses that made sense, doctors and specialists who had dealt with 'this kind of thing' many times before, pills and schedules and seemingly magic remedies to the problem. The annoying thing was, in all other respects, he was the best dad. I never felt like I lacked my mum's presence. I'd never known her. I had my Dad's mum, Nanna, and a couple of aunts and uncles to help me grow up.

Dad made breakfast and got me off to school until I could make my own way, was ready to help with homework, hung out and watched TV with me, asked me how my day was and vaguely told me about his, and was there for every end-of-term show with my drama club. I could even sometimes talk to him: get advice and another perspective, and it seldom felt like he was judging me. He was a great dad.

He was, however, convinced that something was wrong with me... And when young, it had taken me a while to realise it was all to do with Edding.

While I couldn't remember my mother at all, I had no recollection of ever being without Edding. By the time I was able to fully form memories, he'd already been around a long time, and I was very used to him. He was a little boy, about the same age as me. I had no idea how I knew his name, because he never spoke. Perhaps he told me some other way, before I learned to remember things. But at first, I used to say 'we' to Dad. Maybe that was why I hated it when other people used 'we' when they didn't mean it; because I harked back to asking Dad if 'we' could go out and play, if 'we' were having dessert or what 'we' were all doing tomorrow. Dad seemed curious and cautious at first. "Who's we?" he said jovially a couple of times. I went to tell him, but then I felt Edding's hand on me. Depending on where he touched me - my back, my shoulder, my arm, hand, elbow or even hair, I learned quickly that this was his main method of communication. And whenever Dad asked who it was I was talking to, I felt the odd sensation of a hand, millimetres in front of my mouth. And so I never said Who. I would say My Friend and I. And Dad settled into the comfortable idea that as an only child with a slightly different family dynamic, I had naturally come up with an imaginary friend.

At first, Dad could not have been more accommodating. Dad occasionally talked to himself as he went about the house, so I never thought of it as being odd when I talked to Edding. We set extra spaces at the table: one for Mum, next to Dad, and one next to me, for my 'little friend'. Edding never ate, but then Dad never gave him any food. Nothing that wasn't just scraps anyway, when I complained that My Friend would go hungry. We'd play in the garden and have races. Dad always said I won, even when My Friend did. I even told him when to stop reading bedtime stories, because sometimes My Friend had fallen asleep, long before I had, and Dad would shut the book, kiss the top of my head, try and kiss My Friend when I insisted – he usually missed - and said goodnight. They were happy memories, from when I was still little, and I had no idea Dad ever had any reservations.

Then there was the day we went to the beach. Dad had packed the car with towels, wind-breakers, inflatables, and various other beach-going things in the boot, that spilled over onto the back seat, next to me. When Dad sat in and turned the engine on, Edding was standing outside, looking forlornly in through my window. "Daddy, is Edding coming too?" I asked.

Dad whipped his head back to look at me, a frown on his face, and he said nothing for a long time. When he spoke again, the world changed. "What did you just call him?"

I repeated Edding's name, but when I looked out of the car to where he had been a moment ago, he was gone.

We drove to the beach in silence. It was a glorious day, and it was the most miserable one I've ever known, when it was just Dad and me. I tried to have fun - I ran into the sea for a paddle and vague doggy-crawl swim with my arm inflatables on, while Dad sat on a beach towel a few metres back on the sand and did nothing, saying nothing all day. He seemed to watch me with narrowed eyes, his lips occasionally moving minutely. But apart from a quick, lacklustre game of frisbee, he didn't even interact with me the entire time.

A few days after that, I had my first doctor's appointment.

It seemed I didn't live my life by birthdays after that day. Nor by seasonal celebrations or even personal achievements. I lived them according to when my next appointment was. Meanwhile, Edding and I got on with it as best we could. After the day at the beach, he was around me almost all of the time. Even sometimes when I didn't want him to be. Sometimes I could send him away, with a look or a strong feeling. Sometimes I couldn't. Like my first kiss. It had been with my long-time crush from the year above in the empty sports hall at the end of the day. We seemed to have been waiting to have it for ages, and my cheeks were hot like fire when our mouths touched. Then, suddenly, Edding was in the doorway, glowering at me... and the moment was over. My lack of enthusiasm mistaken for disinterest, we never kissed again.

Bits of this, I related to specialists. Some, I'd learnt to leave out. But everything I said went into notes and files, and things I'd said and experienced years ago might come up in a conversation with a new therapist or doctor. They were always so eager to talk about events as well, as if the things that happened in the real world were more important than the fact I had a more tangible imaginary friend than anybody else ever had.

*Did I remember the glass jar full of stones and shells that my mother had made?* It was only a matter of time before they came back to that one. Dad probably kept mentioning it. Well, I remembered it happening, but not exactly what had happened. I remembered the shock of the smashing sound, quite close by and unexpected, as the jar met the stone flags at the bottom of the mantelpiece. I was shocked into still silence. I remembered Dad standing over the pieces of glass and broken, scattered shells, bits of stones and pebbles rolling into odd places over the floor. I remembered the colour of his face, his telling me, harshly, not to move. I remember Edding was a mixture of angry and upset. However, I don't remember how it fell. I remember Dad sweeping it up, morose and complaining – my mother had apparently put that jar together, collected on their many beach trips, each item a tiny reminiscence that could not be replaced. I don't remember anything else, except that I tried to explain to Dad that it hadn't been me. If it wasn't him, and it hadn't been me, then it must have been Edding.

And I didn't have an explanation for that more than anyone else did.

*Was it an accident?* Yes, I always said, it must have been. And Edding, without saying a word, would glare at me. Somehow, I knew that it wasn't.

"Ralph tells me you still speak to your friend," the specialist announced, and I was suddenly back in the room, having been absent only for a moment or two. "But that you've been hiding it from him for a great while. Is that the case?"

My fists clenched. "My Dad perceives a lot of things. Maybe he's the one who should be in here, talking to you."

At that, the strangest thing happened: she laughed. It was a shimmering, summer's evening type of laugh. Not the kind you hear in a clinical environment, with clipboards, biros and childish drawings on the wall, pandering to the younger children with 'real problems' that came here. It was almost flirtatious, which confused the hell out of me. Then Edding's hand fell upon my shoulder. His grip was firm but not painful. I wished he could speak. But he didn't need to. His grip, with something like a heartbeat pulsing through his palm, into my shoulder and up into my throat, gave me all the words, the impressions, the knowledge I needed. That shimmering summer's-evening laugh was because of my dad. Because she knew he was on the other side of the mirror. And so she had perfected her carefree laugh, curving out of her mouth like her curls of hair, cascading like water all about her, until she was a river nymph.

"You're on first name terms with my dad," I observed.

Her laughter instantly died, but she covered well. Her face betrayed no worry. "We've been talking about you a lot," she said, and now her voice was made of honey. "Your father is still very worried about you, and wants me to help you get well. But you're going to have to trust those who wish to help. So, if you can – now, or soon, I want you to be as honest with me as you can."

Edding's grip changed on my shoulder. There was something genuine in what she said, yet there were layers of sediment lying under her words. Edding and I regarded her. Had she been able to see both of us, she'd have seen our heads cock to the side in the exact same way, in the exact same moment.

*You don't just 'want to help'*, I thought as I stared at her. *You want my Dad. You're just like Helen. She wanted Dad. But she didn't want me.*

Dad didn't date anyone for a long while. I started encouraging him when I became a teen, and he went on a couple of dates. Then, suddenly, he introduced me to Helen. Blonde, immaculate hair. A glamorous sense of style which hid her age. And at first, an almost girlish, instant friendliness with me. I'd never had that before. This encouraged Dad to see her more. It was odd, but the closer she got to my dad, and the more settled they seemed as a couple, the less she seemed to like me. She loved Dad, but I could soon tell she wasn't interested in me at all. She'd make a big show of being so in front of Dad from time to time, but for the rest of it, she tried to make it so it was just the two of them as much as possible. She started saying things quietly to Dad as I left a room, or stopped whispering to him abruptly if I entered. Dad started asking strange questions, and looking confused. We'd started withdrawing from each other somehow. This left more time for him and Helen, however. She wanted to move in. Dad said it would be better after I'd left for uni. Helen didn't like this answer. She became convinced that I was making it all up, that there was no Edding, that I saw no one when she thought the two of us were alone... She tried getting me on tape, but Edding found the phone she'd hidden. She blamed me when it went missing. She blamed me for a lot of things. For the puncture in her car tyre. For the tummy bug she picked up, when she clearly hadn't prepared her food properly. She probably blamed me in her explanation to Dad, if there was one, when she finally just upped and disappeared overnight after an argument where it seemed she was handing an ultimatum to Dad. Dad didn't take the bait, but it was the loudest I'd ever heard him shout. And I could hear my name mentioned, used like a weapon back and forth between them.

We didn't have the telly on in our house for a good few weeks after she left. Edding and I wondered if that was some kind of unspoken punishment.

And now, here comes another one, I thought. *Well, let her try,* I answered silently to Edding. *See how long Dad puts up with that laugh. See how long it takes her to realise it's about you and me, and not about her. See if she likes it when she realises. And even if she doesn't, we'll be away soon.* We'd already put off university a couple of years, and I was eager to get there. I wanted normal. I wanted situations wherein I could have fun and Edding could do as he pleased, but not infringe upon me all the time. Some part of me hoped that Edding would soon be like your older sibling who had moved away, but you got to see every now and again. That would be healthy. And if that could work, well, who cared if Dad dated, got a long-term girlfriend, or even a new wife? Who even cared if Helen came back, if she hadn't gotten her claws into someone else in the meantime? I wouldn't care by that point. As long as he just stayed my dad, but the rest of this nonsense, these appointments, these pills, these endless stupid questions, just went away.

I was coping. But I knew I wasn't going to get better.

In the car on the way home, I sat next to Edding in the back. I felt ridiculous that Dad still made me sit in the back, but it was one of his slightly odd rules. I had been very careful all day. I hadn't referred to Edding. I hadn't looked at him. I hadn't even mentioned him, not openly. My hope was that at some point, Dad would just forget I'd ever had an imaginary friend for longer than most kids.

"What do you think of Carly?" Dad asked.

I felt Edding shift in his seat. That had been the first name we'd seen on the badge of the specialist.

"I don't know," I answered honestly. "I suppose she's trying different things, but... We'll see."

"How is it now?" he asked.

That was Dad's way of asking if we were alone, and I had perfected the art of lying to him about it.

"Everything's fine," I said, leaning forward. "What is it?"

"Well, Carly suggested I have a talk with you," he said.

That was scary. We barely ever talked. The odd conversation, sure, but to actually Talk?

"What about?"

"About... How we do things. She's been talking to me – via email," he clarified, as if seeing through my curiosity. "She's been very eager to hammer home that there must be a lot of honesty between you and I. And we have to start being... very honest with ourselves as well as each other. Do you agree?"

"Very honest," I repeated quietly, half to ourselves. "You want me to be very honest now?"

Dad didn't answer.

"I hate these stupid things. These sessions. These pills. I don't want to do it anymore." I still felt like a teenager. I had wings on my back, tucked between the back of the chair and the seat, waiting for some proverbial cord stretching between my father and myself to be severed, that I could at least feel their span, and what it was to fly above the clouds.

"You know I don't like these things any more than you do," he dourly replied.

Silence for a little time. Edding started kicking the empty seat in front of him. I let him. I had to. I couldn't tell him off, not in front of Dad.

Eventually, Dad cleared his throat. "Do you think Edding is ever going to go away on his own?"

The silence following this was a choke-hold. A fist, or a boot, even, silently, slowly increasing in pressure on my neck. What was the right answer? Yes, I'll make him, someday? No, I know he's not?

"I don't know," I said at last.

My dad hit the steering wheel. He'd never done anything so spontaneously violent before. "Aren't you ever going to answer any question put to you with something other than 'I don't know'?"

"I *don't* know!" I fought back. Edding was leaning forward, and Dad had sped up the car. "I can't answer what I've no idea about."

"He's here now, isn't he?" he demanded.

Edding's hand reached over my mouth. *Don't tell*, it was saying. *Don't say I'm here.*

"Ask him what he wants to go away!" Dad insisted.

I'd asked Edding that very question, a few years ago. I'd been seventeen. I was almost desperate to have sex. It seemed like everyone else in the world had, except me. There'd been someone else, not from our school. One evening, I found myself at their house, alone. I told Dad I was at a different friend's. Fifteen minutes and half a Pepsi later, we were on the bed. I wanted to be good, but I didn't know what I was doing. Thankfully, I hadn't been laughed at, and the pace was slow; almost romantic. Then I opened my eyes and Edding was there, standing by the side of the bed. I'd learned to block him out as much as possible, but he stood and peered, as if curious. I wanted to push him away, to have just one thing that was mine, mine alone. I'd looked up at him and mentally asked him what he wanted just so that he could go away. Edding just moved his head until it became a shake. He didn't want anything, I realised. It was not, and would never be a transaction between us; never an exchange. This was a permanent arrangement. There was nothing I could give him, because I was real, and he was not. I could fall in love and have sex and eat food and interact with others and sing and swim in the ocean, and do any number of things he wanted to do, but he couldn't. And the only way he could even begin to know what any of this was, was to watch me go through it, when I was desperate for just a few minutes alone.

It can make you feel a bit crazy, trying to focus on someone making love to you, when your grown-up, imaginary friend is standing in the room, staring at every second of it. Sometimes, while it was happening, he'd sit in the corner and cry. Sometimes, he'd even sit on the bed and watch with great interest, as if he were watching a movie. Because of that, I could never concentrate, so I doubt I was ever much of a lover. Or a partner at all.

I couldn't commit to someone else, because I was already fully committed to. By Edding.

"He doesn't want anything to go away, Dad," I informed him, the memories racing through at a few thousand frames per second. "It doesn't work like that."

"Well, he's going to have to bloody well take something, and learn to like it," Dad said, spittle landing on the steering wheel. "Tell him – do you hear me?" He raised his voice. "You are not welcome. Do you understand me? You are not wanted and you are not welcome. I don't care what she thinks or what she tells you - leave us alone."

The car sped up a little more. Dad had never spoken to Edding before. My heart felt like someone was tipping rocks into it, slowly adding to the weight, moment by moment.

"Tell him we have a chance," Dad careened on. "Tell him we've got an opportunity to be a family at last. That he can't have anything else, and he's been with us long enough. That you are going to get well, and there is nothing he can do to stop that or to stop me. Tell me what he says."

Edding's hand reached through into my body, past my ribs and between my lungs. I felt my heart crunch as he took hold, those tiny rocks spilling out in all directions, catching my breath. "Dad, what's going on?" I demanded.

The rolling hills that stood between the institute we'd come from, and home, stretched out in every direction as Dad pulled the car over. The roads before and behind us were deserted, and the green countryside only interrupted by a peppering of interspersed buildings. Dad sat in the driver's seat motionless, but breathing heavily. The clouds overhead were almost exactly the same shade as his jumper as he got out of the car.

He shut the door, his hands steepled in front of his face and he dragged them down over his chin and jaw, then interlaced them behind his head in his hair. His odd curled silvering hair would look oddly beautiful when entwining with the specialist's blonde, sea-nymph locks as he kissed her temple. What a strange impression, but I wanted to know if they had already gone there? Was I the only one that was left behind? And then I felt Edding's hand on my shoulder again. But instead of staying with him, I got out and went around the car to my dad.

"What the hell is going on?" I almost shouted.

Dad would not look at me. No. Could not. Wanted to. He tried several times to bring his gaze up, but then would look away. He looked, bizarrely, like a kind of frightened animal. It scared me.

"Do you... know... about Helen?" Dad asked at last.

I shook my head. It was odd he should bring her up when I'd been thinking about her, but maybe Carly reminded him of her too. "What about Helen?"

"Do you remember… that last night, before she left?"

I tried to recall, but what I could remember seemed patchy - it was after my bedtime and I was half asleep when the shouting began. One of their serious talks had turned into Dad trying to calm Helen down, and Helen screaming at him. They'd gone on so loud for so long, I couldn't sleep, and the sleep I eventually had was unsettled, unrefreshing. When I awoke in the late morning, I found Dad sleeping downstairs, slumped in his armchair in the front room, empty beer cans littering the floor about him. I'd never seen him like this. Then he woke suddenly, and took a moment to orientate himself. "Hey kiddo," he'd rasped at me.

Somehow I knew Helen wasn't coming back any time soon.

"I – sort of," I answered honestly.

"Do you remember the police?"

I forgot to take a breath for several seconds. Police. Police? Why would - "No. I don't remember the police." I looked over my shoulder. Edding was sitting very still in the back of the car, staring forwards, as if waiting impatiently for the two of us to get back in.

Dad nodded deliberately slowly. "Like the time you broke the jar of shells."

"Oh for god's sake," I breathed.

"You don't remember it, do you?"

"I remember it," I answered vaguely.

"You don't remember me telling you off before you did it, do you?"

I looked steadily back at him. I didn't really understand him.

"You were upset because I wouldn't let you play with it."

I shook my head. "I don't remember that."

"Why would you?" Dad went on, his voice almost unnervingly calm all of a sudden. "It wasn't you I was talking to."

His resigned exterior was met with my searching gaze.

"It was Him I was talking to, wasn't it?"

I shook my head in growing disbelief.

"Edding's... not like that," I informed him, but my voice sounded strangely unsure.

Dad took a step towards me. I had forgotten that he was still almost head and shoulders above me. "I watched you break that jar, before I could stop you."

My mouth was agape. There was something odd in the wind, like a kind of earthiness I sometimes smell before storms.

"I was worried when we went to the beach. Told myself No, it couldn't be happening to you too. But that confirmed it for me..."

"You think... Edding takes over me? Like...possesses me?" I almost laughed this part out. But Dad's face was unchanged and unsmiling. "Dad, that's ridiculous."

Dad walked off, as if in thought for a few moments. The wind was picking up, locks of my hair caught up in it, some trailing momentarily before my eyes.

"Did I ever tell you how your mother and I met?" We both knew he hadn't, and so he continued. "We were part of a club. Of sorts..." His eyes now met mine, as if he was waiting for me to hear what he hadn't yet said. "Years ago, it probably would have been better known as a coven. And we'd have been called witches."

It was cold, I thought. I wanted a jumper.

"Most of the other members thought it was great fun, and just a weekend laugh. But your mother... She had things she could do," he pronounced very specifically. "I have some too, but not like her. She... I believe... passed some of this on."

"To me?" I asked, my voice hollow.

"And to me," he said quietly. "Somehow."

The cold was all over me, weaving its way through every single thread of my clothing.

"I didn't believe her when she first told me. She said that she had the 'worst and best gift', that she'd had it all her life. She could...take hold... of another."

For the shortest of nano-seconds, like a silhouette cutting through the world, there was a woman sitting in the front of the car, and then she was gone and it was my imagination. It had been so brief, it had to be. I snapped my gaze to Dad, wanting explanations, but unable to ask. He came and stood right beside me.

"You... see her still," I realised as I spoke the words.

The car was empty. Eerily empty. Another place at the table for Mum. Dad muttering under his breath all the time. The ages it had taken for him to date, and then his reluctance... Helen had been jealous – I'd always known Helen was jealous, but I thought it was of me, and my relationship with Dad. Had she had any concept of what she was really jealous of?

"The entire time?"

"I thought... At first... I was just comforting myself. My grief made her seem real. As you started to get bigger, she was a crutch. A coping mechanism, I told myself. Then I realised..."

"That I could see someone too," I finished his sentence. "That I could see Edding."

Whoever initiated it, our fingers entwined, and my father and I were holding hands for the first time in many years, staring at a car that was empty, but wasn't.

"It wasn't an infection," Dad spoke. "I don't know what it was, medically. Maybe an infection of sorts, but she just... gave up."

I wanted a jumper. My god, it was cold. The thunder rolled again, and off in the distance, the briefest of flashes lit up an otherwise overcast, heavy sky, showing up the more silvery hairs in Dad's beard and hair.

"It was a difficult pregnancy," Dad spoke softly, as if he were uttering a prayer. "She was in a lot of pain. She was so worried about you."

The thunder seemed to suddenly pass, as if the storm was moving in another direction. Instinctively, I turned back to the car, but Edding wasn't there. He wasn't anywhere near. I couldn't feel him. It was the furthest he must have been from me in a long time.

"And I need you to understand" - and here his voice finally broke - "your mother loved you. Both of you."

I had an impression, like a set of fleeting, moment-long movies zipping through my head as he spoke. Of a woman ragged with the labours of recent childbirth, teary eyes in a red face, lying in a hospital bed. Dad holding a baby out to her, and she turning away. And by her bed, two empty cots, side by side.

Two cots.

The thunder could've been right over our heads, but it seemed a million miles away. "What happened?" I breathed at last.

Dad's breath sounded like a death rattle. "They called him… a Donor Twin. Do you know what that means?"

Like a smack from a friend, a biology lesson from years ago suddenly snapped into my mind's eye. Five minutes or so of the lesson, that was it, but it had stuck, and I never knew why at the time. Twins. This is how twins work. This is how you get twins. Two eggs. Sometimes, eggs split. Sometimes, conjoined twins. Sometimes, donor twin. One twin stronger. That one takes everything from the other, the Donor twin. The latter are born smaller, usually, more feeble. They might not even survive.

My nails dug into the heel of my free hand. "I killed him," I breathed.

"No," Dad responded. "It wasn't your fault. You didn't know, you couldn't control it: you were a baby."

My eyes were growing misty. I could barely see the car, or him, or even the hills and clouds all about us. "Did Mum believe that?"

A tear fell down Dad's profile. If I was made any less secure, I thought I'd go actually mad. "He lived four days," Dad spoke. "He was put in an incubator almost straightaway. Your mother paced around it night and day, looking in on him. I was holding you, holding you out to her, but she just wouldn't take you. 'I'll hold them both at the same time,' she'd say. Even with everything the doctors were telling us, with it being obvious he wouldn't live, she somehow thought he would."

We stood in silence for what may have been moments, or hours.

"What was his name?" I managed to speak at last.

"He didn't have one," Dad said, a little too quickly. "We didn't even know there were two of you, it was only at the last minute, when she was really weak and in so much pain…"

"He must have had a name," I insisted.

I turned to him, suddenly. An impression again, like a swirling vortex around my father's head, his face, and another face next to him, looking at me across his profile.

"She told you his name," I accused him.

He snapped his head to look at me. "No," he insisted. It was the only time my father had ever actually looked frightened of me.

My teeth clenched. "She did. What did she call him?"

Dad's mouth was open, but no sound came out for a long time. Then finally, voiceless and apparently hoarse and disbelieving, he uttered: "...Edwin."

*Edwin*, the name stuck in my throat. I didn't know that I'd ever be able to say it. *Edwin… Edding…*

As if the revelation of his true name had somehow conjured him, I saw Edding standing before the closed car door, eyes full of furious fire, and he was staring straight at our father.

"I didn't want to tell you," Dad said. "It was my pain, not yours, back then. I always promised myself I would one day, but then..."

"Dad, tell me why you're telling me all this now," I challenged him.

"They found Helen," he said.

The slow dawning of an understanding crept through me like wisps of smoke.

"Think again," he advised me, even more seriously. "Do you remember anything – anything at all - about the night that Helen disappeared?"

Disappeared. That was the word I'd heard often. She'd just – disappeared. But the use of the word was now deliberate, and chilling. She hadn't just disappeared as in left, as in left Dad, as in left us, she'd…

"She - 'disappeared'," I echoed, as if hearing the phrase for the very first time. Rain started to spatter us lightly. I shook my head. "No. I don't even - Is that why we didn't watch the TV?"

"They found her yesterday. What was left of her, now." His voice had dropped so that if I'd stood only a hair's breadth back, I'd never have heard him.

My hands were shaking. "Talk to me," I quietly insisted. "Talk me through it."

"I just remember the shouting. She said all these things. I couldn't explain, of course I couldn't. I tried, but she was so angry, I couldn't stop her…"

Her. He couldn't stop Her. Helen? Or…

"What did she do?"

"I don't remember." His voice was shaking violently, as if the storm had taken possession of it, with its terrible, erratic nature. "I know she hated Helen. She started to make threats. Said that I had to 'deal with the situation', or I wouldn't like what would happen…" Unblinking, his eyes stared at the ground. "But I… don't remember. I had to tell the police that we'd had an argument. That she'd left upset and emotional… I couldn't tell them how your mother looked when she heard some of the things Helen had to say, though, could I? The number of times I have no memory, just this…"

"Impression," I filled in for him. "When something has happened, and you've no idea how…"

His eyes were half-closed. He swayed a little, as if staying upright were proving too much. "I don't remember! Just Helen shouting and then she was leaving and then your mother was there with me, and I was feeling her rage and anger, and after that...nothing." He looked into my face as if I held the answer, but all I could do was mirror the seas of confusion in his eyes. "I woke up surrounded by empty beer cans in front of the TV – you were there. God's sake. I don't remember!"

I darted forward and tried to hold him up, as he swayed forward so violently I thought he might faint. His face was deathly pale, and he was heavy, as if he couldn't hold his own weight up.

I somehow got him in the car and strapped him in. We felt inverted, like I'd strapped my tired-and-angry child in the front seat, and I was calming them through the tail-end of their tantrum, when they were exhausted and confused. He was still breathing heavily when I sat myself in the front passenger seat next to him. I waited a little while as he rested his forehead on the top of the steering wheel, staring at nothing through it. "You don't remember anything about what she might have done that night?" I asked at last.

He sat up, zombie-like, and shook his head. "Nothing. Nothing after I heard her start up the car. Just that she was angry. They both were. Her with Helen, and Helen with me."

"How… how have they found her?"

Dad took a deep breath. "The cliff, not far from your Nanna's. The river at the bottom?" It sounded like a question, but he knew that I knew the place. "She was...still in the car. It was only because of the drought that the water dropped."

"She drove off the edge of the cliff?"

Dad flinched. "They'll ask questions again. They always do… And what if there is something that ties me there, somehow?"

"But you don't remember anything," I probed further.

He very slowly shook his head. "When the police turned up, a few days later, I instantly knew what had happened... She knew, somehow. She wouldn't stop showing me. The image of that sodding cliff."

I took a deep breath. I didn't have answers, but every fibre of my being, and maybe even some of Edding's, felt protective. I had to soothe him. I had to calm the horrific sudden idea that my mother was not the sweet, warm lady I had seen in photographs with Dad. Rather, she might be a storm cloud like those that had gathered that afternoon. Volatile. Over-protective. Vengeful.

Edding's hand reached through the car seat and I felt a wash of steadiness come over me. "You two – had a fight," I said slowly and deliberately. "Couples fight. She was upset and stressed. She wanted to move in, get married, probably have a baby, but because of me, you didn't feel ready. My condition hadn't improved. You told her all this, and off she went. She was angry and upset and you drank because you realised the relationship was over."

"That's what happened," he breathed. I didn't know if he meant it, or was trying to commit this story to memory, but it didn't matter.

"I remember, Dad," I reassured him. "I remember some of the things she said. I don't blame… either of you."

Slowly, his breathing levelled and he kept his eyes locked on mine. "The police might want to talk to you. Now that you're older, I mean."

My hands took hold of his fists, clenched together in front of him. The car windows were steaming up, but then everything, from the outside to into the car to between us, everything went incredibly still.

"I heard the fight. She was mean… She must have been in a terrible state when she left. And it was dark, out here in the countryside. She should have known better."

After some minutes, a car drove by in the rain, and broke us from the bizarre spell. Dad took hold of the wheel, turned the key in the ignition and we silently drove the rest of the way home. We were exhausted. It was as if we'd hiked home.

"Dad," I spoke quietly. "Maybe you could… get some help."

He sighed and nodded. An alarm on his phone went off. It was time for a pill. I didn't take it, and he didn't make me. I resolved that once this storm had passed, we could talk about the pills that I'd taken for years. I just wanted to know if he'd been looking out for me, genuinely thought that I had a problem, or if he had hoped that through me, he'd find a cure for himself. Either way, now I could begin to forgive him.

    Edding wasn't around the next day, and when Dad and I talked, about him, about mum, about so much, there were no extra presences with us. He didn't turn up all that day, or the next. With few withdrawal symptoms, I stopped taking my pills. Dad quietly turned off the alarms on his phone. The boxes and bottles of medication suddenly vanished from the bathroom cabinet. In fact, by the time it came to seeing the specialist, Carly again - which Dad insisted was an appointment we should keep - I realised with a resigned numbness, actually akin to hope, that I hadn't seen Edding for a week, and hadn't needed to take any meds in that time. I wasn't worried. I hoped I'd see him again, but I also liked to think of him and Mum, hanging out, gossiping about Dad and I where we couldn't see. I didn't propose to Dad that maybe, just maybe, Edding and Mum had gone. As in, moved on. As in, for good. And it would just be the two of us now.

    I was resolved to talk about Helen during this session with Carly. It would look odd, I reasoned, if I didn't. Her face was suddenly all over the news again, and being referred to as if the viewer would remember. I didn't, because the TV had been turned off during that time, and now I knew why. I had to talk about my step-mother. I didn't want to implicate Dad by staying too suspiciously quiet. They'd never understand it wasn't him. They don't believe in things like us.

    But how much was too much? What was an acceptable level to talk about?

    "Just be careful," a voice said a few minutes after I'd sat down and Carly had asked her obligatory 'So, how are we doing?'

    I was so surprised to hear this voice, I nearly turned my head. Carly saw it happen, but I played it off as a twitch.

    There was Edding, in a chair close-by, looking, if anything, more real than ever, more assured than I'd ever known him, grinning with fondness, and maybe even pride at me.

    *You talk now,* I thought in Edding's direction.

"You hear me now," he corrected." Out of the corner of my eye, he grinned. "Remember to say it was a tragedy," he advised me. His voice was earthy, and reassuring. It sounded very like my dad's, which would make sense. "Take some culpability for her state of mind, but not too much – you were still pretty much a kid, after all. She was mean, but maybe you were mean back? Don't mention you were worried about losing Dad to her."

Carly was talking and I wished she wouldn't. *I wasn't,* I thought to him quietly.

When I snuck a glance at him again, his grin was wider. "You know you were. We both were. That's why we slashed her tyres that time. That's why we slipped her the gone-off chicken when her back was turned. That's why… You know. Really."

Carly kept on talking, apparently never seeing that I'd held my breath. I had to keep my eyes fixed on her now. I couldn't turn my head. I couldn't look at him as he spoke, as his voice slowly rose until it was all I could hear, and she was somehow cosmically muted.

"She'd have come back, and split us all up eventually. Dad needs Mum, the way you need me. And it's okay. You don't need the memories. The last thing you need to remember is the shouting, some of the things we heard her say to Dad, and how much we hated her then. You don't need to remember getting out of bed. You don't need to remember sneaking into the back of her car. You don't need to remember waiting for the open road and the countryside, waiting for the cliff to be close by. You don't need to remember how it was done. You don't even need to remember the long walk back that night. I've taken care of every little thing that might've got in our way. I had to. For both of us. And if this specialist bitch is going to try and split us all up, all over again, after everything we've all been through, after everything I've done for us, you can rest assured that you won't get any memories you don't want. I'll take care of all of it."

And Carly finished talking, and smiled at me, and somehow, I smiled back.

## The Rope At The Dock

"I hope you're not afraid of ghosts at all," my carriage companion said with something of a chuckle.

It was, in fact, the first thing he had said for the better part of an hour since we'd started our journey, and the bluntness of what he said rather shocked me. With a squint but accompanying friendly smile, I replied: "No, not at all. I don't believe in them."

"Ah!" he said knowingly, but perhaps a tad rehearsed. "Good show."

To my amazement, he then sat back in his seat as if, with this short exchange, the matter was concluded. I watched him for several moments until he realised and returned my gaze.

"Ghosts?" I reiterated. "What made you ask me if I were afraid of ghosts?"

"Oh nothing, nothing," said the older man, waving it away as if it had merely been a passing thought. I let the matter lie for some little time as the carriage trundled on. "Not afraid of anything, I shouldn't wonder, a young, Sure Of Yourself young lady such as yourself," he added presently.

"Fearing a thing that one does not see or understand is not fear, but folly," I responded, quoting vaguely: from where, I knew not. "The fear of ghosts is actually a fear of other things, of things that we do not understand, or the unknown, the afterlife, and whether one believes in that or not."

My companion did not seem to have thought, prior to my stating this, that his anonymous travelling companion may be an amateur student of philosophy or the human mind. He seemed quite amused.

"So you think there's no such thing as ghosts at all then, I'll bet?" he continued, with a touch of fondness and yet, one might almost say, patronisation.

I smiled in return, trying to keep as cordial as I was able. "I've never seen one. I've never heard an account of one that I could trust. No one I have met has seen or experienced one, and the only time I hear any good ghost stories is when a professional writer has penned them." Not wishing to appear a snob, I gritted my teeth and shook my head, bracing myself for something of a story coming, though I had not wished for one. "You have seen a ghost, then?" I proposed, on cue.

The old man was possibly not quite as old as I had first taken him to be. He was completely bald and his face was lined, but there was something of a twinkle in his eye that I hadn't seen in the face of a man any older than, say, sixty. Despite a somewhat colloquial accent, he was well-dressed, in an immaculate black, a cane with him: a beautiful ebony-black creation that my fiancé Lucas would have envied.

"There's no point telling it you," he said, mystically, "if you're not a believer, I suppose…"

"Oh no, do go on," I urged before I could stop myself. "I enjoy a good ghost story, regardless of whether I think it may be true or not."

He smiled and almost laughed at what I said. I began to worry he was merely taking the opportunity to make fun of a young stranger at my expense.

"Are you going to tell me this ghost story?" I asked, flattening down my dress and getting myself comfortable. "You've rather whet my appetite now, and I shall be disappointed if I don't hear some dreadful story as a result of this!"

He considered a moment, and looked off into some far-off distance that he alone could see.

"When I was a young man, I had very little. I wasn't what you'd call a gentleman, you see. I was bright enough, and a hard worker. I was determined to make something of myself. Well, I needed a paying position, and where should I find this, but in an office near the disused docks. The hours were demanding, but I threw myself into my work with the diligence that makes me wipe my brow in memory of it," he said, retrieving a handkerchief from his pocket and doing just that at the appropriate place.

"Well done," I remarked quietly. He did not seem to notice and he carried on.

"There was a young man I worked with there. Young, hot-blooded thing, colleague of my boss. His name was Thomas – that being his last name. I never liked him much, and from what I heard, he was, overall, not liked that much at all by anyone in the office. He could, it's true, be nice and courteous when the humour took him, and he was known by all as a very clever man, but there were too many occasions I can recall where he was rude and arrogant, shouting at both his subordinates and his equals for no real founded reason. I think he must have been from a good family, you know, some people who have had money all their lives and due to their own bad handling, needed to send the young men of the family out to work. Everyone knew that while he was good at his job, he would rather be anywhere than working..."

The old man drifted for a moment, his memories obviously overtaking him. I waited patiently, as our journey's end was still a long way off.

"I had a superior who thought the same as me and didn't like Thomas, but who I respected very much. He seemed a good man. Good with people, even-tempered, always had time for those who had questions or wanted to get on. So when – as I had only a little to do with it all, but knew a thing or two – I thought that there was money going missing from the company, it was he I went to.

"I told him that nigh on £25 had somehow gone missing. Barnes told me to leave it with him and he would look into it – make sure that there really was some money missing and it hadn't been an oversight and then, when he had any evidence or further ideas, he would fetch me for what we had spoken of.

"I don't know how far he got, for he died that night."

I sat up. "Died?" I repeated.

"Not natural," he assured me quickly. "Oh no. Nothing natural about it. They found him floating in the docks. Said he must have slipped and fallen on his way home from the office that evening. Fair enough of a fright to me, for I had walked with him a pace as we left, and so may have been one of the last to see him alive. But there was more than this to be fearful of, for that man was sure-footed. He knew his way back and to that office better than I ever did..."

I nodded, waiting for him to go on.

"I would have liked to have carried on and forgotten about the whole thing, as much as I'd have been able, except...Now, £25, though it seems a lot, may be an oversight and not be so greatly missed. But when £200 goes missing, then people start to take notice. All who worked in our company were uneasy. Except for one."

"That Thomas character," I interjected. But the old man carried on as if I'd not been heard.

"We were all interviewed, one by one, about the missing money. When it came to my turn, and I entered the room where the interview was to be had, you could have knocked me down with a feather if it wasn't Thomas himself, in the presence of other supervisors, with paper and pen before him, head of the questioning into the matter.

"He asked me about the money that had gone. I said that I knew nothing of it. He said another had told him in confidence that they had overheard my speaking to my departed supervisor, Barnes, about the missing £25. I asked who this might be. He answered me, as many might that are born to better stations, that he was to ask the questions, not I. I said it was true that I had told Mr. Barnes, that I had first noticed it. But it was quite impossible that another should have heard us, unless Mr. Barnes disclosed it to another. He in turn tried to goad me. Asked me to show him the sums I had done to prove this first money gone. Then, asked if I was in a home of my own. Had I a wife? Children? Had I debt, now or ever? I knew that he tried to paint me for a base villain, and so answered him calmly and honestly. Seeing that he could not tarnish nor touch me, he himself grew aggravated. And then... My God. He asked me if it were true that Mr. Barnes and I often might walk some way together after the day's work, and our way home included some portion of the docks. Every man in the room, except Thomas himself, shifted uneasily. It might be one thing to say a man was a thief, but another to all of us, that he might be a murderer for it. How I kept my head, I do not know, but I answered him that it was the truth, and I might be the last to see him alive. Yet, with my saying this, Thomas seemed almost to be at ease, and I knew then. I knew the fate of poor, unhappy Barnes and for sure that it were no accident brought him to an untimely end. Now some men may have openly accused him, but with no proof to my claim, I was in danger of being laughed at, or scorned, or even sent packing from my work for the accusation towards a better. Yet somehow, I grew bold, and said, right to Mr. Thomas' face: 'I wish I had stuck with him that night. If I had known aught evil might befall a true friend such as he, I'd have done whatever might have been in my power to ensure his survival, no matter the cost.' He did not look so easy then. And that alone pleased me greatly. Yet in the moment, I realised just how dastardly a character I had made for my enemy, and I knew that he knew. We both knew what the other did."

My companion paused in his oration and took a deep breath in at this point. I wished to prod him, but I was able to contain myself.

"That night, I was eager to get home, as it was getting towards winter time and the nights had stretched, so that it was dark by the time I came to leaving. As will oft happen, a fog rolled in over those docks and despite my brisk pace, I was caught in it. By night, with not much else to navigate yourself, all parts look very much the same, and as I began to second guess myself, with one spot and one rail and one part of the path all looking very much the same as all the other, I soon found myself hopelessly lost. A great fear grew upon me. I knew not what to do, save keep trying to press on, as I dared not go back to the office either…"

"Suddenly, I heard…" He paused and breathed in, seeming a little shaken, "I heard something like footsteps. Light, quick and assured footsteps, close in front of me. I stood stock still, fearing even to call out and see if another were here. They seemed to lead away from me, though I could see nothing and no one in the mist. Unable to see, I simply stood where I was, hoping whoever it might be had not known me to be there. Then I heard them again, but as if this person was in the exact same spot where they had sounded from before. That made no sense, I thought. A man could not walk away, then be back where he had been only a moment before. Growing a little bolder, I called out: 'Hello?'"

"As I'm sure you already know, I got no answer. Instead, after a moment, I heard the exact same thing as I had heard before – the footsteps, a mere few paces from me, moving away through the fog. Much as my heart was in my mouth, I moved to follow them. Then, as they had not done before, they continued on through the fog, always a few steps in front of me, and my eyes never able to make them out in the dark and the mists.

"Before a minute had passed, suddenly the footsteps stopped abruptly. I paused also, for fear of bumping into them in the dark. In what little light there was by the docks, I saw through the dimness that I stood by a large, seaman's rope, tied to a mooring. So close as to cause any to catch their breath, I saw the edge of the dock and the water there below, that had I took one step wrong, I might've been tangled in that very rope and fallen into the water, with very little hope for me thereafter. There was no ship or boat tied to this rope and it seemed to be out of use, for of course, the docks were very seldom used now. Yet the footsteps, my constant companion before, did not begin again. Instead, I was left staring at the rope.

"I was desperate to be gone, for at times I felt that even I was followed, and perhaps there was a lantern off in the fog that followed in the mists so thick but that still I could not see. Yet still, these guiding steps were silent. There was just me, the mooring, and the rope.

"I cannot make you understand what I did next, but the more I looked at it, the more I felt there was some significance in this rope. I picked the thing up. There seemed to be a great sighing in the wind, but there was no wind in the docks, not in that fog. Though it was still attached to the mooring, I reeled in some of the rope and laid it on the path. Not so much, as the rope was wet and so heavy, but as soon as some length of it lay on atop the dock, not a second later I heard those strange footsteps once again, in front of me, and eager not to let them slip away, I ran on behind. I'm sure I need not tell you that not too long after this, I found myself at the edge of the dockland, quite safe, and the fog only behind me. I thought, at one point as I walked away, I heard... a distant cry, like that of a man shouting, in need of help, and my thoughts went back to Barnes and how much fear he must have had, poor fellow, that night when he met his end. All of these things, I knew, were nothing more than the tricks played upon the mind in its own nervousness, I was certain. Much as you are certain that you don't believe in such things..."

Here, my narrator turned and glanced at me, a mischievous glint in his eye. He saw, to what appeared to be his satisfaction, that I was completely enthralled.

"But you *saw* nothing that night," I confirmed with him. "Nothing that would have told you that without a shadow of a doubt, what happened to you was an experience with a ghost?"

He held his hand up. "I'm almost at the end of my tale."

I didn't interrupt him again and nodded, waiting for him to continue.

"I got to work late that next morning, but I wasn't admonished for it at all. I found several worthy men trying to delegate work in a kerfuffle. I asked a good, decent fellow by the name of Goodall what the matter with them was.

"'That Thomas chap, haven't you heard? Drowned in the docks last night.'

"My face might have turned white. 'Drowned?' I repeated. 'What on earth happened?'

"'Some damn fool of a sailor left his rope out on the path last night. Thomas took his leave not long after you, but on his way, - there was fog, of course – he tangles his feet in some rope and falls into the docks. Terrible thing. They're saying: He didn't drown, at first, you see – not from the look on him when they found him early this morning – but instead he was there, all caught up in the rope and then the water started to rise…'

"I did not need to hear any more from him. And I don't know that I cared to think too deeply about that night, but I have, from that day to this, been able to content myself that I could never have known what was to become of Thomas. That if his business had been with me that night, as I suspect, and he had been following me, then so much the better for me, how things turned out...."

At this the old man exhaled one last time, his grin gone, but a tremendous look of relief on his face, as if he had been unburdened of a great guilt through confession. I sat quite still, waiting for him, in case there were more. There was none, it seemed.

"You think…" I heard myself saying, though I tried my best not to lend it too much credence, "you think that you were being 'helped' that night?"

"Who else could have known what Thomas was capable of?" he said, not needing to say the name of the man who he thought had been his saviour in the dark. "How can you explain anything that happened that night?"

I didn't know where to begin. I wondered for a moment if I should tell him a little something about human minds under stress, or how the fog itself can play tricks on eyes and sense of hearing, or how the wind sounds when rushing around walled places, bouncing off water, or even the power of coincidence and possibly a feeling of guilt that he had not yet come to terms with. As I was still considering what I should say or do, I felt the carriage come to a stop and after a moment's pause, the door on my side was opened wide and Lucas, my fiancé, his smile wide and expectant, extended a hand to help me alight. I was so pleased to see him – for I had, in truth, not seen him for the better part of a month by this point – that I quite forgot my companion for a moment and happily jumped down from the carriage, embracing him in greeting. The driver of the carriage started to remove my baggage from the top.

"You're a brave, extravagant little thing, aren't you?" Lucas asked whimsically, as was his way. "Coming across all by yourself."

"Not quite," I informed him. "I had a very good companion who told me a marvellous little story as it happens." I suddenly realised that I hadn't even caught the gentleman's name, or told him mine, and if we were to ever meet in a carriage again, it would be decidedly awkward, if not seemingly rude of me. But turning about, the carriage driver had jumped down and blocked my way, and was seeing to it that all my things had been left with me.

"Strange fellow, that gentleman," I said to him in a quiet voice. "Tells a quaint little ghost story, though, I must say."

Recognition gradually rippled across his face. "Oh! Yes. He loves his yarn, does Mr. Joseph. Tells it to anyone who'll give him time, he will."

"Mr. Joseph?" I repeated. "Is that his name?" And I called it aloud, to wish him goodnight and thank him.

"He won't hear you, miss," the driver said with a resigned expression. "He's told his story." He tried to grin as he shook his head and muttered, jumping back up: "Can't get him out of my carriage for love nor money."

I saw now, with the blind open, that the carriage was empty. It had not tilted or moved with the weight of a living man's exit, and there was not so much as a dent in the seat left behind, where an old man who had told me his ghost story was supposed to have been sitting only a moment ago. As the carriage trundled away, my confused expression following it, Lucas, with his eyes wide and an astonished grin across his face, spoke:

"Bald gentleman, with a cane? What a treat! Do you know, I have made this journey dozens of times, and still the ghost-story telling ghost has never appeared to *me*!"

## The Mysterious Mr. Norton

I do sometimes wonder if I shall ever know what actually happened to me, or to the other women who I happened upon and learnt of during that time, that which I am about to recount. However I have long resolved that, knowing what I *do* know, I will not deliberately pry any further. Oddly, I feel that even now, if I come to know too much, it might be my very sanity's undoing. And God knows, I have come close enough to that before this for one lifetime..

I met Mr. Norton at the end of the summer when I was twenty-seven. I was introduced by a mutual acquaintance, Angela Knightsbridge. She herself was unmarried and pining away after her own older bachelor who seemed to have no eyes for anyone other than an opera singer he had met once. Yet Angela herself was a born match-maker, so she might have credited herself. I must admit, I thought she must know Mr. Norton better than she did, for how she spoke of him.

"Nice sort," she had told me. "He's a widower, if I remember rightly. Lovely man, easy to get along with. Always smiling. He might be good for you, my dear. Very accomplished, and learned. Apparently he has a sizable income and lives off that. I don't believe he works, but are you hung up on having a man who has a career?"

"Oh no," I answered after this barrage of information. "Not particularly. If a man's enough to get by without too much struggle, I'm hardly picky."

"You'd hardly be 'getting by' if you ended up with him, my dear," she said with a grin, and I swore she winked at me. "They say that he hides it well, for he lives very modestly considering, but he's quite a rich man."

It wasn't that that made me meet him. The fact was that many girls my age were getting married. There was a terrible undercurrent in those days – I'm referring to the '20s, of course - a feeling of a sort of run on the bank, except the customers were eligible young women and the currency was unattached men. I even heard some of the older women saying to their daughters, granddaughters and female relations: 'You must act, or all the best men will be gone before your flower has even fully blossomed.' I was a somewhat shy young woman and while I'd had admirers and had also admired myself, it had never really blossomed into anything. So when Angela told me of this nice, established widower with whom she promised to put in a good word and make some kind of an introduction, I was not simply swept away in the moment. I was, in fact, rather excited to see what might come of it.

One evening in the first week of that September, I found myself at the Ritz, one Mr. Norton sitting opposite me. He was indeed, very becoming, discernibly in his forties, but he wore a youthful sprightliness that so defied his age that no one would guess he had left his thirties behind. He had dark hair that was not thinning, but was sparsely speckled here and there with the odd silver hair that no one would notice at first glance. The irises of his eyes were jet-black, from which I couldn't discern the pupils, but I was rather tired of blue eyes and so I found his enchanting. He was taller than myself, and perhaps a little broader, but while I approved of the former, I had no real preference on the latter. I was incredibly glad to see that he was not taking up the fashion that some men his age and older had started, and he had faithfully resisted all mysterious and compelling urge they have, no sooner than they turn forty, to furnish his face with a beard, and so I knew exactly what he looked like from the beginning.

Unlike some men I'd met and knew through my social circles, who droned on about their dull little lives since leaving school, boasting about how their fathers owned this, that, or the other, Mr. Norton offered only bit-pieces of information on himself, and was seemingly far more comfortable asking questions of me, and then listening attentively to my answers. He simply wanted to know how compatible we had a chance of being, and so I answered everything put to me:

## The Mysterious Mr. Norton

I was an only child. I had a mother who was still living, but my father had died a few years ago. My mother and I had inherited a small fortune when he passed and she remained a silent partner at his business, which kept us in a comfortable lifestyle. I had gone away to university, but I hadn't found a potential husband. I had fallen in love, instead, with my chosen subject. I lived with my mother still, in what could almost be called Hampstead, with our modest singular servant, Prudence. I was fond of reading and horse riding, and I fancied trying to write a book someday, but then, so did so many!

He never interrupted me as I spoke, only asked me to go on, or put to me another question to clarify, or continued inquiry in a similar vein. I tried not to let my own stories run away with themselves, and presently felt I might even seem rude, so determined I must turn attention to asking a little of him.

"What have you been told?" he posed with a comical expression.

"Very little," I responded. "That you live modestly, but look after yourself; you don't need to work or otherwise haven't chosen a career -"

"A good way of putting it," he interjected for the first time.

"And that...you were married once."

The awkward silence that I feared would come descended upon us, but still he kept the semblance of a smile, his eyes half-closed. "Yes, that's correct. Or rather... In a manner of speaking I am still married: it just so happens that my wife is no longer with us."

"I am so very sorry," I said. I meant it as well, for his tone carried the weight of unspoken sorrow. "You don't have to discuss it if you don't wish, but on the other hand, I'm more than happy to speak on any subject you find comfortable."

He was quiet for a little time, nodding as if I still spoke and he still listened. Then:

"I'm glad you know it, rather than my having to bring it up, when you wonder why a man such as myself is seemingly unmarried. I have one or two people getting at me to see to it, but I haven't been able to even think of marrying again until just recently... You see, my wife died young and very unexpectedly, for everyone, most of all myself."

The gaiety of the room around us seemed to cocoon he and I, talking low and intimately. "What an awful shock," I uttered quietly.

"It was," he offered. "And I'm afraid to this day, I blame myself."

I kept quiet. I had taken it that the young lady had died of a sudden fever or perhaps even in childbirth, but this indicated not.

"She'd, er, she'd been somewhat ill for a time, but she fought it back, very valiantly. I was very proud of her. I took her to get some sea air to hopefully speed her recovery. They say it's very good for you. Do you know Folkestone at all? Very close to the cliffs of Dover, we could see them from where we were staying. Well, for days, she wouldn't leave the one room and then, suddenly, with a changed tune, one day, she insists on a walk. And…" He stared straight ahead of him and over my shoulder for a moment and I thought in horror how he must be seeing something very terrible in his mind's eye, playing like the moving pictures. "One second she was there, just before me. I was holding her hand. Then the next... she was gone."

The sound of the Ritz was strangely faraway. "She fell?"

"She must have done, though I can't recall it. Or rather, don't wish to recall it."

"How terrible for you." My hand found his on the table and the tips of my fingers were allowed to interlace with his.

"You're very kind. It has admittedly been rather hard at times. I've even thought of quitting my Kensington house and perhaps going to the Continent for a long while, but I shall only be running away from my grief."

"It is brave, then, that you stay." Brave, I thought, and good for me, for I had never seen a man so openly display a tenderness, so unashamedly proffer his vulnerability to another. And how generous to do so with me, a stranger in many ways.

He nodded slowly again and then took in a deep breath. At the end of this, he leant back and smiled at me. "No children, if you were wondering."

He carried on in a mirror fashion, wherein he told me all about himself. His extended family, parents, cousins and so forth, were all 'long dead'. His hobbies were similar to my own, though he also liked orienteering. He was an avid member of a club in town, where he spent a number of his more carefree days, but with this, he again turned to asking more of me. I told him of my favourite books, which he spoke about with enthusiasm, as if he'd only read them yesterday. When I spoke of collecting postcards, he admitted he had thought he was the only person in all the world who did so. Every question he asked, it seemed my answer only confirmed for the both of us that we were a match.

We had gotten a little through the meal when he said to me: "You're a very lovely young lady. Will you permit me to ask if we can see one another again?"

His manner seemed positively old-fashioned, but I was aware he was a little older and so perhaps a little more like his own parents than my generation. I flushed and said I would be very happy to see him again.

After our second meeting, the times between our seeing one another got shorter and shorter. We waited an entire week for our second rendezvous, but hated the idea of waiting so long for the third. That took place four days later. Then a two day pause. Then we made arrangements for the following day. By the time autumn had taken a full grip over the land and everyone was beginning to consider wearing their winter scarves, we were seeing one another practically every day. We found so many things that we shared with one another. We were fond of the theatre and opera, and Mr. Norton was happy to take me out to see performances he had heard of. We went for drives into the countryside on numerous occasions, and usually then walked down a country lane, hand in hand. We exchanged books, he met some of my friends, and in November, Mr. Norton, with rather a lot of showmanship, proposed to me. I couldn't help but say yes.

I have to say now before I continue that even on reflection, all these many years later, those first days with Mr. Norton when we found each other, were some of the happiest days of my entire life. I'd never known happiness like it. I don't know that I ever shall again.

It was unfortunate that just before his proposal, I began to develop health complaints. I had always had something of a lady's constitution and I found it tiresome getting up some mornings out of bed, but then so do we all as we creep ever closer to the grave. It was a little thing at first, to be fatigued still after a long night of good sleep, but when every morning I found it more and more difficult to drag myself from bed, even to keep my eyes open after the sun had risen, I suffered quietly, to keep from my new fiancé anything of my illness. I was conscious, eternally, of his late wife's last year and would have been mortified had he begun to worry about my silly, trivial problems in a similar way. I went several times to the doctor, but there was nothing he could find that was the matter with me – nothing wrong with my blood, nor any of my organs, so I was told, and I was able to demonstrate that I was a mentally fit young woman. When asked to elaborate on my symptoms, I could only answer vaguely: "I'm just so tired and parts of me just - ache."

On the first of December, Mr. Norton came to visit my mother and I. It was quite charming and again, an old-fashioned ideal of his, but he insisted that in order to continue to show my mother he was an honourable man, in private, we ought to always be accompanied whenever possible. He didn't want people to talk, as he said. My mother set her eyes by him, for I don't think she imagined I could bring such a lovely creature home.

I wish I had had more time to talk it over with her, as she seemed happy enough. But on this visit, she too was somewhat ill.

"No improvement?" Mr. Norton commented.

My mother was wrapped in a thick shawl and sitting next to the blazing fire. Anyone well would have moved away in a trice, even though it was winter. "None, sadly," I answered quietly.

"Prudence looking after you both?"

"Of course, very well."

He fiddled with his empty teacup as if the contents might rematerialise within. "Why don't I come and live with you? I mean, straight away. I could shoulder some of the Care burden."

"Oh I couldn't ask you to do that!" I said. "It's very kind of you, but what a thing that you should move in to look after your fiancé's mother!"

"Soon, therefore, to be my mother-in-law," he reminded me with a grin. "And it would be a pleasure. It's not as if you would be keeping me from much."

"But what about your Kensington house? You promised me I should see it soon, and I still have not!"

"I'm glad about that – I don't want you to see it. I wouldn't want you to like the place, because I've decided to give it up."

"Give it up?" I reiterated in surprise.

"Yes. I'm going to let it, and come and live here with you, if you'll have me a little sooner than anticipated."

"Well – well, of course! But -"

"No! I think you'll find I'm actually quite headstrong when I've made up my mind, and that is what I've done. I'll send for some of my things."

Over the next few days, Mr. Norton, without much fuss, came to live in our house with us. My mother was overjoyed, evident even through her illness.

"When will you two be married?" she asked one evening over supper. Her sickness had enfeebled her voice and she spoke almost like a lady twice her age.

"Spring, I hope," I told her. "I want to be married under an apple blossom."

"Nonsense," cut in Mr. Norton in good humour. "Blossoms falling all about you would make you look far paler than you deserve. I think that snowbells and crocuses would suit you far better."

"Snowbells and crocuses? But they grow in February at the latest, and January usually!"

"My point exactly," he said with triumph.

So our wedding date was set for early January. It didn't even occur to me to argue down his enthusiasm - who would quibble over the weather, I thought, if one were wise enough to recognise when they had met a spouse so perfect as I had? Besides, Mr. Norton was paying for it all, not wanting me to fritter away the sum my father had left me. Furthermore, Mother began to deteriorate. As winter's icy grip closed fist-like all about us, she grew frailer and frailer by the day, 'til her skin was wrinkled and papery thin, and her once glorious hair came out in clumps, 'til it seemed she rather wires on her head than hair. When our own doctors gave us no answers, I sent for doctors from further afield, with specialisms and alternative methods, but very few of them offered any real hope and those that did, I fear, were charlatans to a man. My own condition improved with the focus I placed upon her through caring, but as the days passed, the horrible possibility that I might have to be married without her loomed ominously over myself and the entire household, like an open secret that no one dared speak of, in case the speaking gave it power. Mr. Norton was wonderful, and arranged for another servant to come into the house to look after her needs better. He looked after us impeccably.

Then in mid-December, I met, quite by chance, an old school-fellow of mine – Charlotte Fitzgerald. We were both out, I having forced myself from the house despite my tiredness, when we recognised one another, and fell upon each other with gushing enthusiasm that took us to a local restaurant for tea.

"Is there a stork coming your way soon?" I asked.

She giggled and smoothed down her dress. I had heard it, but had not been sure 'til I saw her. "Oh yes. We have the names all picked out! But what about you? I heard marriage is on the cards! Who's your lucky devil then?"

"I fear I am the lucky one entirely," I corrected her. "He's the most frightfully doting chap; a widower, you know, slightly older than us. His name's Mr. Norton, he's from South Kensington."

A slight change came over Charlotte as I said this. I daresay she tried to hide it, but I saw how she stopped and looked at me, blinking only once in what felt like a minute. "Norton!" she said, trying to appear only half-interested. "I see… He's not an orienteering sort, is he?"

"Yes!" I said cheerily. "You know him, then?"

She grinned, but it was a forced grin, which the eyes did not support. "Yes, I know the gentleman. Or rather, I knew his wife while she lived."

"Really?" I was going to ask her about this previous Mrs. Norton when Charlotte carried on -

"When's the happy day?"

"January 18th," I said.

She did blink at that. "Quite close," said she. "A winter wedding!" Here she leant towards me and enquired very quietly: "You don't have your own unexpected stork on the way, do you?"

"Oh good grief, no!" I blushed about as red as a pillar box. I had forgotten how forward she could sometimes be, for all her well meaning. "No, not at all! Mr. Norton simply thought it made sense to have it sooner rather than later."

"Ah, his idea?" she reiterated. "Well… It's nice to have a man so eager. Has your mother met him?"

"Oh yes," I said, "they adore each other. He lives with us now."

"Ah," said she. "How very nice... How is your dear mother, anyway?"

"Not so very well, sadly. She's very frail and overly delicate just now. She has good days and bad days, but mostly I grow more fearful for her by the day."

"I wish her a speedy recovery... And you, my dear? How have you been? I mean, when it comes to your own health?"

It seemed an odd way to ask it, but I answered stintingly: "Well I'm better by far than Mother, but I often don't feel it. I too have good and bad days, but do you know, I simply couldn't bring myself to leave the house for days, I felt so weak recently."

"Ah, my dear. I am sorry for it... Well, I hope that if you have only one more day out before Christmas, it will be to come to a Yuletide Soiree I'm having. In fact, I insist upon your coming and will brook no argument. It's this coming week. Here, I'll write you down the address. But it's, er, a lady's night if you see what I mean. Just us girls. We have to have something all our own, don't we?"

I explained as much to Mr. Norton later that day – that I wanted to attend a soiree with an old school friend who was a lovely girl, but it was a Ladies' Event. He chuckled at this. "I wonder sometimes if you don't think more of your school friends and their bidding than of me," he teased. "'Come to a soiree just by yourself' they'll say, and there'll probably be half a dozen young men there to steal you away. Besides, I'm not happy with your colour just now, is it wise for you to go?"

"My colour?" I echoed.

"You know you're paler than you should be," he said. "While I understand it, I don't appreciate your keeping from me that you're ill, like you do your mother."

"I didn't want either of you to worry."

"Nothing but complete honesty between us. We promised, don't you remember?"

"Of course I do."

"Well, I suppose I can look after your mother while you're out for the evening, but personally, I don't like it. Not so close to Christmas either, it's not the kind of thing I'd have chosen to do at all."

"I'm so sorry, darling. Perhaps you're right. I won't go if you don't want me to."

I remember then he looked at me, as if trying to decide upon something he wasn't willing to air, and then his look was calm and happy again, and he came over and kissed me. "No. I'm probably being old and fusty. If you want to go, you should."

I almost didn't, but now, I'm very glad I did.

The soiree was on a Friday, and I arrived a little later than I meant. By that time, everyone was already helping themselves at Charlotte's buffet and Charlotte herself was having a gay old time. When her eye fell on me, she paused everything, forcing her smile once more. "You must meet a friend of mine," she said.

She grabbed the wrist of an older woman over my shoulder and took us into an adjoining room, away from everyone else and then spoke, in a rather quieter voice. "We all have a mutual acquaintance. Sara, dear, this is the lady I was telling you about. The soon-to-be Mrs. Norton."

The lady now standing on the other side of Charlotte was, on first glance, a slightly older lady, a docile, sweet little thing but with a face that meant to be well-meaning, but instead simply looked sad. She looked as if she might be slightly foreign, but I could not have placed her just by looking at her. The lady's face fell even further than it had been before. Her lips parted as she looked at me. She took in a deep breath and said: "I can't turn you away from marrying him. I know I can't. But I beg you, please, hear me a little to know what may become of you."

I was quite taken aback and more than a little insulted at what she had said. Charlotte calmed me. "Do as she asks. If you are my friend, give this woman five minutes of your time this evening. Five minutes, that's all."

Flustered, I acquiesced for Charlotte's sake, and she sat us down in three armchairs in this little room, and Sara began to speak as if telling a story:

"The sad truth is I know you will not believe me. Not this time. Not now. In time to come, you will see, but only when, I think, it is already too late. It always is the way.

"When I was young and foolish and lived back in my country, I met a man, an Englishman of perhaps forty, who had come to the quiet region where I lived, to recover from bereavement – his wife had just died…. He called himself Mr. Norton."

I struggled not to scoff, as it was quite impossible that this forty-year-old man was anything to do with my Mr. Norton, though possibly an unfortunate relation to mine, but Charlotte's look told me not to interject.

"There was no one to show him the beauty of our country in the region and so he took me into his pay. We spent much time together. He took me with him on excursions, brought me into his rooms, even cared for me when I fell ill. The two of us, we…we fell in love.

"Some months after his coming, he decided to travel onwards. He invited me to join him. I had no father to ask permission of, and only a married sister who had not met him, for she lived in another town. Being a good Catholic woman, I said it was quite impossible, no matter how much I wished it. He had then said that if that was all that was preventing me, then we should marry…"

It took Sara only a day or two to realise that her request to her English admirer for more time had been taken as an outright refusal, and, desperate to reclaim her love, she went to his rooms, only to find he had already left without saying goodbye. With visions of a heartbroken man leaving the Continent to forget a painful relationship, so soon after becoming a widower, Sara was beside herself to correct the wrong and despite patchy health, she made the bold decision to follow him to Great Britain, and declare through gesture her willingness to go ahead with the marriage. She arrived perhaps a week after the two had last seen one another. He had spoken of his home in Scotland, in Ayrshire, in great detail, and so she found it very easily. She had presented herself on the doorstep, only to be greeted by an old woman.

"I asked for Mr. Norton. 'Mr. Norton is my husband,' the old woman said. 'I am Mrs. Norton and while I'm not in the best of health, you may say to me anything you wish to say to my husband.' I told her it was a misunderstanding and it must be her son I knew. 'I have not yet been blessed with a son', the woman told me. 'What is it you want from him? What business have you here, madam? Why do you plague my husband?' Of course I thought this woman had grown quite mad with her old age… She was quite rude to me, but then Mr. Norton himself came and saw what was happening. He took the old woman away, telling her that all was well and then came to me. He told me that his mother had grown increasingly confused in her old age, and sometimes could not remember him at all, and thought his father, her husband still lived, for they looked so alike. He asked me what I was doing in Scotland. I told him I had come to marry him, as he had asked me to. I went to embrace him, but he stopped me. He told me he had been thinking and while he wished to marry me, there was

## The Mysterious Mr. Norton

business he had to attend to and he would send for me soon. I asked to stay with him, as all my worldly goods I had left behind me, and could only make a little money as a translator if I was wise. He said my presence would confuse and upset his mother. So I set myself up at a hotel, very close, to be sure he could come and visit me whenever he wanted. What a fool I was."

Though I was not sure how this Scottish Mr. Norton had any bearing upon me and my own Mr. Norton, I couldn't help but feel for the lady. She was obviously greatly moved by her experiences from long ago. "And did he take advantage? When he came to see you?" I asked cautiously.

"No! No he did not. He left me that at least. No, sweet girl. Instead, I never met him again."

"Gracious! What on earth happened?"

"I still don't know, not entirely. I waited for weeks. I sent letters. I tried to come to the house on occasion, but each time, Mr. Norton was not at home. Perhaps the fifth time, I arrived as a funeral was taking place. When I asked who had died, they said 'Mrs. Norton', his mother. I waited perhaps a month for his grief to subside, sending more notes on my condolences, but I had never received a reply in all this time. When I next went to the house, a stranger opened the door. She explained that the last resident in the house, possibly the 'Mr. Norton' whom I asked for, had sold the house the very day after his mother's death, and he had moved away, to set up his new home with a fiancée in Kensington."

At this last piece of information, I was the most baffled, out of anything I had heard. I was sure by now, of course, the insinuation was that this Mr. Norton and mine were perhaps one and the same, but that was impossible. Sara took out a handkerchief and dabbed at the tears lining her face. There was seemingly no more for her to say.

"I'm sorry for how you were treated," I stammered. "This does indeed sound like a horrible turn of events for you, and I am so sorry for it, but... I don't understand. When did all this happen?"

Charlotte answered: "Twelve years ago, give or take a Christmas or two."

"Twelve years?" I echoed. I stared at Sara, who had described herself as a foolish 'young' girl at the time, when she had quite obviously been a fully grown woman. But it was not this I alluded to. "Twelve years ago, my Mr. Norton would have been a young man, in his late twenties or possibly about thirty. Nowhere near forty, as yours was. And he's never lived in Scotland, and I've certainly never heard him talk about Scotland or Ayrshire. He certainly doesn't sound like he's from there. I also find it completely out of the question that he would treat anyone such as your Mr. Norton treated you."

Sara sighed and turned to look at Charlotte. "I have done as you asked. I have told it all. The rest is up to you and her."

In bewilderment, I watched as the shadow-faced woman stood and went to join the rest of the party, as if the outrage of the implications and the questions with which she had left me were as nothing to her.

"What on earth does this mean, Charlotte?" I demanded. "What a strange tale! You don't seriously believe this lady's story – if there is any truth to it at all - is about my fiancé, do you? For god's sake, you've met him. You knew him, and his wife."

Charlotte stood and adjusted her hair in a mirror on the wall, but was palpably deep in thought. "I honestly don't know what to believe, my dear." She looked at my own reflection in the mirror, and so her echo stared out at me from the cold glass. "Do you know anything about his late wife, Clara?"

"No," I confessed. "I never asked. I didn't wish to upset him."

"It's funny," she went on, making for the door. "When she first told me about him, she described him as a widower. Odd that a man should have so many late wives, or that all Mr. Nortons seem to be widowers," and she left the room.

I stayed as long as I could stomach at the party but in truth, my mind was working against itself, trying to work the thing out, even on the way home. The thing was quite impossible. The two Nortons simply could not be the same man. The times and dates were all wrong. And what had her Mr. Norton hoped to gain from taking advantage of a young Sara? His actions towards her were concerning indeed, but also made no sense. And surely, I would have heard my Mr. Norton refer to Scotland before, if indeed his mother was a Scotswoman and his family had at least lived there for years. Mr. Norton surely hadn't already had two long and happy marriages, and he would have certainly mentioned it had he been a widower twice.

And yet, Charlotte and I having known each other a long while, I had never known her to be dishonest. It wasn't in her nature. In some way, I felt she was trying to help me, but her reasons and her concerns were elusive things.

By the time I arrived back in Hampstead, I resolved to think no more about it. It was all coincidence. Charlotte had got it wrong, perhaps. Sara had mistaken Norton for an unpopular name. If any of what I had heard was true, it was because there were two if not three Nortons who all happened to have met other people after becoming a widower. Some of them were doubtless lying, but not mine. I had seen the look on his face when he told me of his late wife's death. And I knew he would never lie to me.

I forgot it entirely when I reached home and saw Mr. Norton in the doorway, looking quite pale.

"Are you alright?" I demanded. "Darling, it's gone midnight, what are you doing out?"

"My darling," he said, and took my hand. "Prepare yourself. I'm so sorry."

I knew before I had even gotten into the house... A few hours ago, Mother had gone to sleep before the fire, looking frailer and older than she should've, tucked into her blanket. Prudence came in to ask if anything was needed before bed and was unable to wake her cold form. Mr. Norton apologised to me profusely, as if it was his fault, saying she might have been sitting there for minutes at a time where something might have been done, but he hadn't been in the room.

"Oh God, I forgive you, though there's nothing to forgive," I told him, beside myself with my sudden, horrible grief. "Don't you know I don't know what I'd do if you hadn't been here with her? I wish I'd never gone to that awful party. This is truly the worst night of my life."

Mr. Norton was up early the next day making all the arrangements. I stayed in bed partially because of my malady, partially because I was so desolate at her untimely loss, and the doctors still unable to give me any reason for her death beyond old age. I had heard of people dying of old age when they were in their seventies and eighties, to be sure, but in one's fifties seemed strange to say the least.

Christmas morning was plain miserable. The funeral was set for the

30th, in the same church where we were to be wed. I couldn't bear the thought. Mr. Norton tried to pick me up from my melancholia with gifts, but it was no good. Over Christmas Dinner, with an empty chair at one place, I suddenly put down my knife and fork.

"I can't continue as if nothing at all has happened. I'm sorry, dearest, but we shall have to postpone the wedding."

"Oh darling," said Mr. Norton, "don't say that. What better reason to stick to it, than it would surely lift us from our sorrows? And your mother would have wanted us to be married, and you looked after well. She'd have been mortified to think anything she did might put it off."

"Yes, I'm sure she would," I agreed. "All the same. Let's get married in the spring instead, as I thought we might."

"But darling," he protested, "what of your health? You know you're not as well as you could be. Your mother's death with this has had a tremendous effect on you. What if it were to deteriorate further? No, I think we ought to have some excitement sooner, give you something to keep your mind occupied."

"I'll be fine," I insisted. "I've quite made up my mind, dear. Let us set a date in April or May. I can't go through with a marriage in a few weeks, darling, I really can't."

"April and May are a long time away," he observed. "I really don't think we should put it off as long as that!"

"It will be all for the best," I reassured him. "It will give us ample time to arrange things beautifully. We could have the best day."

"And the best honeymoon," he said, sliding his hand across the table and winking at me.

I don't know to this day why I then said what I said or did what I did, but let us say that curiosity, if it kills cats, is an imposing mistress on human beings as well. "Yes. A lovely honeymoon. I know it's all the rage to go to France and things, but I was hoping we could stay closer to home."

"Really?" he chuckled.

"Yes. Strangely enough, I was wondering what you thought of Scotland."

He paused. It was so slight and quick, anyone else might have missed it. "Scotland!" said he. There was the due surprise, but something else was there in his voice. "Are you sure? I hear it's bitterly cold in Scotland at the best of times. Not much of a business to have a honeymoon there. What's made you think of Scotland?"

"I don't know. A friend of mine was talking about it recently. Ayrshire, she mentioned as a perfect place, and I've never been before." I stared at him. "Have you? Been to Scotland before, that is."

He looked at me oddly and for a moment - only a moment - I could have sworn I saw something dart behind his eyes, something not altogether pleasant and not even very human. For a brief moment, it was as if a mask had slipped, but it had disappeared a moment later, and I put it down to my imagination. "No," he answered. "No, I don't think I've ever been to Scotland at all. Certainly not - what was it? - Air-shur?"

We sat at the dining table staring at one another and then at some point, we started to attend to our meals again.

My health, while it did not improve much, thankfully did not deteriorate. There were some days which were worse than others, and some when I felt nearly no fatigue at all. I encouraged Mr. Norton to go out into Hampstead and beyond and enjoy himself without me on my bad days, which he was keen to do. He would come back and tell me of his day and ask how mine had been. On my better days, we stayed at home together.

Then Mr. Norton started to go out even on the days when I was feeling well. I offered to come with him, but he cited his fears that if I was truly on the mend, the chill air of the winter might force me back into my bed and future prospects of wellness might be bleak. So I dutifully stayed at home, attempting to arrange a date for our wedding. Every time we came to it, however, there was some problem in the way. The church was not available, or certain necessaries unforthcoming at that time. I grew rather frustrated, especially as Mr. Norton took to going out every day by himself, sometimes for a day or two at a time. Occasionally I would only know of his return at breakfast when I saw him, and he would apologise and admit that he had met a friend at his club and the time had gotten away from them. My health gradually started to improve, but Mr. Norton only noticed in passing.

Then, one day, he didn't come home at all. I don't mean he was very late. I mean, he never came home after that.

On the first of March, Prudence reported she had knocked at his door many times about breakfast, but receiving no answer, at noon, she had gone in to find his bed unslept in, but everything else left as if he had only just left the room. Between then and the fourth, I grew increasingly worried. There were no calls, no notes, no letters. What if something terrible had befallen him, I reasoned, and here was I worrying about my own health when all the while he could be in a ditch somewhere? I contacted various mutual acquaintances, none of whom seemed to have seen him if they responded to me, or others simply did not reply. I was quite beside myself. I even went so far as to show up at his club, asking for him, but was turned away with a kindly, if confused confession that no one in the club had seen him for a great long time. I eventually called Scotland Yard to help me look for him.

It all made no sense, I told them. He had brought so little with him from Kensington, but he must be wanting his things. The search, and my dedication to finding him wore on my strength again, and I felt more like a ghost than a living person. My habits became unhealthy, and the search took all of my attention. I wrote several letters everyday, and had some notices put in the newspapers. I called every constabulary within twenty miles every day for weeks. With weeks passing, and still no sign, I took to riding on the Underground railway system and combing the places we had been together, in case I should find him somewhere along the way. He would turn and see me, and on finding I had been looking for him all this time, he would explain and it would all make sense, and he would have done what he had to do, which I knew nothing about, but in some way, it was for me, and I had taken his love so for granted and ought to be ashamed of myself. I was. My god, I was so ashamed and desperate. How could I have been so careless and inconsiderate in so many ways I'd never even realised? How had I even entertained the bizarre stories I had heard of him, and through doing so, lost the man that surely God himself had picked out for me?

And then, quite unexpectedly, on the 28th, at seven o'clock in the evening, Charlotte and Sara were on my doorstep.

Charlotte, now a new mother, swept into the room in her furs and shrugged them off, looking at me and tutting. "You look terrible my dear," she said sullenly. "Though with what Sara has been telling me, I'm not surprised in the least. Have you somewhere we can sit and talk?"

I took them through into the drawing room. Prudence brought in some tea and they asked me, politely, how I had been. I burst into uncontrollable tears and told them everything. To my amazement, while they were quite sympathetic and said all the right things one can to someone who is in distress, they seemed not a bit surprised. Eventually, when I'd regained my composure, Sara, sitting close to the firelight, began speaking.

"I know you did not believe what I said before, or maybe thought there must be two Mr. Nortons, but perhaps you will listen to me now. Most of what I tell you, I have found out only in the past few years, and I don't say any of it to upset you. I say it to help you.

"Twenty years years ago, maybe even more, there was a Mr. Norton who came from London to Scotland to live with his new wife in the large family home in Ayrshire. She was the youngest of three otherwise unmarried sisters, who lived with their parents and an ageing grandmother. The family doted upon Mr. Norton, though I do believe there was much jealousy from the older sisters. And then the grandmother died. Then the next year, the father died also, of old age."

"Oh gosh! He must have been greatly older than his wife then."

She shook her head. "The grandmother had been HIS mother."

That was odd, I thought. To die of old age only a year after one's mother has died.

"And then," Sara continued immediately, "after maybe eighteen months, the mother followed her husband. Then the two sisters, one after the other, one death every other year, following a wasting disease. Doctors came and could not understand it. And then, finally, the wife. She died last, and, I found, despite what I was told, that she died after I met Mr. Norton. It is my belief that the woman who first greeted me at his house in Scotland was telling me the truth: she was not Mrs. Norton his mother, but Mrs. Norton his wife."

My mind was racing. "I'm sorry, I'm completely confused. Do you mean to say it is your belief that Mr. Norton, in some way, was making these people, this family, ill? Poisoning them or causing this – as you say - wasting disease? Remember my Mr. Norton would have been a very young man twenty or more years ago."

"I don't know the answers, truly. I don't have answers that would satisfy others or myself to this day. But…" And here she leant forward.

Her eyes looked old and wise and sad in the firelight. "Do you know how old I am?"

I didn't like to say. Then Charlotte touched my arm.

"I'm sure you'll think as I used, that Sara has many years on us. In fact, there are only five years between she and us."

I was taken aback. Rather than putting her in her early thirties, as Charlotte intimated, I might easily have put her at fifty, or even older. Though it would tie in with what it seemed was being assumed had become of this Scottish wife....

The room became very close suddenly and a great feeling of dread crept over my shoulders and shot like lightning down my back. I stood, going to the mirror in the hall and peered into it. I stared at the echo of myself in its glass, peering at my face, my eyes and the skin around them, my jaw, the corners of my mouth as if I had never seen any of it before…

And perhaps I had not. Not truly, not recently. My illness, and my current worries had taken my health, my youth and vigour away from me, but I knew eventually, when it was over and the balance of my life restored, I would recover. However now, as if a veil had been silently lifted, I gazed with horror. Age had come upon me, faster than it had any right. I had always prided myself up to this point in looking youthful and charming, but now I saw that I looked noticeably older. Older than my years. Perhaps not by very many, but I could see it. These changes were not the result of recent tiredness, or the strange illness, or the search itself. They were permanent and unchangeable.

Sara and Charlotte followed me into the hall. They saw the look on my face as I turned from the mirror towards them. I parted my lips, but I knew that while they could present me with the facts, they knew as much as I now did.

"Consider, my dear," Charlotte said. "My friend Clara was a great strong girl. Large, full of life, a true sportswoman. When everyone else was ill with a cold, she never had a touch of it, not her entire life. Then she got married. It was the first time I've ever known her ill. But there was some kind of problem, I think. Towards the end, I don't believe she loved him any more. And, in case you were wondering, I might be in the minority, but I don't for a moment believe all this 'there one moment, gone the next' nonsense." She donned her coat and the two left with never

## The Mysterious Mr. Norton

another word.

The next morning, I received a young policeman from Scotland Yard. "It's a Mr. Norton, formerly of Kensington you had us look for, isn't it, miss?" he asked gingerly in the morning room.

Though I was still reeling from the odd and rather damning admissions from last night, my heart leapt. "You've found him? Is he alright?"

He looked a little lost. "Oh, yes, miss. Mr. Norton came to us yesterday, but I can tell you he's quite well, and of course can advise that he is no longer a Missing Person, as it were."

I kept my eyes on him, and he looked back, his lips closed, when surely there had to be more. I felt my brow furrow. "Is that all?"

The young man rifled through his notes, looking almost nervous. "Er… Yes, miss. We thought it best to tell you in person."

I looked at the young man's face, as if that would give me more explanation. "I – I'm not sure I know what you mean," I stammered. "Mr. Norton is my fiancé. I haven't seen or heard anything of him besides this for a great many weeks now. Did he give any indication when he'd be home? What has he been doing, where has he been?!"

The policeman swallowed and again consulted his notes. "I er… The gentleman had come that day from Chelsea, miss. He told us to tell you he's quite well, but he asks that you don't look for him any more."

I couldn't answer. It was the last thing I'd expected to hear.

The young officer removed his hat and his wrist rubbed alongside his temple. "He's asked, miss, that you don't contact him either, and that it's for the best. You see, his wife, she won't like it. She'll either be very jealous, or she'll take a funny turn."

"Wife!" I repeated, barely able to breathe. "No. No, it's impossible. You must have got the wrong man! My Mr. Norton is not married. He's engaged – to me!"

The young policeman, in decided awkwardness, could no longer meet my gaze. "I do think we have the right man, miss. Answers your description, described yourself to us… He saw one of your notices in the papers he said, and wanted the whole thing… Well, 'tied up' was how he put it , before his wife got wind. The young lady's health is not the best, so I'm told, and he didn't wish to put off their wedding, but it might have been she'd have took a funny turn, had she found out the confusion."

## The Mysterious Mr. Norton

I collapsed into the nearest chair, all the breath gone from within me. "He has married..." I uttered. The words made no sense. They could not be true. Yet an officer of the law, for all his nerves, was confirming them as perfectly true. 'Confusion' was the word the officer had used. Mr. Norton had no doubt used this word with him. I was 'confused', and my weeks of worry, of searching and even the promise that we would be married was nothing more than a side effect: part of my 'confusion'. "He has married…"

"Newly, miss," the young policeman reminded me, with an unspoken apology in his voice, as if his sympathy was more with me than his need to carry out this particular task. "He told me to thank you for your many kindnesses to him in recent months, but he knows in time you will come to understand."

I looked sharply up at him. "Was there anything else? Anything else he said. Come along, man, think!"

He fumbled for a moment, then brought a piece of paper out of his pocket, colouring red. "Yes, miss. I didn't think it appropriate to read the words he actually spoke -"

"Never mind that!" I argued hotly. "Tell me. At once."

He cleared his throat awkwardly. "The very words he wished me to say to you are the words: "I shall never forget you, and know that you shall never forget me, but we left it too long to marry, and knew each other too well to become husband and wife. I have seen you become deceitful and dishonest, and your mind, like your mother's towards the end, is not under your control any longer. As for me, I'm sure you know as much as you want to know."

I said nothing, and Prudence eventually entered and thanking him, hurried the young policeman out. I think I cried, and if I did, I must have cried for days at a time. I wasn't sure who for. But I think I did.

I ignored Mr. Norton's bidding initially, and sent him letters. Some, I shame to say, pleading and desperate, some irate and demanding, some nothing but an endless stream of unanswered questions. I sent them, probably once a week or more, for months – right through the spring and into summer, until they were returned to me in a single large bundle, some opened, some never having been so, with a simple scrawled note at the top saying 'Write no more'.

But after that, I did write one last time. One evening, I started writing this very story, trying to make sense of it all, and started to see and notice things that I had not before. And from that, I put aside this story, and took up my letter-writing pad and wrote something very similar to this:

*My Dear Mr Norton,*

*You'll be very pleased to hear that this will be the very last letter you ever receive from me. You were in fact quite correct: I knew as much of you as I wished to, and all the extra information upon you I have come across is of no consequence.*

*In order to help syphon some of the more outlandish and ridiculous tales about your person that have pervaded during recent times, I have just today agreed to help Scotland Yard in their enquiries into several mysterious deaths over the years, all connected - by pure coincidence, I am sure - to other widowers bearing the name of Norton. I was hesitant, but my friends Charlotte Fitzgerald and a lady by the name of Sara have convinced me, and I am now, as payment for the many kindnesses you once showed me, determined to clear your name by establishing in a court of law that there is no possible way that you were the same Mr. Norton.*

*I apologise in advance if they seek to speak to you and your wife. I know she is of a delicate disposition: from what I hear almost fully as frail as my mother was after you came to live with us. I invite you, for her sake, to consider removing to a place where Scotland Yard and its affiliations presently hold less sway. If your wife is truly possessed of a lady's constitution, might I recommend you leave the poor lady behind to lessen her suffering? The stress of travelling well might be too much for her, and I fear that the newspapers might get a hold of such stories, and when it comes to people knowing far too much for their own good, you know what might become of them - there one moment, gone the next.*

*I feel I do know you well, and therefore I am assured you will do the right thing. My apologies once again, and I wish you the very best of luck..*

*Yours sincerely*

*Etc. Etc..*

Prudence sent it by the next morning's post. But it seemed I was already too late. Only a few days later, if I had not been a believer before, all of my horrors were confirmed. I read of the death of one Mrs. Norton, whose new husband, in 'uncontrollable grief', had decided to quit the country without even staying for the funeral.

I made myself known to the family doctor. Doctor Heygate was a kindly older man, with tightly-curled hair and small eyes behind spectacles, set in a large, friendly face, who nevertheless impressed upon me that he could not divulge certain things about his patients, but I was insistent.

"If it's possible Mrs. Norton contracted anything up from her husband, there is a likelihood I was exposed to it also. Maybe even my mother, who died of old age at not even sixty! For my own health, please tell me what you know."

He relented. His twinkly eyes behind his round spectacles gazed at me from under a furrowed brow. "I don't know the disease which the young Mrs. Norton died from. It's certainly not like any disease I know, but from my own examination, I cannot say that she was poisoned in any way. Nor can I say there was anything external that caused her death. But... if I didn't know better…"

"If you didn't know better," I cut in with urgency, "you would have said that she just withered away, wouldn't you? As if she grew old in her young body suddenly, and simply withered away? How old did she look when she lay there, Dr. Heygate?"

He sighed heavily and shook his head slowly. "And yet I brought her into this world, not twenty-five years ago."

The injustice of it all was unbearable. I went to a police station but it was with great restraint that the officers who listened to me did not laugh. I tried my best to explain that lives had been claimed – my mother, this new wife's, numerous late wives before. Was there any chance of poisoning? No, I didn't think so. Where was he living now? I didn't know. To all reports, he was on the Continent, but that was all I could say. Was he receiving the full sum of these women's money on their deaths? I didn't know – he certainly wouldn't have gotten all that much from me had I died, and Sara was nothing but a devoted country girl with a bit of pluck. Yes, he'd married women with money before but that didn't seem his main goal. So, why should he kill them?

And what could I say? Even I wasn't sure what the answer was. All I knew was what happened to us before he did.

## The Mysterious Mr. Norton

There are two final parts to this story. Neither of them are a happy ending, and prompt even further questions than they provide answers. But they must be included, for they are the only things to shine any light, now that you know the story, on what it might mean, and frustratingly, neither provides any absolute answers. In fact, they both provoke yet more questions.

The first is an admission and an experience that happened only the once, but I hope it shall never be repeated. If a young lady is determined enough, she can find out certain things. Addresses, names of tenants, that kind of thing. Without incriminating myself too openly, I can tell you that exactly a year after I had met Mr. Norton, I sat in what had once been my father's study one evening, with a book in my lap and a single lamp shining on its dusty, handwritten pages. Just inside the first page were initials, indicating the owner and writer of this account. These were 'C.N.' And this, from memory is what I read inside:

*February 25th*

*A little better today. Dr. Gomm befuddled, no idea what it could be. Intimated might be in my mind as opposed to in my body. Have been reading: Juliet's brother recently had a book published about his research into mythology across different cultures. Well within myself, just uncontrollably tired. N very sweet. Hoping when fully healed, we can try for a child.*

*March 22nd*

*Several bad days. Fighting as best I can. Lost all my most recent tennis games with Charlotte - v. annoying. Racket a dead-weight in my hand yesterday. So horrid. Reading about spirits and demons takes less energy, though. N annoyed at me. Thinks he knows what is best for me, but he can overstep sometimes. Tries to monitor a lot and always talks about the expense of getting a doctor or trying something new. Never knew he had so much money! Try not to wonder, but perhaps things mightve been better had we waited longer after his wife's death. Told I make too many excuses for him.*

## The Mysterious Mr. Norton

*April 4th*

Caught sight of self in mirror. Look positively repulsive - look like my own mother, rather than my age! Hope they find what's wrong with me soon. Almost finished mythology book now. Must ask Juliet to congratulate her brother on a wonderful read.

*April 19th*

N and I not speaking. Real row last night. Said I'd become so obstinate and pigheaded, he wouldn't marry me now. Got in a few blows myself - told him I preferred mythological creatures of my book than having to deal with his moods and strange relationship with the truth. Then he struck me. Never done that before. Tried this morning to make it up with breakfast, telling me as I ate that everything he did, he did for my benefit alone, and our love. Told him, finally, I no longer believe him. If he wants divorce, can have one. Almost thought several of his hairs turned grey there & then. Said I didn't mean it. Said I did. He left room. Night now. Feeling a little stronger. Perhaps this was coming. Am not so above getting divorced. He'll be as much to blame as me. Don't think I love him any more.

The next entry was somewhat different, or at least, the handwriting, while belonging to the same person, was markedly different. It looked as if she had either written it in very dim light, or that she'd been writing so fast she hadn't even looked back over what she had written. Perhaps it was both. It took me a while to decipher, and I still could not be sure if I knew exactly what had been written:

*May 5th*

God help me. I am either doomed or have gone mad, and what is the difference? Keep going back to the book to check, wish he'd written more. Does he come from the West, where the Indians of the American plains say creatures live through us? Or perhaps just a demon. On the surface, he does everything to make me love him again, but I know too much now.

## The Mysterious Mr. Norton

*I know it's for show.*

*Oh God. I think he knows. I think he knows what I know. From the book. I was a fool. Left it open a few days ago. He snapped it shut when I came into the room. I cannot even describe the change that came over his face, like something darting behind his eyes, like something behind had seen me, like a predator seeing its prey trying to escape, just like Papa used to talk about in hunting...*

*Haven't left house for weeks. Only Charlotte has come to see me and said I looked better. I tried to get across to her that I needed help, that I had to be taken away, but she didn't understand. Why would she?*

*He's taking me away tomorrow. Says what we need is a holiday. He pretends still that all is well, but I'm so afraid. Now that I know, now that I no longer love him, I don't think he has a use for me.*

*If anyone ever reads this, for God's sake, say a prayer for me!*

I shut the book, and I did. I prayed as I quietly wept for her. There one moment, gone the next. He'd had no choice, as far as he was concerned. She obviously knew too much.

On the one side of my father's study was a great window which had no curtain – never had, for my father liked the sunshine to stream into the room when he first entered it to work. But this was the middle of the night, and the darkness that lay beyond the window was far more ominous. I found myself looking at the glass, at its almost curious, unending blackness beyond. For a fraction of a moment, as my eyes continued on the spot, the lamplight seemed to flicker. In the window, apart from the darkness and yet part of the darkness, I realised there was something moving there, out in the night. Quite impossible, on this raised floor, with nothing beyond the window, and yet...there was a face, looking in at me in silence.

My heart ceased. The eyes that I could see glared at me, wide and impossible. The face that framed them had dark hair, and the skin was… Of a colour I cannot describe for I did not know that such a colour existed in nature. Yet I knew who it was. And at the same time I knew that while he could not be there, beyond the window, he was also definitely right there.

This was all only for a mere few moments. I might have told myself my eyes, tired and weak from the lamplight, were playing hideous tricks on me, had it not been for the voice I heard, loud and clear in my head:

"No one's going to believe you. No one ever does."

I screamed and jumped from my chair. I ran out of the room in search of more light, in search of anything but that face, that voice, and Prudence, herself horrified at what might be happening, rushed up from downstairs to ask what on earth the matter was.

But by the time we had returned to the study, my hysteria beginning to subside with the brandy Prudence provided, there was, of course, no face beyond the window. No voice still audible in my head. Even the book that I convinced myself I had been reading had vanished. Despite my asking Prudence what she did with it, she faithfully pleaded all ignorance, and I never saw it again.

A number of years passed. I never did marry, but I knew it wasn't for me. Instead, I took up good works. I didn't like to think of all the evil and terrible things in the world, but I feared them and their effect less from doing what little good I myself could.

One autumn, Charlotte Fitzgerald got in touch with me. She asked me to meet her out at lunch one day in Piccadilly, which I did. She was a mother a number of times now, and it suited her. After we had dined and our empty plates transformed into cups of tea, a silence fell over us. I wondered if, as I first had when she'd asked me out, we were going to discuss that which we seemed to be deliberately avoiding. Everything else had been talked of and exhausted. Now, nothing lay before us in looking back. Except That.

"Sara has died," Charlotte told me.

"Oh no," I responded. "What happened?"

"Old age," she responded with an unreadable look.

I didn't echo her in my surprise. I simply waited.

"She had me down as her next of kin."

"Truly? What of her sister, back home?"

"Yes, truly, and I don't know. I had to go into her flat and sift through all of her things."

After a moment of staring into her teacup and taking large gulps, she reached into her handbag and drew out a newspaper clipping that was much older than anything I'd ever seen. There on the ageing black and white page, which was almost falling apart at the edges it was so old, was an artist's impression of a couple of the time.

"You must consider yourself very lucky," Charlotte said. There was quite obviously a lot of pain for her on this subject: first Clara whom she did not know needed help, now Sara, nearly me. She started to get ready to leave, even with the remnants in her teacup still warm. "You have been able to make a life beyond him. Sara was never so lucky."

The newspaper couple were obviously of some standing in society given their mode of dress, and an entire page was dedicated to the apparently newly betrothed man and woman. The man looked distinctly familiar.

"Where did you get this?"

"It was in Sara's rooms, among all her things." She paused and sighed. "You should have seen it. It was like a shrine to him. Things like this. Articles across the years. Photographs – no idea how she got them. She never gave him up. Not truly. It wasn't until I walked into those empty rooms of hers that I saw and understood. Somewhere, deep within her, I'm quite sure that even though she knew what he was, better than any of us ever will, she was convinced that someday, he would return to her. Perhaps she even did me the favour of helping you simply to put him off another marriage."

"He was the love of her life," I noted. How many years had she not only given away to his strange powers, but given away purely in loving him? What kind of life had their crossed paths created for her?

"You can add her to his list," Charlotte sneered, rising and putting her coat about her in that elegant, glamorous way that only Charlotte could. "What's the date today?"

"30th."

"The full date," she snapped.

"Er... the 30th of October, 1931."

"Just so," she said, and leant forward, her hand over mine. "I know that you and I wanted answers. Now, my dear, you should simply be happy and count yourself very lucky that you will never have them."

She swept from the place. It was rather queer. I turned back to the newspaper page. There he was, still looking, according to the artist, as if he were just approaching his early forties, sprightly and youthful with dark hair, and those eyes with pupils one could not quite see.

I skimmed the words on the page beneath the picture: 'Lord and Lady Bridlehurst announce the engagement of their daughter Annabella to Baron Norton. The date given is understood to be Midsummer, 1782.'

## The Audience Member

She had come to my show!

There really was no mistaking her. There she was on the front row, in the coat she kept for best, watching me from the audience. She turned and spoke to the lady next to her. I couldn't tell, from my own concentration and the music what it was she said, but her grin was wide and proud and knowing what I knew of my mother, her words were probably going to be something along the lines of: "That's my daughter, you know."

A few years after my daughter Abigail's birth, I was ready to take to the stage again. I had been away from it for what certainly felt like a long time, and was rather nervous. The first job we set up was coincidentally not too far from my hometown, possibly an hour's drive away from where my mother still lived. I was excited about this comeback performance, and chose for it a beautiful black ball-gown that shimmered in the light, and in order for it to look truly spectacular, I had my hair done up by a local hairdresser, in a large elegant bun. Abigail's eyes shone as she saw me at the hotel, ready to leave, for she hadn't seen me quite so elegantly dressed before. To her, it was usually jeans, shirts and maybe a large dress to help me forget the lumps and bumps she had given me that had taken so long to shake off. Now, for the first time, she might see me as I used to see my mother in my mind's eye. As something more than simply 'Mummy'. As a creature with a life that went beyond their tiny, important world.

Though I did wish my tiny world had been a little more important to my mother at times.

Just as we were about to go, the hotel room phone rang and Arnold, still working his way into his jacket, answered it.

"Hello?" He blinked a couple of times and moved the receiver a little. "Hello?" he said again. I looked up and watched him wait for a reply. After a moment, he bemusedly put the receiver down.

"Could be from the venue," I suggested, handing Abigail to her minder. "All that internal and external ringing to sort out."

"Yes," Arnold mumbled, and we went out to the car. The snow had started falling again and even though the hall wasn't all that far, I could hardly walk there in my dress and high heels. We parked in our designated spot and Arnold didn't get out at once. "...You know I... I think that might have been your mother trying to get through to us."

"Really?... Why, did you hear her say something?"

"No," Arnold replied, as if he were having a quiet argument within himself. "It might not have been her. She'd have to have the number for our hotel, know which one we were staying at..."

"Cedric might have told her," I said quietly. "What makes you think it might have been her?"

Arnold shrugged and opened his door. "I'm not sure. It was just a feeling."

And I don't know why, but I thought he was probably right.

For the first few years of my married life, I heard not a thing from my mother. She did not come to my wedding. Every year, a Christmas card would land on the mat, or perhaps a birthday card, but nothing personal was written therein. Around the time we were expecting Abigail, the phone calls started. Arnold was always the one to answer the phone if I was playing; I did not want to be distracted. She'd ask curtly to speak to me, and as I had told him to, Arnold asked her to leave a message instead. Invariably, she left no message, swore at him, and put the phone down.

My mother hadn't wanted me to marry Arnold. She warned me that if we had children, they'd turn out similarly – lazy and with a predisposition to be unkempt. Whatever my mother saw in him that was to his deficit, I either couldn't see it, or it didn't matter. Not long after my twenty-fifth birthday, and my first slew of professional performances, Arnold proposed.

## The Audience Member

I was very, very happy.

My mother, on the other hand, was furious.

"You don't think she'd come tonight, do you?" I said to Arnold's reflection in the dressing room.

"I don't know," he responded amiably. Why had I even asked him? Hortense never got to know him very well, so he in turn, only knew much of her from me, and I had hardly spoken of her over the years.

Several times I tried to apply my lipstick, but kept smudging it. Each time made me more minutely angry.

"Would it be terrible if she came?" Arnold asked.

I shrugged. I didn't mean the shrug.

"You probably won't even know she's there, if she does come," he added gently.

"Probably not."

"Do you want me to go and check the tickets list?"

"No, thank you."

"What shall I do?"

I looked at him properly. This was the reason I had married him. Full of nice ideas of how to support me. My biggest musical fan, absolutely. Yet always ready to be told what would help, in order to do his best for me.

I'd never been able to tell my mother what I needed.

I felt myself begin to smile. "I think you should enjoy the evening," I replied.

His own grin was fond and charming. I'd never stood a chance. "You'll be absolutely fine. I've no doubt this will be a comeback to remember."

He stopped at the dressing room door. He had a slightly annoying habit of pausing, as he had in the car for the drive over, when he wanted to ask and know something, but wasn't sure how it would be received. Perhaps he was always wary that there was a chance I might someday explode. It was in the blood, after all, that was probably his background concern.

"Do you blame me?" he asked.

I stood looking in the mirror at his turned face. "No," I said quietly and honestly. "You didn't do this. She did."

Reassured at least some way, he opened the dressing room door and went out.

For a few moments, I let myself think of it. That horrible last day I'd seen her in the flesh, years previously. I normally tried to pack those memories away, and stack other, happy memories on top. Just for now, though, I let the images come.

I had inherited from her one particular thing: my mother was a great lover of music. She'd not been particularly wealthy when younger and so hadn't learnt an instrument. Almost as if in compensation, she was adamant I learn, and I stick to something classical. I would have liked the violin, but in the end, she plumped for the somewhat more affordable piano, and my lessons began when I was five. It was soon obvious to my tutor and mother that I had some talent. The fact that I was good at something grew on me, and by the time I was twelve, I was practising two hours a day, around school time and homework. By the time I was sixteen, I had decided to go to a conservatoire, and begin a career as a musician. This being the one thing we seemed to bond over, my mother was thrilled.

She'd come to see me while I was away studying, just after I turned nineteen. Out of the blue, she called me early one morning to say she'd be there by the afternoon, and then, there she was. This was completely typical of her. Yet what wasn't was that she was very calm when she arrived. None of the usual excessive busy-ness that I had, to an extent, also inherited. In comparison to her normal humours, she was practically serene. She smiled and embraced me when we met, asked me all the questions a parent will ask of a child who has left home, but of course, she never seemed bothered with before; then she sat with me over a cup of tea in my little student flat. She was smiling so much, and didn't talk excessively or complain or fill in the silences as we sat talking. She told me that she knew I was going to make a fabulous career of my music. She'd woken up that morning, completely convinced, having had a dream of me onstage in a dark, sequinned, cocktail gown, playing on a grand piano to thousands of people, crying a little and saying to the bemused lady next to her 'That's my daughter, you know.'

I had worried whether she believed in me or not. But it seemed she did. The one lovely thing ongoing about our relationship was that she never once wavered in her belief that I was going to be a successful pianist.

But on the whole, she was too unpredictable. Our relationship was far too based on what her moods in the moment were. So I wouldn't go back to those days. Not now. Not with a little one to think of as well.

The concert hall had once been something else, but had been claimed in the name of classical music and larger scale local productions for some time. Its mock Victorian facade with royal boxes lining the edges of the stage, was beautifully offset by row upon row of scarlet seats. Not that by the time I'd taken to the stage, I could do any more than vaguely take in this impressive beauty.

There was but one seat left in the whole house, towards the front. As all things were, it was something of a formal affair, and I entered, bowed and took to the piano.

Towards the end of the first piece, quite oddly, I felt compelled to look, just briefly, into the audience. And in the same seat that had been empty before, now sat my mother.

She grinned up at me, as if to apologise for her lateness, but she was, in fact, grinning from ear to ear. It was a shock to see her. She'd changed a little. Even from here, I could tell there was an age about her I hadn't noticed before, and I almost went wrong with my fingering a few moments after noticing her.

Throughout the show, at opportune moments, I cast glances towards her, trying to make it appear as if I didn't see her. She sat in the seat near the front, her face practically alight with pride, smiling the whole way through. She had brought herself possibly an hour out in the car to come and see me. And when I realised this, I wanted to cry. I wanted the performance to end quicker, so that I could go and embrace her afterwards, and see if she would come back with us to the hotel, and briefly meet her granddaughter at last.

The performance finished, and I took my bow, then swept from the stage. She was probably waiting for me by the stage door even now, or maybe even attempting to talk her way into the dressing room.

Backstage, Arnold was ready to hug me. "Is my mother back here?" I asked.

"Your mother?" he said, sounding surprised. "No! Was she in the audience?"

## The Audience Member

"Yes, I saw her," I told him, and realised I was smiling.

We waited a few minutes as people started to file out, but she didn't make an appearance. "Are you sure it was her?" Arnold probed.

"I'm certain of it," I said. I recalled the picture of her I had in my mind. Yes, of course it had been her. Hadn't it? Or had I been thinking about the possibility of her coming so hard, that I was suggestible? Since when had I ever been able to tell anyone in the audience with those lights shining so brightly from the Gods? "I know it was..."

Arnold nodded. He was trying to stay positive, at least on the surface, but we both knew it wasn't like her.

"If it was her," Arnold said as we walked back to the car, "she was probably too embarrassed to actually come and speak to you. It has been a long time after all.... She might've called by the morning, you never know."

But I'd given up hope, and my bent head quieted him as we drove back to the hotel.

"Do you want to talk about it?" Arnold asked as we lay in bed, hushed voices to keep from waking Abigail.

"I don't know."

I did and I didn't. I loved my mother, but she was my shame as well.

"Tell me what you're thinking of," Arnold whispered. "Just talk, if you need to."

I did and I didn't. Arnold had seen her at what was, in all our minds, the worst.

After I had gotten engaged to Arnold, the late night phone calls started. My mother called me, sometimes drunk, sometimes just in a viciously bad mood. Arnold was going to ruin me. I was throwing my life away. What was she going to do? Since my father had left, she had Cedric and I. What was she going to do? Did I even care?

I put up with them for a few weeks. Then I stopped answering the phone after it got to a certain time. The date of our engagement party grew close and I even thought of uninviting her, but at the time, I thought that was the worst thing I could possibly do. I'd been wrong.

She turned up already drunk, having driven herself there. People around her started looking uneasy fairly quickly. She'd told several people

## The Audience Member

I probably had a drug problem, having lost weight in the lead up to the wedding. When she was refused service at the bar, she started screaming. Shouting. Every swear word imaginable came out of her mouth. It was different to have her like this, in front of other people. I thought it was the Her that that only Cedric and I saw, but apparently, when she was angry and hurt over nothing enough, she didn't care in the end who saw her.

I'd dragged her to one side and said if she carried on, she was not only going to be thrown out, but wouldn't be coming to the wedding.

She barked at me. She wasn't coming to the wedding anyway. Why bother coming? I'd only get divorced in a few years. Then I'd be the one needing my children to look after me, and it would be everything I deserved if they never even came to visit me, and never thought of looking after me, and went off to live and have babies with never a care for me.

"Mum," I had said, trying to get some sense into her. "This – is not my fault. This is yours."

And she hit me across the face, so hard that I felt the sting and everyone seemed to gasp. Arnold had managed to manhandle her out of the building with the help of a few others. I could still hear her shouting and doing God knew what else as friends darted about me with ice cubes and serviettes trying to bring down the redness on my face.

"She did go too far," I mumbled quietly.

"From everything you've told me, she went too far many times. That just happened to be the time that mattered most."

"What should I do?"

Arnold kissed my temple. "Sleep on it now. You'll know better what to do in the morning."

It was not yet seven a.m. when the hotel phone rang. Slightly early for a social call, but then it might have been someone in the hotel looking for us, so for the first time in many years, I answered the phone myself.

"Hello?"

"Lydia?" said a hollow voice at the other end.

"Cedric," said I. "Bit early, isn't it? What's the matter?"

There was a long pause. "Lyddie, I've got some rather bad news. Are you sitting down?"

I sat up in bed. "What is it?"

"Did you have a show last night?"

"Yes. Yes, I did." I gave him the name of the hall where I performed.

"That explains it," he muttered.

"Explains what, for god's sake?"

"Lyddie... Mum died last night."

I couldn't bring myself to break the silence for possibly near half a minute. "Are you there?" I heard him check.

"She... she died?"

Arnold stirred, and sat up beside me.

"I'm sorry to tell you like this. Her car was found about two hundred yards from a phone booth. When they got to the phone booth..."

I tried to keep the invading, horrible images from my mind. "What happened?"

"Heart attack, they think," Cedric said, his voice sounding suddenly distant in its own way. "She had the phone in one hand and she was just lying on the ground. Looks like she had some kind of car trouble along her route and went to call for help or something and maybe the stress of it... Anyway, that's as much as we can tell. And Lyddie... she had a ticket for a show at that place in her coat pocket. She hadn't told me anything about it, but... I thought you ought to know."

The tears started to well up at the bottom of my eyes. "Cedric, she'd just come from my concert!" And I could barely get the words out.

Cedric waited until the heaving gulps of air in my disbelief and sudden sense of loss had begun to subside. "Are... are you sure, Lyddie? I don't think she could have been at your concert."

"She was in a seat near the front row. I thought she'd stop behind to talk to us."

"No, Lyddie, I don't think that she made it to your show. Her ticket was intact – it hadn't been torn or anything. I – saw it myself you see."

The horror of it dawned on me, but the other fact made no sense. "She was definitely there. I saw her. I was unsure, but -"

"I really don't think that can be right, Lyddie," he said, in his tone that was so very like Daddy's – matter-of-fact but rather sure of himself. "The police called me at eleven, but she'd been lying there where she was for maybe four hours?"

That was impossible, I thought. Two hours before that time, she'd still have been sitting watching me play, where I'd seen her.

"She'd been dead for four hours?" I echoed.

"Yes," Cedric went on. "'She was gone before you'd even played a note."

It was all fairly easily explained after the shock had worn off. After the coroner confirmed that my mother had indeed died around the seven o'clock mark in the evening, before my show began, I started to see the reality of it all. I had been thinking of my mother beforehand, given the strange phone call. I was highly nervous. There probably had been a woman, a latecomer, with a resemblance to my mother sitting in the seat that I had originally thought was empty. Maybe I had so wanted it to be her, I convinced myself that it was. There was possibly even a certain amount of guilt on my part that went into my illusion. I tried not to think too much about it, for the whole thing was quite awful, and now, of course, I'd never be able to introduce my mother to my daughter, or see if there was anything at all left of us to salvage.

Cedric and I went to my mother's house some time later to get her affairs in order. There were a great many things we had to decide to sell, keep or put into storage. It would not be an easy task, but it had to be done. I decided to stay at a hotel instead of the house. I didn't like the thought of staying there, somehow.

The lady behind the hotel's front desk seemed to look at me as if she were trying to place me and on learning my name, realised that she'd seen me perform at that same concert months before.

"It was a wonderful show," she congratulated me. "You're from 'round here, aren't you? Your family must be very proud."

"Thank you," I said demurely. "I hope my mother would have been. She would have loved to see me that night."

"Oh she really enjoyed it," said the lady with enthusiasm, not seeing the colour drain from my face. "She was sitting next to me. Of course, I didn't know it was her at first, but after the first piece, she turned to me and was so proud, she said: 'That's my daughter, you know'."

## The Horse, After Midnight

"Well," said Robert, pulling the large, heavy curtains back across the ageing windows of the hall, obscuring the view of the outside world. "That rather settles it. It's appalling out there. There will definitely be no going home this evening for any of us. The rain is too bad and this storm seems to just be beginning, so I doubt it shall let up for at least a few hours."

The other gentlemen of the room were in agreement, and were not put out by this announcement. The storm outside had slowly been getting nearer and louder over the course of the evening as the four of them had dined together, played cards and backgammon, drank and then pulled closer to the fireside as they smoked side by side, and now the sound of the wind and rain lashing at the ancient beams of the country manor house was near impossible to ignore.

"I thought as much," said Arthur, the eldest of the four of them. "Our apologies, Edgar," he addressed the youngest of them, "but it seems you must play host overnight as well as this evening."

"My dear chaps!" Edgar, the youngest in whose home they sat, declared, with nothing short of a delighted grin across his young, pleasant face. "No need for apologies! In honesty, it was my hope there'd be an excuse for you to stay a little longer. I even planned for it, and there are beds made ready for you all."

There had been little thought that any of the three guests might go home tonight anyway. The nearest, Marsden, lived a whole hour away by carriage, and it was rather after ten o'clock by now. Even had the weather been good, it was highly likely the guests would have remained.

These four gentlemen sitting in front of the fire, their chairs turned towards the hearth and away from the table, had been friends for a great long while now, though this was possibly the first time that they had sat about in each other's company in so deliberate yet relaxed a fashion. Arthur, the eldest, had in fact been a friend of Edgar's late father and occasionally would come to see him, keeping a parochial eye on him for the sake of his departed friend. He was about 40, or so he claimed, though the middle two were certain that he was nearer 45. The middle two were young men in their twenties, Robert and Marsden, both still as yet unmarried, their own fathers having been friends with Edgar's father, and despite their host himself only just having turned 18, got along very well with him. The house in which they were currently sheltering from the storm was Edgar's ancestral home, in which his family had reputedly lived since before Henry VIII. Supper now long over and backgammon no longer holding its initial allure, the group debated the best way to keep themselves entertained. All four of them were still quite wakeful and none but Marsden had the slightest inclination to go to bed yet.

"Come along Arthur," Edgar said presently in his customary good natured if slightly blustery way. "You must know a good one!"

The oldest of them looked up, as if he had missed a great part of some conversation. "A good what?" he asked.

"Why a ghost story of course!" said Edgar.

"Ghost stories?" Robert echoed, taking out his pipe. "Are we at that point in the evening already?"

"I don't know any ghost stories," Arthur answered quickly. Almost, one might have said, a little too quickly.

"Oh dear," Marsden said with a sudden nervous look about his face. "I feel I'm terrible when it comes to ghost stories. I could tell one if I had the nerve to, but it's one of the few things that I find utterly terrifying."

"Never mind that," Edgar grinned. "You have the rest of us here and besides, Arthur knows a good one, don't you Arthur?"

Arthur stared at his young host for a few seconds before finally answering: "I suppose I know one. I never really thought it a thing for public consumption."

## The Horse, After Midnight

"Hang it all, man, we're not the public," said Edgar in great disgust. "My father said you knew a very good one about this very place. You've dodged me for years when I've asked you, but now you have a full audience, I dare say you cannot escape it any longer."

Arthur again was silent for a little while, pretending to minutely examine his pipe. "It isn't that good."

"I knew it!" Edgar sang, adjusting his chair so that it faced Arthur.

"Good gracious. Did it really take place here?" Marsden asked. He was trying his best to hide the slight tremor that had already crept into his voice, but the others merely ignored it out of kindness.

"It's just a story, Marsden," Robert put in helpfully.

At this point everyone might have expected Arthur, not only the eldest but undoubtedly the most sensible and wise of the four of them, to echo Robert's thoughts. That what he was about to relate was indeed nothing but a story. But for his silence and the suddenly unfamiliar look in his eye, they might have gone on waiting for some while.

"Well," Arthur began with a heavy sigh, "It was of course a long time ago now. And yes, Marsden, it did take place here. It was actually pretty similar to the way it is now, when it started. Not stormy or raining cats and dogs, you understand. I mean it was the latter part of the year. Summer: very much a distant memory. Latter end of October if I remember rightly."

"Yes, yes, yes," Edgar cut in impatiently, "we understand the setting, tell us the story itself!"

It would be prudent at this point in the narrative to tell the reader or listener a little more about Edgar's ancestral home. It was a good, solid, Tudor build, long and winding in places, lavish without necessity in others, and with many rooms that, with the passage of time, had been rendered all but useless, given their original purpose. Many such rooms had been turned into guest bedrooms, or, for their separation from other rooms that served a similar purpose, were locked and left to gather dust. Edgar occasionally remarked that despite nearing his 20th year, he had likely only been in half the rooms in his house. As Arthur began to talk, he could not have asked for a more perfect setting to tell his ghost story, with the breezes of history whipping their way through cracks in doors, and the storm raging fit to turn into a full gale sounding all about them.

"I was a young man at the time. possibly even of Edgar's age. I had not long met Edgar's father Hector…"

"Hold on," Robert interrupted, knocking his pipe more out of habit than need. "Do you mean to say this happened to you? This story, to you personally?"

Arthur pushed his lips together in an unhappy smile. "I could not confidently account for any of it otherwise," he supplied.

Each of his three listeners leant forward towards him without even realising it.

Arthur spent the first minutes after announcing this reminiscing, as one can begin to do at his time of life, and his talk touched briefly on how he and Hector, Edgar's father, had met, their instant friendship and how delighted Arthur had been to be invited for the first time to his home. The other young men knew most of these peripheral circumstances, but supportively kept quiet and attentive while their storyteller got into the spirit of the thing.

"...It was the very first night of my stay here, and the two of us – Hector and I – sat alone together in this very room, just as we do now: after supper and all the servants long gone to bed. I don't recall there being a storm. In fact, I'm quite sure there could not have been or else I never would have heard it."

Marsden shifted uncomfortably in his chair.

"Hector didn't believe in ghosts or anything like that, I don't think. He didn't even mean to tell me anything like a ghost story. It was simply late at night and the two of us were sharing stories with each other of our families, our upbringing, and the strange tales that establish themselves in every family."

All the other young men smiled or nodded slowly to themselves.

"Hector's was this: In the 17th century, the plague was rife and particularly pernicious in this part of the country. It was not quite so bad in these out-of-the-way places as it might be in London for example, because then, just as now, it's plausible there would be no need or opportunity for you to see anyone outside of your household or the locality for some great while. The patriarch here – Edgar's ancestor, I should say – was by this time an elderly man and had by all accounts lived for longer than anyone had expected him to, but there was something rather wrong with him. In his advancing years he had become increasingly paranoid and at times, very irrational. Hector informed me that once, this patriarch had held his own daughter-in-law by the throat and leant her back over the gallery railings there -" here he pointed to part of the hall high up in the wall, where indeed a long wooden banister served as a railing around the gallery, "because he had it in his mind that she was his older sister who had tormented him in childhood, but had died decades before. This was apparently not even the worst of what he had done prior to the story he told me, but he omitted these details."

"I say!" Edgar declared with quite out-of-place cheerfulness. "You are doing me great favour this evening, Arthur, telling me all these fascinating things about my family I haven't the foggiest about! Do go on."

The other three men smiled, as seeing it in such a way was very much Edgar's characteristic way of looking at things.

"Well," Arthur continued with another sigh, "as I have said, this story he told me was not even the worst thing that the old man did. Hector said he didn't quite believe it before he told it me. You see, when news of the plague reached them here, the old man became quite obsessed with it. The family tried to leave and go into seclusion somewhere, but the old man refused to go, and what was more, he insisted his eldest grandson stay behind to watch over things in everyone else's absence, and the young man was only too happy to oblige…" Here Arthur paused. "If you wanted to know what the grandson, this young man looked like, he's over there."

It was a half-hearted gesture, but all three pairs of eyes keenly followed where Arthur pointed with his pipe, to the opposite end of the room. Edgar, entertained and newly obsessed with this subject, snatched at a nearby candlestick and marched across the hall, holding it aloft until Arthur nodded.

The portrait was of a young man, barely out of his boyhood. The other three could almost instantly see the family look between he and Edgar, though while Edgar might have been described by some as handsome, the only word to describe this boy was beautiful, with large eyes and a slim face. "I've caught myself more than once standing before that very portrait," Arthur said dreamily. "I hope the artist was well paid, for it is a great likeness."

The full effect of these words took a few moments for the rest of the party to understand.

"What!" Robert was the first to say. "But he – I mean - When did - Do you mean to say you - ?"

"Not at first," Arthur replied. "But then, I'm getting ahead of myself…

"The rest of the family eventually agreed and left, the old man and the grandson staying behind. The mother of the young man wrote to him often, asking him for word on how he and his grandfather were. He wrote back for a little while, but as time went on, his letters grew less and less legible, less coherent. Then the grandfather wrote to the family and said that his grandson had gotten the plague.

"The young man's mother, naturally, rushed back to tend to her son, but of course, took days to get here. When she arrived, the old man said the boy had left very suddenly one night with never an explanation, and hadn't been back since. Not being able to rely on the old man's memory, the mother tried to find out when he had left, if he'd said where he was going, but no one seemed to know anything at all. He'd simply – gone."

"What, he absconded entirely?" Marsden posed.

"What a queer thing to do," Robert noted, "especially if you do have the plague."

"Well, the poor chap might've been brain-addled, mightn't he?" Edgar proposed, thumping the candlestick back in its place. "Look here, though, Arthur, this doesn't sound like much of a ghost story to me, rather than a bit of family shame I didn't know about."

"Do be patient, Edgar," Arthur breathed. There was a tone to his speech that made each of his listeners very still and attentive very quickly. "Now I will say that I was tired, in an unfamiliar place, desperate to make my own good impression upon Hector as a man I -" he faltered. All the other three had quietly come to their own conclusions about why Arthur had reached his age and never married, but even the occasionally-brash Edgar did not break into what he had imagined Arthur was going to say. "A man I - wished to maintain a good opinion of me," Arthur finished, and that which was so intricate a part of him remained undisclosed to his friends. "But you see, it was at this point that I heard the horse."

The storm railed. The audience didn't move, and neither did Arthur for a moment or two.

"I wasn't sure at first. It must have been by this time after midnight but not quite 2 o'clock in the morning. So when I first heard what sounded like

## The Horse, After Midnight

a horse being taken from its stable under protest, I didn't mention it to Hector. Then the thing grew louder, as if it all was just happening outside that window there, but the curtains were drawn, just as they are now. Then I heard a man's voice. He was shouting: nothing in words, but rather he was simply calling as if angry, making a noise enough to frighten any animal. Frightened me with the odd, inhuman guttural noise, and so loud. I heard the horse become yet more distressed, such heartbreaking sounds, and then its hooves against the drive, and its appalling shrill cry as it tore away from here.

"I looked at Hector in the fire light and declared something like: "What on earth is all the commotion? Has that man lost his wits?" But I could tell from the way Hector looked back at me that he did not know of what I spoke. Perhaps this was a common occurrence of something I did not understand, but then surely he would have offered me an explanation so as not to alarm me. I asked him what on earth that awful treatment of the animal was, yet his answer was to simply ask me what I meant. 'The horse', I must have said, 'that dreadful business outside with the horse. What else should I mean? You naturally heard it.' He looked at me now as if I was quite out of my wits, but in his good nature, he strode to the window, parted the curtains and we looked out into the darkness. I was quite befuddled to see nothing at all there: no torches, no man, no sign of a horse, and no sound of either. I told him exactly as I had heard it, yet at this he declared that indeed it was far past any decent hour to be out of bed, and we should retire immediately.

"I was so embarrassed about it, and so confused that I simply bid Hector goodnight and took myself to bed. I didn't hear it for the rest of the night, though I stayed up for a good while after. I retained the sounds in my mind, as I do now. I could almost envision the horse, taken against its will from its stable, then taunted horribly. Then that horrible voice, guttural and throaty and making no sense whatever, vicious to the ear. How could I have conjured this into my brain?

"I mentioned it to neither Hector nor anyone else the following day. I did not wish his thus far good opinion of me to waver. By midday, I had in fact quite put it from my mind that anything extraordinary had happened the night before, and for most of that day, Hector indulged me by showing me the grounds and telling me even more history of the place."

"Nevermind history," Edgar said suddenly. Marsden visibly moved in his chair at this interjection. "Back to these horse sounds in the night!"

For the first time in a while, Arthur smiled somewhat. "There's the first part of the mystery, I suppose. For while I am quite convinced that I heard them, I never heard them again. Not during that particular visit nor at any other time, Not to this very evening."

"Oh," said Edgar, his posture suddenly crumpling with disappointment. "You don't mean to say that that is the story in its entirety? I say, it really isn't very good."

"No no no," Arthur said quickly, but seemingly not in a hurry to continue. "No, I fear there is more…"

Again Arthur was quiet for some moments and his eyes drifted across the hall to the dim portrait. "Nothing happened for the rest of my first visit here, or else I might never have come back at all. Hector wrote and invited me again in spring, and so I came. As the cab came up the drive, I could see Hector standing on the bottom of the steps, having heard the horses' approach, waiting for me."

"By Jove, yes," Edgar declared, with both fondness and the touch of gravity and his voice. "The number of times that his sharp ears had him knowing the guests would be arriving even before they knew."

"Quite," Arthur agreed. "When I caught sight of him on the steps, however, my eyes did not rest with him. My attention was caught by someone standing at a window, a guest, also watching my arrival. Hector always had people staying. I got out of the carriage and embraced Hector, my head fully over his shoulder and I was turned towards the house. It was only now that I glanced up again towards the window and I saw this guest's face. I knew somehow it was familiar, but I could not place it. The figure looked straight down at me, gave a sort of smile, then turned and walked away, so I could not see him. Hector bustled me inside and we sat down to some food together. It was then that I looked up and got the shock. For the briefest of moments, I thought the young man at the window was in the room with us, but instead it was simply the portrait you see there."

Silence reigned supreme among the three other listeners, as if the storm itself was forgotten. Even Robert's pipe was forgotten and all that might have been heard in the room was Marsden, chewing at his nails.

"I asked Hector who else of his family was in the house at this time, only to have him say that the rest of them were all on the continent, and that the only servants at his disposal were those that were in the room with us at that time. I shame to say that I suddenly became quite ill, and it took me a good full hour to recover. Hector, always the wonderful host, had me put to bed until I overcame it, though I was so embarrassed as it was so obviously not fever or malady, but rather that I had simply fainted. Eventually of course I came around, and Hector suggested some fresh air might do me good.

"He had me sit in that awful chair with wheels that he occasionally pushed his own mother about in when she got older, and we took in the gardens. But you see, here is where it got quite awful. It was not dark at all, we had only really just had luncheon, and yet as Hector slowly progressed with me past trees and hedgerows, out of the corner of my eye, I saw that same figure of the young man again. He might've been at the other end of the gardens one moment, then the next...much closer, almost as if he were playing some macabre form of hide and seek with me. I became quite convinced that just as on my visit before, Hector was oblivious to what was going on. I was still not quite certain that he wasn't simply playing some elaborate and terrible prank on me, and so on several occasions I directed his attention to exactly where I saw the young man. His disposition was calm, and one can tell when someone is trying their best to keep up a prank, but he was not. I knew that I could see what he could not, which was the figure of this otherwise invisible young man."

"I say," Edgar interrupted yet again, which was becoming a habit and, if you had asked the other two, rather spoiling the effect of the story, though Marsden might not have minded. "You must have been asking yourself questions, old man. This young buck had gone away long before, hadn't he? If he was, as I'm sure by this point, long dead, and he is your ghost, why exactly was he haunting the family grounds?"

"I'm coming to that," Arthur replied as patiently as he might, and again the rest of the party fell silent in anticipation.

"He did not appear to me all the time, I hasten to add. I stayed with Hector for a fortnight, and there were several days where he did not appear at all. On these days, it was easy to tell myself that it was all mere trickery of the mind. But on the times that I saw it, I knew it could be no such thing. I tried on occasion to ignore it. Once, I was sitting next to Hector, almost in exactly the place Marsden and Robert are now -

"Oh God," Marsden said quietly, then swallowed loudly.

"And I had been ignoring the thing all day. When I looked towards Hector, I saw the young man, very still, peering down at me from the gallery. I continued to ignore him. When I looked again, he was on this floor, near his own portrait over there. I told myself it could not be and did not look again for some minutes. Then when Hector arrested my attention to ask me if I was wakeful or not, I looked up and saw him, standing next to Hector, his eyes on me."

The sound of the storm was still raging but even as Arthur dropped his voice, his listeners were with him.

"And each night I kept hearing the same thing. The first night it was a simple knock, though a very soft one. I thought that one of the servants had come to my door to ask if I wanted anything, and I called through that I was quite alright. A moment, and then the knock came again. I called again that I was quite alright and there was nothing I needed. Even fainter on the 3rd time I became convinced it was not the servants, but perhaps it might be Hector, and so I got up and went to the door. There was, as you might be able to guess, no one on the other side. Nothing but the darkness of the corridor. And then I heard it again, with the door wide open. With the appearances I had been seeing, I was unsettled to say the least. It had only ever appeared to me before. It had never spoken and I had never heard an accompanying sound, so I attempted to tell myself that the two were unconnected. I heard it a fifth time. It was still faint, but I realised now with better attention that it was not a quiet, near knock of propriety. Instead it was rather a distant knock of urgency, but from whence it came, I could not fathom and even knowing the house a little, I could not imagine who it might be, whether it was one room or several rooms away or if such a knock had a meaning ascribed the household I didn't know. I called out 'hello' several times but was never answered. There would simply be another short silence, followed by a knock. I declared aloud, to Hector, that I had had enough of these terrible, unfriendly games of his, and marched to his room to get some kind of revenge, I suppose. I was able to convince myself that it was all an elaborate ruse as I went down the corridor, only to find his door unlatched and he within, sound asleep in bed! I cannot tell you quite how horrified and very alone I felt at that time."

"I made my way back towards my bedroom, with only candlelight to guide me. All the servants were taking themselves to bed or were indeed already asleep. Each room I passed through, to a different degree or at a different volume, I heard the knocking, more urgent than before. Had the elaborate seances been quite in fashion then as they are now, I might have tried to explain it away that perhaps the servants were making fun of me, or trying to make a Believer of me to make an impression upon Hector, but deep in my heart I knew then as I know it now that was not the case.

"I heard the knocking every night. I would be given at most perhaps an hour in bed wherein I might sleep, but following this, the sound was relentless all night until a little before dawn. At times, they even lulled me into a false sense of security and I would think they had stopped, and begin to sleep, only to be woken not half an hour later, and I got very little good rest.

"After perhaps a week, Hector remarked at table that I did not look very well, and suggested it might be better we go to my house instead, or even into town if the air there suited me better. But I did not wish to appear weak in front of him. I told him I had several things on my mind and that kept me awake at night. I did not tell him about the knocking. I knew it was just the same as the appearances. He saw and heard nothing. I was alone in the haunting."

Robert pushed back against Marsden who, whether he was aware of it or not, was fully leaning against his friend as if for comfort.

"Finally on what was to be my second to last day, I brought Hector back to my room just as night was falling. We passed some time there, though Hector thought it odd. Finally, I heard the first knock. I looked at Hector. He heard nothing. I asked him if he was aware of anything, what he could hear. Remember that these were faint knocks anyway. He listened very keenly for some time but told me he could hear nothing apart from ourselves speaking. He had not failed to notice that my behaviour had grown increasingly odd since my arrival and asked me if..." He took a breath, not in fear, but rather as if some deep emotion were mixed with that fear, "if anything he had done or perhaps that we were not as great friends as I had hoped we would become had affected me. I wished I had answered him more delicately, for his observation and love, but I said that I

## The Horse, After Midnight

had expected nothing, and no, it was nothing he had done. The knocking came again. I begged if he could hear anything at all. He was quite worried, and insisted that first thing in the morning, he would send for the doctor. I told him that if only I could find out what was happening, I felt certain I would be well again and would he undertake anything that might help me reach that end? He, as true a friend as any man could ever ask for -" here the passion was unmistakable in Arthur's voice, "said that he would do whatever it took within good reason to ensure my health. So I picked up a candlestick and with him at my side and some boldness along with us, I started to trace the source of the knocking."

Arthur was here quiet for some little time. The others dared not interrupt him now.

"It took us some time before we came to where, to me the knocking sounded quite loud, as if someone were knocking upon a wooden wall quite close. I asked Hector now if he could hear anything. It was almost maddening that he could hear not a single thing, and I daresay he was beginning to believe I must be quite mad. At least now, though, I knew I was close. It struck me in a terrible way that while we had wandered through the house, I had not all evening seen the image of the young man that occasionally appeared to me and my thoughts flew to him. My mind was working keenly and without even arranging my words in a subtle or proper way, I turned on my host and said:

"Hector, is there anything that you have not yet told me which might be a sort of...ghost story, of anything that has taken place in his house?'

"He laughed but almost as if to make light of a horrible situation. He said that one or two of the servants, in his own living memory, had left their employ quite suddenly because of 'disturbances' of an unfathomable nature. One local woman of good reputation had left the house in hysterics, claiming that a young golden-haired man followed her wherever she went. I asked him plainly if there was anything else pertaining to this that I should need to know. He thought for a moment and seemed during this time to become almost pale. With the knocking that he could not hear, as if it were only a foot away from me, he said that there was something among the locals that he had overheard when he was a boy, about his house. That on some nights, people would see a horse run through the village as if scared out of its wits, riderless. There was also talk in the village of two workmen who had undertaken some work in the house for which they were handsomely paid, but they refused to speak of it, or to ever come and work at the house again.

"With that, I launched myself at the very spot from whence the knocking sound came. Hector cried out, asking me if I were in my senses, but I knew he could not hear what I could. And so, I kept at it for several minutes, until parts of me bled and some of the servants had even come forth from bed, but there beyond the crumbling wall was a doorway. The door itself had long rotted, and the room was exposed. I took hold again of the candlestick that Hector held aloft and thrust it through the hole and into the room… and just as I suspected, there he was and had been all along. There was the young man."

With that Arthur sat back in his chair, the other three staring at him open-mouthed.

"My god," Robert said quietly in horror. "Behind a doorway that had been walled up? So… how long had he been there?"

"A very, very long time," Arthur said gravely, his jaw leaning against his curled fingers. It was not quite a fist he made. "Unless you have seen such things, it is impossible to impress upon you that there are many ways one can tell that a body has been dead for a long time." He was still and silent for a while.

"Yes," Edgar cut in again, almost suddenly enough to make Marsden jump. "I'll bet! First of all, the thing would be in the process of crumbling away to nothing, wouldn't it? Then there would be the clothes, and they would be practically ruined at worst, and noticeably completely out of date at best. Was there dust everywhere? I'll bet there was. Besides, if this all happened around the time of the plague, well that was in the 17th century, the 1660s, wasn't it? I remember - the great fire of 1666 knocked a lot of it out of London, and here we are living under Her Majesty Queen Victoria more than 200 years later. And also, Arthur here isn't quite that old, so I suppose this was not even 30 years ago."

"There was very little of him left," Arthur said suddenly quite clearly, but as if he had not heard half of what Edgar had just said. "He was leaning against the brickwork. His jawbone had fallen from his skull and lay some little distance away on the wooden floor. His flesh and all else had deserted him, but some of his hair remained." He gulped as if the worst he almost could not bring himself to say. "He was turned towards me and you see, it had been so long, his eyes too were quite gone... "

"That must have been an awful shock," said Robert sympathetically.

Arthur nodded slowly. "But I didn't see him as he truly was at first. You see, for a single second, at most two, when I first opened the way and thrust the candle through it, I saw him at once. And he smiled at me."

No one spoke. Edgar grinned momentarily, as if the nerves were even getting through to him.

"There was brickwork with wood all about, and the room was very narrow. One could tell that no one had been there for many many years. But he was leaning up against the wall, just as I had seen him before, with his short blonde hair, his pale face, and his white tunic shirt. He looked more alive than anyone I had ever seen. He looked at me and smiled. I think I must have smiled in return. He was breathing heavily, for the air was very oppressive in that room. I heard him utter the words "I knew you'd find me," and then he uttered no more and it was all over. It was only then, in the moment directly after, with the impression of his words still loud in my ear, that my eyes closed briefly to adjust to the light and that was when I saw what truly lay before me."

More solemn silence in the room, that an hour ago would have been described as anything but solemn.

"Not a living man," Robert supplied quietly. "Just... what was left of him."

"Did you... ever find anything else out?" Marsden inquired in spite of his nerves. "I mean, about the particulars? Could it be known what had really happened?"

Arthur did not seem keen to send the silence away and only after another great pause did he answer. "Yes I did. His name was Guillaume, or nowadays we might be more readily disposed to call him William. When I recovered from this shock a week or more later, Hector came to see me. There was a young woman who..." At this, Arthur sat himself slightly differently in his chair and appeared to put on all the expected indications that this next news was good. "He had been fond of her for a while and he wanted my opinion on his asking her to marry him. I thought they would make a good match."

"Quite right too," Edgar said, thankful for some cheer, "otherwise I

## The Horse, After Midnight

might never have been born."

"But," Arthur continued unperturbed, "he asked during his stay if I wanted to know what else he had found out. He said he would never be able to understand exactly what I had experienced, but that knowing more might put my mind at rest. He had spent some time, it seemed, interviewing certain people in the local village and the various hereabouts. What he could garner from half-remembered tales and whispers passed down, that sort of thing, was that the young man, the grandson, had had a… Someone," he said very deliberately, "who lived nearby who he had been very much in love with. The grandfather found it out. When the young man would not give up his love, it was after this, when the whispers of the plague's return was abroad, that the grandfather sent the rest of the family away. William was often seen about the village at first. He would come on his own horse and meet his love. But he had not been seen for a great while when many weeks later, the workmen were asked to the house. They did their work and came away again and never breathed a word of what they did… Apart from one. On his deathbed, unable to get the priest to his house, the ageing workman had confessed to his son what he had done. When he arrived, the old man had moments of lucidity and sense, and in the next, moments of what might be lunacy. He put them to work bricking up an old room, but they were not to look within the room. Still, they did. Inside was William. He had been subjected to…what might have been weeks or even months of terrible torture, tied to a single place there. The old man, finding out they had disobeyed, threatened to accuse them all of thievery, which might've seen them all hanged, and besides his grandson was dying of the plague. But these men knew even as they completed their awful task – for similar has been done to those still living, yet close to death with the plague, I hear tell – that William was to die from his mistreatment. And from what they did. Hector also tried to find out about William's beloved, but could only ever find the vaguest of news. It was thought and retold in the village that the lover had died not long after William disappeared. Hector found a name. A single name. That was all. He couldn't be sure if it was a Christian name, or a surname, but he was fairly certain…" Arthur here, for the first time, almost laughed. "It was a Christian name."

"And the name was….?" Robert asked.

Arthur exhaled. "Arthur."

Each of the other three reacted quietly, but then were contemplative and quite still for a while. Arthur seemed to remember himself in the moment and pulled down his waistcoat and came more fully to his senses than it seemed he had for the past hour. "Of course, that side is all hearsay, so no one will ever know."

"That old Devil," Edgar remarked, with no more observation for the fact that the patriarch of whom they talked was his own ancestor, than anyone who had only just heard the story. "What a bloody thing to do. I say! Do you suppose he wasn't really going crazy at all in his old age? What if he was completely compos mentis all along, and was just sort of play-acting?"

"Who can say?" Robert posed. "It's conceivable, though more depraved than anyone would like."

"All because of this Disapproved Love," Marsden spoke quietly and mournfully.

At this, the younger three slowly raised their heads to look at Arthur again. He was unaware – his look was wistful, and each of the three considered in their own quiet way the sufferings that he had gone through that would have been more protracted than this mere pamphlet out of the tome of his life. It might have occurred to each of them then, or perhaps at a later time, that more had been spoken of and accepted that evening, through a frank, long and deep experience with their friends, than had come to pass at all in any of their recent years. Even Edgar seemed strangely moved.

It was Robert who finally ended the evening's exchange. "That was a capital story, Arthur, old man," he said with as much enthusiasm as he could manage at such a late hour. "I for one am glad and grateful that you shared it. If we get stormed in another evening, then one of us could return the favour, though I doubt we shall be able to tell a tale as wonderful and necessary as yours."

Arthur, never having felt the need for flattery, smiled humbly and nodded in thanks. With very little further discussion, it was soon concluded that the night's reveries had come to an end and it was indeed time to go to bed. Inside of 10 minutes, the fire was very nearly out, the candlesticks had gone off in their respective directions to wherever the gentlemen were spending the night, and the hall was silent and empty.

## The Horse, After Midnight

Marsden found the ticking of the clock in his room quite a welcome companion as he first settled down to go to sleep. He was pleasantly surprised that in spite of the overall horror of Arthur's tale, his nerves were not so wrecked as they otherwise might have been, and his head hit the pillow without his needing to double check the door was shut or locked. Presently he slept.

The clock in his room however, did not sound the hours as so many other clocks do. And so he had no way of telling exactly what the time was when he heard the first soft tap, like a knock.

It was quiet and nearby, but not quite of a character of someone knocking at the door. It sounded different somehow. The first thing the young man did on opening his eyes was to keep his body as still as possible and listen as keenly as he might. Silence for a second. Two seconds. Three. He had just counted the 9th second when the sound came again, slightly louder, as if only a few feet away from his head, through the wall next to him, insistent and unmistakable.

He sprang from his bed as if there were a snake within it. He felt he should call out to the others, but his throat was quite dry and the sound would not have carried. In a panic, he felt a way along the room wall until he came to his own belongings, his waistcoat hanging inelegantly over the edge of the cupboard door. Furtively, with shaking hands, he searched the shallow pockets, until his trembling fingers found the thing he was looking for and he drew out a match. He struck it. In that same moment he wished he had not. For at the glass of his window, he made out a face - framed by blonde hair, pale and familiar, its eyes looking straight at him.

The match fell from his hands and might have set the whole place alight, but by some act of Providence, he was able to pick it up again and put the burning end to the wick of the candlestick on his bedside table. Gasping for breath, he turned again towards his window. Why had he formed the habit of being awoken by the rising of the morning sun, so that even now he would not close his curtains in a haunted house? He held the candlestick up.

All at the window was still. There was very little to make out. There was darkness, and perhaps a moonlit outline of a tree in the Gardens, but nothing more. Certainly not a face. All the same, it took him at least a

## The Horse, After Midnight

minute and a half to calm his breathing before he could even consider turning away from the window and sitting back down on the bed again.

Nothing there, he told himself. Nothing at all.

And yet - what was that sound outside? In the stillness of the countryside and the sleepiness of the house itself and all its residents, he could hear a noise. This was not knocking, however. This was something different. It sounded in an abstract sort of way like hooves upon the ground. A horse. Surely it was a horse, though why one would be being taken from the stables at this time of night he could not fathom.

His heart grew cold. What was the first thing that Arthur had heard, on his first night in this house? Had he not heard a great commotion outside like horses, a horse being frightened out of its wits? As if in answer, he heard a horse neighing as if in distress. His hands trembled again. What could anyone be doing to the creature? No, it all had to be a trick of his mind, or perhaps Arthur had decided he would not spend another night in the house with so many memories and now with the storm cleared and the rain stopped, he was seeing to his own horse so that he might leave immediately. But surely, Arthur was not such a brute to make his horse make such terrible pitiful noises. Not Arthur. And surely, that voice that he could hear was not Arthur's voice, low and terrible, not speaking so much as snarling and making a noise as if specifically to frighten the creature away.

Marsden could barely breathe. He saw it now: The old man had sent his grandson's horse away, to make it look as if the boy had left of his own volition, so that no one would look for him. But now both he and the boy had returned and were taunting him with knocks and snarls and appearances in windows, and for a brief moment, Marsden looked again, and saw the face of the pale boy at the window: animated, eyes wide, mouth moving as if trying to scream through the window at him, but Marsden could hear nothing over the sound of the Horse and the Snarl.

He picked up the candle and ran from the room. He might have called Arthur's name as he ran down the passage. He might have called his own best friend Robert's as he came to the stairs. He might have called for Edgar, or the name of a servant he knew, or indeed anyone's name as the sound outside grew deafening, and the front door stood before him as he ran to it in his nightgown, barely catching his breath, but by God, he had to be away. Out and away from this dreadful, awful, terrifying, godless, haunted possessed house! He had to get away!

He flung the great door open, ready to run out into the night if necessary, if simply to be away from it all. The terrible noises suddenly stopped, and there was nothing but the young man with the blonde hair on the step in front of him, his large eyes staring at him, shaking, his skin almost blue like a newly-buried corpse restless from its grave.

Marsden fell back and finally shrieked at the top of his lungs, candlestick and candle clattering to the floor. The figure's brow furrowed as its wide eyes followed him. Marsden forgot to breathe. What did the young man want from him? Why appear to him? Why was he now mixed up in such a nightmare? It just stood there looking at him as if annoyed and confused and then finally parted its lips to say something terrible and said:

"Get out of the way, dammit, Marsden, let me in before I perish. Damned freezing out here! Don't you know it's nearly November?"

The figure spoke with the voice of Edgar and the pieces did not fully fall into place for Marsden until more light started to come into the room with accompanying people, raised from their beds at the sound of Marsden's horrifying cry. Edgar stepped into the house and righted the candle Marsden had dropped before it could do any real damage to the floor. In the next moment, Marsden heard the comforting voice of Robert on the stairs behind him, even though he was shouting.

"What in hell are you about, the two of you?" he demanded. It was really quite the angriest either of the two had ever seen him in their lives, and he was obviously not a man who appreciated being woken from his bed before he had had a full night's sleep. "It's not yet 4 in the morning - what in God's name is all this noise? Screams and knocks loud enough to wake the Dead!

"It's nothing," Edgar insisted with his head bent. "I got locked out, that's all."

"Locked out?" Robert bellowed. "What in the name of everything that is Holy were you doing outside at this time in the first place? And what the devil were you screaming about, Marsden?"

Marsden, now a little more in his senses, gingerly picked himself up off the floor and tried to make himself as tall and respectable a height as possible, which was somewhat difficult, given that he was shorter by 2 inches than Edgar, and by at least four next to Robert. "I heard... I heard knocking," he reported, feeling stupid. "Then the young ma - Edgar appeared at my window. And..." Realising now it had been Edgar all along, his voice trailed off as Arthur finally made his way to the top of the stairs. He was far too embarrassed to offer any kind of explanation to him.

"What the hell were you doing, Edgar?" Robert demanded.

Edgar folded his arms across his chest and started to look a little annoyed. "I was... I was trying to scare Marsden."

"You were doing what?" Robert tried to clarify. Arthur looked even less impressed than Robert. Edgar avoided their gaze and his face started to go a funny shade of pink. Marsden wondered now how he ever could have mistaken Edgar for the beautiful boy in the picture, as he'd never looked further from him than right at this moment.

"I was trying to scare Marsden, alright?" Edgar spoke to the room at large. "I saw Arthur's story made him nervy and I just wanted to have a little fun, give him a little scare. I climbed out onto the ledge by his window, tapped on his wall until he woke up and then meant to get away before he could spot me. I would have owned up to it the following morning. As it happens," he continued grumpily through clenched teeth, "part of the wall that I used to climb up didn't take my weight very well, and I nearly fell. I had to go all the way around the house to the front here, and I've been out here long enough to Catch My Death!"

"Well," said Robert hotly, "I don't think that any of us would say that it wasn't deserved under the circumstances. For god's sake, what if Arthur had heard you?"

"Oh don't be ridiculous," Edgar snapped almost viciously. "I knew that Arthur wasn't staying in that side of the house. If I had thought he would have heard me, I never would have dreamt of it. Look, it wouldn't even have been a big scare for Marsden," Edgar tried to reason with them. "I just wanted to shake him up a bit and you never know, after realising it was me he might have given up on his idea of ghosts altogether! I could have cured him of a great fear! - Oh," he faltered, looking at Arthur as if he had only just realised that he had put his foot in it. "Not that I don't believe you're a very compelling storyteller, Arthur. I really do, and you told it very well, you had us all going the whole way through – didn't he,

## The Horse, After Midnight

chaps?"

"Why don't we all just go back to bed?" Arthur spoke for the first time.

The staff began to go back to their bedrooms in various states of wakefulness. Shame-faced, Edgar walked up to join the others, Marsden walking somewhat dreamily behind them.

The other three, beginning finally to cool from the night's alarm, had reached the top of the stairs when they noticed that Marsden was still standing at the bottom step, his breathing shallow, and his expression one of sudden and supreme horror.

"The horse," he uttered. He looked up at Edgar. "How did you make the sound of the horse?"

There came no answer. Edgar stared blankly back down at him. "Horse?" he repeated. "I did nothing with a horse."

"Nothing at all?" Marsden demanded, sounding a little bolder. "You didn't drag it from the stables and taunt it, making snarling noises to scare it?"

"No, of course not," Edgar spoke sullenly, as if somewhat offended. "What should I be doing messing about with horses at nearly four in the morning? Even for a prank."

No one else had come in from outside, and all the servants had come from their rooms in their nightgowns. Marsden now caught the eye of Arthur. His face too was pale, and he could tell from the look on the younger man's face, with recently-visited horror, that he spoke the truth.

"Snarling, but a human?" Arthur whispered. His voice was hollow. "You say it sounded almost as if someone were 'snarling' at the creature?"

Strange questions that none of the men could answer passed wordlessly between them. What should be done? What could be done? What did it mean? Why had Marsden heard it where none of the others had? Marsden's eyes followed Arthur's as he turned once again to look towards the wall where many of Edgars' ancestors had their portraits lining the walls. This time however he was not looking towards the young beautiful William that had so stimulated their imagination that evening. Instead, he was looking at another portrait which was only just visible in the flickering light from their candles now. It was of an old man of advancing years, his face locked in some kind of almost ridiculous grin, and his staring eyes really quite unnerving to look at. One might almost have wondered why the painter would even paint such a subject. But then it was likely the poor artist hadn't any choice. Especially not if the sitter had been the patriarch of the family at the time.

## The Forgotten Boy

Mrs. Huggin sat opposite me with an old-style handkerchief stretching between one gripped hand and another. Despite a formal outfit and an almost business-like attitude about her, she looked nervous. Not of me: I was, after all, there to help, not make anyone intimidated, or I was never going to get my full counselling qualification. Large round eyes peered from behind almost perfectly circular glasses, and her grey suit, complemented by similarly toned moccasin shoes, and very well-kept hair, told me much that I had already read on paper of her.

Mrs. Huggin was fifty-nine. She was a divorcee of several years, though had kept the 'Mrs.' moniker, and had attended, and then later worked all her adult life at the same school: a large, imposing building I knew by reputation more than sight on the outskirts of the city. She was, I knew, in no way a frivolous or un-sensible woman, and yet the conversation we were having had led me to question this. I found it nearly impossible to understand why Mrs. Huggin was so very convinced of what she had seen, but obviously not really seen.

"I never thought," she began hesitantly, "that it would be anything like what it was. You hear many different stories, don't you? In some, I suppose the ones I believed a little more easily, I remember hearing that one could not really tell the difference at first. Between a real person and a..." The word hung unspoken like a misty vapour between us, not to be caught, and she avoided committing to the admission by drinking the water I offered all my clients. "But I wish I had never heard those stories," she continued at length. "They obviously don't know. Not people who think you can't tell. They didn't in any way prepare me…"

She drifted and said no more. "And how many times have you seen it now?" I asked with as much softness as I could.

She blinked rapidly and gathered herself again. "I reckon this is the… fourth time. Third for definite, but it might be four. I think I saw it once, but… I couldn't be sure, that first time. You never think it'll happen to you. I suppose everyone thinks that about anything." Again, she grasped at the glass of water, and her face was turned away from me as she spoke, as if connecting with me might make her experience far too real. "But when I saw it… I didn't think for a moment that it was a real little boy. I knew when I laid eyes on it – I knew that though he was looking straight at me, that he was dead. He looked dead, you see."

I paused and resisted the urge to make notes. "When you say 'He looked dead'…"

She struggled to find the words. "He just looked – not alive," she attempted. "You know. You know the difference. He wasn't living, not any more. He was – Dead."

"Let's go back," I tried, pushing my glasses further back up my nose and over my ears. "I want you to start from before the illusion actually happened."

Her face darkened. "Illusion?" she repeated. "You think it was an illusion. As in – you don't believe me?"

"It's a turn of phrase," I tried to cover for myself quickly. "Would it make you happier to call it an Apparition?"

This seemed, in the moment at least, to satisfy her, and she rested back in the chair.

She described to me what, by her own admission, had started like any previous morning she'd ever had in her working life, with painstaking attention to the minutiae of her established routine. She had risen before six and had an unhurried morning getting ready for work. She'd showered, put on the radio for the news, drunk coffee and had breakfast in a nightgown, then dressed, did her hair and makeup and drove the approximate fifteen minutes to the school, arriving as usual, the first one to the school grounds at about 7.30 a.m. She had put her things down under the tall reception desk just inside the second set of large double doors, and switched on a lamp.

"Then I looked up. I just saw something out of the corner of my eye, and looked up."

She stared off past my shoulder, taking nothing in and seeing nothing that was before her.

"He was just… standing there. Six or seven feet away from me. Brown hair. Dark eyes, though I couldn't say... The circles all about his eyes were dark. And he wasn't dressed like a normal, 'modern' boy. And he was staring straight at me." She hadn't blinked during this description, as if even now, she was afraid for her eyes to close even for a moment.

"And how did he leave?" I asked, my voice even softer than before.

She swallowed. "He stood there for what seemed like an eternity. Probably was only a few seconds, but it was a long time to me. Then he turned and walked away."

"He walked away?" I clarified. "He didn't disappear?"

"Oh no," she confirmed quickly. "No. Thank God he didn't. He just sort of turned and walked off down the corridor towards…."

She trailed off. I was still quite convinced that no matter, with how much conviction Mrs. Huggin said that she had seen this little boy who was Not Alive, she was either the victim of a clever prank by some of the schoolchildren, or else there was something within her that had dictated that this moment happened. I'd read before that many patients would have episodes that seemed abstract, but were actually linked to something that had happened in their lives, a manifestation of that trauma. However, I had also heard from an aunt, long ago, that when a friend of hers kept seeing his late wife, his doctor had prescribed him bananas, and with the uptake in potassium, he'd never suffered visitations again.

"I'm glad you were able to tell me," I said. "Now, let's talk a little about the past. Just a little about your upbringing, shall we?"

She didn't look impressed at that. "Why? What's that got to do with anything?"

I was going to have to learn to phrase myself better. My first week unsupervised, and I was already doubting my abilities as a counsellor. "Well, some events that happen early on in life trigger episodes like this later on. Do you have any events that this in any way reminds you of?"

"No," she said quickly, regaining her confidence. "Nothing. The only bereavements I've ever really suffered were my own parents about a decade or so ago."

"Brothers and sisters?"

"No," she replied, seeming to see where I was going. "I was an only child. And, before you think of it, my ex-husband and I never had any children. One of the reasons we divorced, in fact. He decided one day he wanted them, but I'd spent my life around them by that point, and my mind hadn't changed."

A dead end, it seemed, for want of a less pun-like description. No deceased son or younger brother, nothing like that. "Was there – ever," I tried cautiously, "ever a story about a child that made a great impression on you when you were young? Of course, you may not remember it specifically, but you'd be surprised how susceptible children are."

"No, I wouldn't," she replied darkly. "Not with a father like mine, I wouldn't. Any stern man can make any child susceptible, suggestible to whatever he wants, I know it."

I nodded. "Something of a difficult childhood, sometimes," I spoke diplomatically.

"Oh no," she countered. "No, I wouldn't say 'difficult'. I suppose...Well, I was scared of him, my father, as was my mother. But he never caused me what you might call – what's the word – trauma?"

*Nothing that you'd recognise as trauma, anyway,* I noted to myself.

"But to answer your question – no I don't recall anything, no story of a child."

"Locally, or in the papers? Or even perhaps – an urban legend, at the school? Something other children talked about when you were there."

She shifted her weight slightly in the seat and sat up a little straighter.

"No," she said, her voice lilting upwards at the end.

"You're quite sure?" I asked delicately.

"No. I can't say as any come to mind. I've forgotten most of what our stories were when we were in school."

"Of course," I nodded. I didn't believe her. "So, in your own words – take your time – what do you think the boy represents?"

She cocked her head. "How do you mean?"

"I mean… let's say the boy appeared to you to tell you something..."

She interrupted me: "I don't know what you mean. Tell me something? What would some little boy who's obviously passed away have to tell me? You think I'm daft, don't you? You don't believe a word I'm saying."

"Mrs. Huggin," I tried again, "I believe everything you've said. But if this thing has appeared to you, it must be for a specific reason. Quieten your mind for a moment, and tell me if you can think of this apparition, then tell me if any feelings are becoming clearer."

Mrs. Huggin, obviously beginning to think that the entire session was a farcical sham or just a complete waste of time, nevertheless closed her eyes with a frustrated sigh, and obliged. "I don't want to think of him," she confessed.

"Just let the feelings come. You need only begin to think about it and they should be right there."

A thin line formed between her brows, and her lips were held tremulously together. She was already in discomfort.. "I don't know. There's a feeling of – sadness, I suppose?"

"Good, good, well done." I waited for more suggestions, but nothing came. "What else?"

She concentrated very hard, then snapped her eyes open. "Nothing. Nothing else at all. There's honestly nothing to tell. I'm the simplest woman you could meet. I also make sure I do what's right, what's allowed, you know, so I don't see how and why I should have any such feelings."

"What's right and what's allowed?" I repeated.

"Oh, you know. Well, I suppose you don't, your parents no doubt brought you up very diff – As I said, my father was a stern man. Strict, I suppose you'd call him. Fair, but strict. He believed in Spare the Rod, Spoil The Child. He had a very…" She winced. "Swift hand, I think it's called. He put the fear of God, and himself, into me and my mother. So I've always been a good member of society. Not like children these days. I made sure I was always a good child, and I rather think I'm a good person now, maybe even because of that upbringing, so I'm not ashamed of it."

She seemed so insistent on this, all I could do was smile weakly, and nod.

"But I'm not here to talk about my father," she added hurriedly, not realising that it was she who had brought him up, twice. "That's all irrelevant. I want to know how and why I saw… what I saw. Can we at least talk about that next time?"

I made myself a cup of tea when Mrs. Huggin had left. I was rather annoyed, overall. Jess, a mentor that I was working under, had assigned her to me. I'd had a career break the other year and decided I wanted to retrain to be a counsellor. Most cases that I was on were voluntary, as I was only just beginning, though I was enjoying the work. I didn't think Mrs. Huggin would have come had she known I didn't even have the appropriate letters after my name, and frankly, I was rather angry at Jess for leaving me with someone with issues I had no experience in. What was I supposed to do with her? The woman was convinced she'd seen a ghost, several times. That was the unsaid implication that had hung like a transparent vapour in the room. This woman didn't need some mature student who happened to wear a pair of glasses trying to pull all available fragments of my learning together for her problem. She might even need psychiatry, and I resolved to tell Jess as much when she got back from holiday.

I didn't see Mrs. Huggin, and, except in passing, didn't really think of her for the next few days. However, about seven-twenty a.m. on the Friday, my mobile started ringing. I picked it up and at first it seemed there was no one there. Then, a voiceless whisper:

"It's happened again."

The unnerving voice shocked me into wakefulness. "Mrs… Huggin?"

"It's happened again. Just now!"

As people will invariably do, I unnecessarily mirrored Mrs. Huggin's hushed tone. "Mrs. Huggin, I don't think you should be at work, given what you're experiencing."

"I can't leave! I might lose my job if I leave!"

"Is there anyone else at the school with you?"

"No. The headmistress will be arriving soon, but not for another fifteen, twenty minutes or so."

"Alright," I reasoned. "Go and sit in your car until the headmistress arrives. Then, once you've spoken to her, you're going to have to call your doctor, who will write you a sick note."

"But – but – what if he doesn't give me it? I'm not ill, really."

"But you are very stressed, Mrs. Huggin," I tried to tell her. "These appearances have you very stressed, anyone can tell."

"Can't you come with me?" she asked. "If you came, they might know I'm telling the truth."

"But you are telling the truth," I reminded her. I was, as before, as certain as I could be that Mrs. Huggin completely believed in her experience.

Somehow, within the hour, dishevelled but functional, I found myself telling the headmistress that Mrs. Huggin was suffering great strain at present, and could do with some emergency time off. Ms. Wainwright agreed and Mrs. Huggin was signed off for a week, with no need to get a sick note, which she seemed very relieved at.

I took Ms. Wainwright to one side after this, and asked if there were any CCTV in the school. Showing Mrs. Huggin that there was nothing on a screen might go some way to shattering her morbid illusion, but Ms. Wainwright informed me that there was nothing throughout the school – only a camera in her own office, and one in the finance room. It had been a long shot, but I thanked her all the same for understanding.

A few days after this, Mrs. Huggin was back in the room with me. She seemed a little better even for her few days away, and announced promptly that she wanted to be getting back to work. I gently tried to convince her to at least take the rest of the week, but even though she was obviously still somewhat shaken when the subject was brought up, she staunchly dictated that the school simply could not do without her – a familiar idea I had encountered with others whom were also very – supposedly - sure of where their place and importance in the world was.

Once the pleasantries had passed us by, I got back to the matter: "Was it different this time? When you… saw what you saw."

"No. No, not at all. I looked up, thinking someone was there, and there he was. Dark-eyed and looking straight at me. He stood there, then turned very deliberately, and went down the corridor towards…"

This was the second time she had stopped short. "Where was he going?"

She tentatively played with the handkerchief again stretched between her palms, which served, obviously, as a kind of safety blanket for her. "The rest of the school," she answered with no conviction.

"Specifically?"

"How should I know?" she asked, but I sat patiently watching her and waiting. Her resolve finally failed and I heard her mutter: "Maybe the boiler room."

"The boiler room? Is the boiler room nearby?"

Her words were without feeling, as if presenting me with facts of bare bone. "No. It's downstairs, you can only get to it by going out through the playground, if you have a key to the room itself."

"Oh. I see...So why might he be heading for the boiler room, and not any other room? The canteen or a classroom, maybe?"

"Don't know what makes me say that," she said, her body and face trying their best to turn away from me. "It's just a feeling... And if there's any place in the whole school where such a... Thing Like That might go or come from, you can be assured it's that terrible, bloody place." At her own swear word, her cheeks and tips of her ears started to go pink.

"Doesn't sound like a nice room at all."

"It's not," she agreed, her voice strangely reverent. I couldn't quite tell if she wanted to talk about it, or would rather the whole thing was dropped. "Worst room in the whole school. Always was, even when I was a girl. Can't stomach it, not even to look at the door."

"That must be quite horrid. To have a place of work as lovely as the school, with the memories you must have, but to have that horrid room there as well. What kind of feelings do thinking about it prompt?"

"Awful ones. Claustrophobia for one. And a sense of...danger. Fear. It's large but with a low ceiling. Big, awful pipes, and huge machines like old engines. And there's all these huge holes in the floorboards. Young child might fall through and get their leg trapped, if they got in and weren't careful. Smells awful too – I'd know the smell of that place if I'd been retired fifty years. Haven't had to go in decades now, thank God. School's a listed building, you see, so they can't change anything without permission. Not fit for purpose, I don't doubt, but Ms. Wainwright is insistent on keeping writing to the council to have it all redone. I don't know if they even get her letters, but they never reply."

"You know it rather well, this room, for saying you hate it so much," I noted.

She seemed defensive again. "No. Not at all. We all knew to stay out of the boiler room when we attended school. Someone went in and got found out, and then they were expelled, so I never thought to. You know what my father was like. I'd have got the whipping of my life if he found out and if I'd got expelled..." She shifted and her eyes clouded. No trauma, she had said. But her generation hadn't been gifted with the knowledge of what real trauma was.

"So when did you see it?" I asked. "The boiler room?"

"I don't remember."

"Was it frightening when you were a child?"

"Must have been, I've always hated it. But look – does it really matter? Like you said, how am I to know where he was going? If you don't mind, I don't want to talk about that bloody place again."

I don't know why I said what I said next. "Maybe it would be an idea to take someone with you, maybe Ms. Wainwright and just pop your head around the door someday soon. Just to have a look at it. Just to confirm that yes, it might be a horrible room, but you'll probably find it's not quite so awful as your mind's told you it is. What do you think?"

I watched the colour flood and then swiftly leave her face. "What will that achieve? Make me sick, that will. Can't stand that place, I told you. Now for God's sake, is there any other way you can help without dragging up the one thing I hate more than seeing little dead children in my place of work?"

We were getting nowhere. I steered her away as much as possible, but she had been right: Mrs. Huggin was a simple, straightforward, no-nonsense woman with a strong idea of where her place in the world was, and what was allowed and what was forbidden. She wasn't dissatisfied with her life or her lot whatsoever. In fact, she said she felt very lucky – she worked at a place she loved. She was respected in the school, even by the children. She owned her own house. Her husband and she were still friends of a sort, and she could afford holidays and personal treats now and again. Her mother, she said, would never have been able to dream of living a life like hers. No, indeed, despite this recent problem, she was very lucky.

"But am I too lucky?" she said, just as the session was coming to a close.

I couldn't help but smile at the familiar Northern attitude I knew very well. "You think it's possible to be too lucky?"

"Well, there's got to be balance," she said forlornly. "Spare the rod, spoil the child, my father believed. I don't know why, but I know somehow that he'd never approve of the way I did things. He'd say I didn't deserve it." She lifted her head and looked into my face. "And you know, I'm not sure I do."

I made a heavy note to come back to this subject at our next session, but sadly, I never got the chance.

It was six-thirty p.m. a few days later, and it was the time of year where it was already dark. I should have already gone home, but I lost track of time and liked doing a little paperwork in the building to avoid the mental weight of taking it home to do. I was eyebrow-deep in another case study when my mobile rang, and I was so tired and determined to finish something, that I didn't look at the number. I simply answered: "Hello?"

Silence. Just a vague, somewhat distant-sounding breath. It reminded me of prank calls when I was a child.

"Hello?" I tried again. Still nothing. I checked my screen. "Mrs. Huggin, is that you?"

Nothing for a second. Then a sudden, quick beep. A button being pushed.

"Mrs. Huggin, are you alright?"

No answer. I could only just hear her breathing.

"Has it... Has it happened again? Is that why you're ringing?"

Beep.

"When? Can you tell me?" Inexplicable excitement rose within me. "When did this happen, can you talk?"

Silence. An odd lump seemed to be sitting over my heart.

"Has it just happened?"

Still silence. I took a slow breath in and suddenly felt rather cold.

"Is it – right now? Can you see him right now?"

A moment's pause and then -

Beep.

Perhaps it was the time of day, or the time of the year, but in that moment I didn't think about telling her that it was all an illusion or a trick of her mind. Or even about needing to refer her. I stood, my other work and deadlines forgotten. "I want you to wait right there, do you hear me? I'll be at the school as fast as I can. Are you the last to leave? Is there anyone else there?"

No other noise.

"Don't worry," I reassured her. "I'll hurry, I'll be there soon."

A quick, plaintive Beep.

I was in my car less than a minute later and must have broken the speed limit several times on my way. I wasn't even thinking what I was going to do when I got there and confronted this poor woman who was seeing things, but I was eager to jump on it. Even the drive over there didn't curb my enthusiasm. It was unethical, but I wanted to try and show her that none of it was really happening. She might be able to start healing from then. If not, then she definitely needed better help than mine.

When I reached the school, I worried that Mrs. Huggin had left without me, though her car was still there. The place was in complete darkness. It's a strange and, in itself, very eerie thing, a school without children and teachers in it, especially at nighttime. As I parked my car, I suppressed a shiver as I looked up at the building. In the daytime, with its bustle and talk and movement everywhere, the school made sense. However now, with its gaping silence, its tall, unshuttered windows betraying only more darkness, and the stillness… My goodness, the stillness was the worst of all somehow. It seemed wrong. As if there must be things, otherworldly and unnameable, tramping up and about the corridors with not a care for mortal sanity, yet though we might be able to feel something of them, we would never truly understand them. Yes. The stillness was the worst.

The two large double doors were unlocked, of course, though there were no lights on within. It took me a moment to find the main switch for the lights in the foyer, and I blinked under their sudden harshness.

Inside the building, with a light nearby was a vast improvement, though my eyes played tricks and I ignored my mind telling me that there was naturally something, some being just beyond where the light extended to, in the nearest darkness. I had tried never to do so, but I found myself judging Mrs. Huggin even less now that I was here, to see what she had to come into each morning, and leave behind each night. After a lifetime in such a building, it seemed reasonable even, that one might be convinced that this echoey, sprawling, unnatural place must be haunted.

I called out for Mrs. Huggin, but the school answered with only a continuation of its gloomy, lifeless quiet. The place was large, I reasoned, and if she was further than the next room, it was highly unlikely she would hear me. At the tall reception desk her handbag was on the floor, open, tucked in beyond the wheels of her chair. I cast a quick glance for her mobile, but all I saw were several scrunched up papers, stuffed within so that it was almost overflowing. As my foot touched the handbag, one fell out and rolled away.

I picked it up to put it back, but my fingertips fell on decent paper, which had an odd feel when crumpled. Embossed, but in reverse, I could see part of the school's emblem. Unable to resist, I unfolded the paper, and saw it was an official school letter, addressed to someone I didn't know, citing the 'untenable' maintenance of the current issue with the boiler room. At the bottom, it was signed in ink from Ms. Wainwright, the headmistress.

I wondered how this got scrunched up and put in Mrs. Huggin's bag, when surely it should have gone out with the post.

I saw a flash of something through one of the panes of glass at the top of double doors on the other side of the foyer. It seemed like light, going on and off. Making sure I could identify where all the light switches might be, I followed where it seemed I should go.

The boilers really did need seeing to, I decided as I left the reception area. The place was freezing. I saw my breath in the air as I entered a high, long corridor, with many different doors off it. I gauged how far the light had seemed and opened the swinging door to the staff bathrooms.

The light within was on. "Mrs. Huggin?"

There was a very, very faint noise in one of the stalls. I pushed against a few, and they opened, but the last, did not.

"Mrs. Huggin, are you in there?" I asked.

"Is he still there?" came a terrified whisper.

This was worse than I could have imagined. This had gone from occasional sighting to full blown psychosis. I weighed up calling an ambulance immediately, whether she wished me to or not.

"No, Mrs. Huggin, you're quite safe," I answered. "There's no one here but myself."

There was a slow, reluctant sound of movement. The old-style bolt shot back and timidly, Mrs. Huggin looked out.

She was decidedly different from the last time I had seen her. Her usually-neat-and-orderly hair was almost wild. The makeup around her wide eyes was greatly smeared, as if she had been crying hysterically. She kept blinking and I noted the frightened tremor in her chin.

"Mrs. Huggin?" I said again, in quiet alarm, blaming myself for not contacting Jess, holiday or not.

"He was out there. Just then. When I called. Thank God I had my mobile in my pocket. I was about to leave for the night, when I turned to the door... " She was on the verge of tears again.

"Would you like me to drive you home, Mrs Huggin?" I offered. "I can call someone, if you'd like - "

"No!" she said in alarm, darting back and forth behind the edge of the door. "No, I can't leave. I know now. I know he won't let me. I know it... I know what it means."

I sensed that I wasn't going to like whatever 'It Means', but nodded to show I was listening.

"He won't let me leave any more," she said in a hollow whisper. I had one of those creeping shivers shoot from my tailbone right up my spine and into my neck. "That's why I called you."

I really, really didn't like this, and felt so ill-equipped to help her.

"There's nothing for you to do but come home now, Mrs Huggin. It's gone seven o'clock."

"But I can't, I can't!" she insisted. I would have to call Jess tonight at this rate, and Ms. Wainwright too. "He gets closer and closer... And now, I can't leave. He's waiting for me."

She wasn't making sense, and being here must be the last place someone in her state needed to be. "You can leave any time you want," I assured her. "I'm going to walk you out to your car, and then I think I'll drive you home, to make sure you get there alright."

"No!" she said, and her surprisingly strong grip for such a boney-looking hand took hold of my wrist. Something akin to resolve started to spread across her face. I tried to show nothing of my inner fear, but I almost wanted to go back to the foyer, and deal with the unseen creatures of the dark, instead of being here, with this poor, unhinged woman. "I've got to tell you." She impressed upon me.

Keeping her hand on my lower arm, she led me out of the bathrooms. She seemed to momentarily lose her nerve, but at my suggestion that we should probably just leave, she started moving away from the foyer, down the long corridor, with me in close tow. Through a set of double fire exit doors ahead, a light shone from above on what looked like an outdoor play area.

This, I realised, must be the way to the boiler room.

We traversed the length of the corridor, dropped down a few steps and by use of keys Mrs. Huggin had about her, went out into the playground. It was odd, but even though it was dark now, it seemed warmer outside than in. No wonder Ms. Wainwright was eager for the system to be fixed, if that was what they had to look forward to as winter was setting in. I couldn't see where I was going, but Mrs. Huggin knew exactly where she was and only half a minute after walking across the paved ground, she opened another door to a very different part of the building. I braced myself. Either I was about to show Mrs. Huggin that there was nothing in the boiler room to be frightened of, or I was about to see that this woman needed help far beyond what myself and Jess offered.

Or… Or….

This small attachment to the main building looked as if it might fall down if someone so much as sneezed at it. Mrs. Huggin's hands were trembling so much as she opened the three heavy padlocks on the boiler room door, I thought we'd never get in. But finally, with an agonising creak, louder than you might expect, the door swung slowly inward., and Mrs. Huggin ducked behind me.

A wall of strange odour met us, oddly familiar and yet sickening, reminding me of fetid water and forgotten places where the sun could never reach. I instinctively lifted my long-sleeved arm to cover my nose and mouth as Mrs. Huggin reached around and pressed something into my other hand. A torch. I clicked it on and shone it into the boiler room.

I could see instantly why Mrs. Huggin wanted to avoid this place altogether. In daylight, it must have been fairly horrid. In the dark, it was terrifying. I'd never seen a boiler system so large, or so old. Gargantuan, squat, ancient machines that would not have been out of place in a museum sat eerily still feet from us. I shone the torch's shaft of light here and there. I wanted, of course, to say to Mrs. Huggin: "See? There's nothing here. They need to do a lot of work and I can see why you feel the way you do, but – It's fine." But every time I went to open my mouth, I heard a noise over my shoulder. Just a thin, commonplace type of noise, but made by neither of us. And once, I thought I saw something like... a figure, I suppose, that ducked behind the end boiler just before the torchlight reached them.

The floorboards seemed ancient, and weighted with dust. And there were, as Mrs. Huggin had described, large holes here and there, that gave way into... who knew what beneath? Listed building, it may be, I thought, but this was ridiculous. No matter how far out in the styx any school might be, to let their heating system be this archaic, if not altogether dangerous, was horrendous.

It had taken me probably all of five seconds to decide that Mrs. Huggin's fears probably all stemmed from being in this room at some point, past when anyone would want to be, and that I myself really didn't want to stay here. To use a phrase, the place didn't feel... 'right'.

"This is appalling," I said aloud. "This whole thing should have been updated... God knows, years ago, if not decades! How has this been allowed to stay like this?"

Mrs. Huggin's face was turned away. She was right in the corner of the room, close to the door, looking as if she couldn't decide whether she needed to stay, or was going to bolt at the first opportunity. And I suppose it was her face being so definitely turned away from me in that moment that got me thinking, and remembering that letter. That crumpled letter I'd seen in her bag, that seemed to have a number of brothers and sisters. And a thought occurred to me.

"Mrs. Huggin, who deals with the letters for having all this done up? Emails and phone calls? The letters Ms. Wainwright writes to the council or...whoever it is who'd come in to do the work?"

Mrs. Huggin didn't answer. She dipped her head and looked up at me, the run mascara giving her a macabre look. It seemed she was trying to ascertain how much I knew. I understood, without needing to ask again, it was she who was in charge of such correspondence, and for some reason, despite her obvious detestation of this terrible place, she had been making sure the letters Ms. Wainwright kept sending about the boiler room and never left the school. It wouldn't surprise me if nobody concerned outside the school even had a clue.

"Who comes to maintain the boilers?" I asked.

Mrs. Huggin didn't respond.

"Who?" I said more forcefully. She almost started.

"Mr. Huggin," she said under duress. "He was responsible. But he's retired now. I can't get him to come back, no matter how much I plead with him."

"Mrs. Huggin, this is very dangerous," I said, wondering that no one had realised how bad she might be before this. "If no one's coming in to check and update any of this…"

I felt for a few horrible moments as if I'd been drawn into a trap. Or perhaps that I'd stumbled across more than myself or Mrs. Huggin had meant me to. Surely there'd be a system in place. Surely people had to come and check such things by law. How had she avoided that all this time? What was going on?

My sympathy started to fall away, and I felt frightened again. Not just of the room, but of whatever it was that was going on beyond, but because of this room. "Carmen," I said, using her given name for the first time since we'd met, "I think it's time you told me what's – really going on." My voice shook as it left my mouth. An icy cold chill, like I hadn't experienced in a long while, gripped the dead centre of my chest and for a second, I forgot to breathe.

Mrs. Huggin looked at me for a while, and in that time, strangely, it was as if the vast majority of her years fell away. Her glance was sideways and upwards, as if she were a small girl anticipating being told off, and I couldn't help but feel sorry for her. It only lasted a few moments, but I remember it even now.

"I really wanted to say something. But you see, I couldn't. I was frightened. My father… He was a fair man, but he got cross quite easily."

I didn't interrupt her. She seemed to grow even frailer in the dim light as she continued.

"His name," Mrs. Huggin said slowly, "was Francis," and I realised she wasn't talking about her father any more. "He was eight, I think. He was in my class. Quiet boy. Barely ever made eye contact. There was only…

me what talked to him. I was his friend. But for me, he should never have spoke to anyone his own age, he was so shy. He was smarter than me. In fact, I think he was smarter than most of us, even those in the years above. Did nothing but read. Wouldn't play, not if he had a book. I tried my best. Some children could be quite mean to him. Steal his books. And he was so even-tempered, he never got angry or screamed or cried. He'd just sit there, saddened.

"One day, I found him in the playground with half a book in his hand. An older boy had grabbed it and ripped it right in two. He was so upset, but he wouldn't go and tell anyone. I offered, but.... He just asked me to help him."

She paused. "Help him with what?" I prompted.

"Find somewhere quiet, where he could just get on and read. He wasn't allowed back in the classroom during lunch or playtime, and there were no nook or crannies that would afford him peace in the playground, so I told him about..."

Again, she paused. This time, I waited.

"I didn't DO anything on purpose," she insisted. "My father was always warning me what would happen if I got into trouble, but it was supposed to be our den. The caretaker back then, he never locked anything but the main doors. We come in and it's our little hideaway. I was so excited, but I kept telling him we couldn't tell anyone. If anyone found out... I was so frightened... I just kept on talking. He tries to read, but I'm too distracted, trying to figure out how we don't get caught. And he gets angry and I'm still talking and then he uses the book to hit me. Not hard. Just to tell me to be quiet. And I was so angry. Angry like my father could get sometimes. And I hit him! So hard!"

My torchlight fell where her gaze did. A large hole, large enough for someone to lose their footing in. Large enough, I thought in horror, for a rather small boy to fall through.

Mrs. Huggin's head shook slowly side to side. I realised my wrist was unsteady as I deliberately shone the light further down into the hole. Nothing but darkness, and bits of debris.

"After break time, we went back to class. We were asked if we'd seen him after the register and I stayed quiet. I couldn't come back for ages.

Just couldn't. And I had to bring in little bits of what I found, to put down the hole, bit by bit."

I wasn't looking down the hole now. I was looking her full in the face. I was waiting for a moment that I knew must be coming. Decided had to come... But might not.

"Each time I heard him mentioned, I knew I should say something. Each hour. Each day."

My heart dropped. She hadn't only left him. She hadn't said a word. 'Days' had gone by and she had said nothing. The moment wasn't coming.

"His parents.... It was in the papers, 'young boy missing'. Even then, I truly wanted to say something, but the longer I left it, the more I knew I'd go to prison. All the awful things my father said, it would all happen."

Her voice was almost explanatory now. It had happened to someone else, but the reasoning, the rationale, surely, these were understood, her voice said. My voice, in contrast, was difficult to find.

"Did he... die... when he fell?" I asked.

She may as well not have heard me. I wondered if that had even been important to her, for even a second. The sickly smell in the air was going to make me throw up.

"You didn't say a thing," I spoke quietly. "Not ever, did you?"

A crooked smile appeared on her face. "Yes, I did. Just now."

My free hand clenched into a fist. I was not usually this emotional, but all I could see in my mind's eye was a tiny little boy, frightened and in pain from a fall, shouting for help. Mrs. Huggin, almost as small and young, peering down into the hole, weighing up how heavy her father's belt would feel, and then leaving him. Keeping quiet. Later, tipping things down into the hole, until he was duly covered. She felt, sometimes, the urge to say something, to confess. Not to help the boy, this Francis, but for herself. And every time her father threatened her, had assumed before this great crime that his daughter was 'bad' somehow, she had become more and more resolved never to speak of it. She had stayed here to make sure the secret was never discovered. Long past her school days. Long past her own father's death and the threat of his physical punishment. Long past when it must have been just a thought she hurried aside, while carrying out her otherwise dull little life, when she had, by accident or self-preservation, ended the life of a bright little boy.

I was trembling, in a mix of disgust and rage. It was no longer a question why she was haunted, rather why it was only now.

And just as I was thinking this, something changed. Mrs. Huggin's face dropped and her eye line swerved to a little in front of me, about level with my waist. I followed her gaze, but couldn't see a thing.

It was happening, I realised. She could see him. He was apparently right in front of me.

She opened her mouth and started crying. Nothing she said or tried to say made sense. I couldn't see a thing. There was nothing there. I couldn't even force myself to breathe. Was he there? The little boy? Was he there? Could she see something I couldn't? *This must be what going mad actually feels like,* I thought.

There was a noise, sudden, sharp and loud all about us, unlike any noise I'd ever heard before. Part breathy sigh, part creaky door closing heavily and part high-pitched, echoing scream. We both jumped out of our skin, my hands protectively going over my ears, my torch clattering to the floor and going out, the sound of a battery popping from its case. I stood, half crouched towards the floor, as if bracing for impact.

Then it was over, and it took me a moment or two to recover from whatever it was, and reach out, grab at the torch and put the battery in again and stand up, somewhat gingerly.

I looked across at Mrs. Huggin. She was staring straight at me, into my eyes. Her mouth was open as if in a silent scream. Her eyes were wide and her posture almost contorted. I stared, my own horror returning, as a slow, awful realisation came over me.

I was looking at someone who was dead. That sounds strange even to read back to myself, but I knew it. A basic instinct within me told me that this woman was no longer alive, somehow.

She stayed in that strange, unnatural stance for a few moments. Then, like a puppet with its strings cut suddenly, she collapsed. Her mouth was exaggeratedly agape. Her body looked broken. Her eyes were wide open, though they did not see me any more. And without question, she now truly was dead.

I paused to stare at her. Then, unable to turn my face away, I backed out of the room. I wiped the torch and threw it back towards her body. Her keys were still on her, I realised. But why wouldn't they be? If she was still in the building, nothing was going to be locked. As I retraced my steps carefully, wiping with the different edges of my coat cuffs anything that I might've touched, I remembered Ms. Wainwright telling me that there was no CCTV. Not anywhere I had been anyway. She had made a call to me on her phone, which I could later say, truthfully, hadn't been a conversation as much as a series of beeps. I felt almost safe in a macabre fashion as I got out again into the night air and saw my wonderful little car waiting for me, to take me home and enable me to forget about all this.

I was quite calm, oddly. I stared at the school, sitting there in the darkness, looking back at me with its many windows and pervasive, dangerous shadows. I glanced up and down the street. No cameras I could see here either. I unlocked my car and sat inside, but then I stopped.

No, I realised. I would not repeat mistakes. I could not do as she had done.

This might've ended my career before I'd even begun it, I feared, but I couldn't just leave her there, not like that. I dialled a number everyone knows and waited for them to ask me where I wanted to be put through to. I answered. Quickly, a voice asked me what the emergency was.

"Yes," I responded, impressed with my own detachment. "I'd like to make an anonymous tip, I shan't be telling you my name. There's a woman who's had a heart attack at Grey Stones School near Copham Edge. She's very much dead, I'm afraid. Also in the boiler room - you might need to do some digging - you'll find the body of a little boy somewhere, I believe. About eight. He's been there a good while, maybe fifty years or more, so I'm not sure what's left, but he's there."

There was disbelief, and I hung on just long enough to make sure they had got all the relevant details, then knew I had to get out of there as soon as possible. I leant over to put my phone away, and turned on the lights of the car before the engine so that I could see better. That's when I saw the little boy.

My heart stopped. Everyone says when they suffer a terrible, immediate fright that their 'heart stops', and I never took them literally until that moment, when it really did happen to me.

Standing right in front of my car in the beams of the headlights, was a little boy, exactly as Mrs. Huggin had described him. A little boy who happened to be dead. He stared at me and I stared back.

## The Forgotten Boy

I didn't breathe, not a breath, as he turned and slowly walked around the other side of my car, opened the door and sat down next to me, in the passenger seat.

I'd forgotten how to blink. My whole body had stopped working. He looked forward, over the dashboard at first, as if waiting for the car to move, then turned to me. His eyes were there, but so hollow they might not have been.

A voice, tiny and thin, that must have been mine, finally broke from my mouth. "What do you want?" I asked.

He said nothing. He just stared back, unblinking at me.

I had to leave. They were going to arrive any minute. But there was a dead boy in my car, looking at me with expectant eyes.

"You want to go home?"

He said nothing. He just stared, unblinking, back at me.

"I don't know where you live," I reasoned quietly, tears filling my eyes with fear, and likely something else as well.

Again, nothing. And his look, now that I saw it in the glow from the lights outside, was not as frightening as I thought it might be. Sitting in the seat, without daylight or direct lighting, he might have just been another very pale, slightly off-colour little boy.

"You just want to leave the school," I spoke with a voice that was little more than breath.

He nodded. And that was all he gave me.

As if I did not have a little dead boy sitting in my car, I started the engine and pulled out of the school car park. I turned down the road, back the way I had come and drove in silence through the outskirts of town.

Considering I was so aware of him, it's odd to me now that I didn't notice him leave. I certainly didn't stop, and the car door never opened. I paused at traffic lights and realised then that he had vanished. He just wasn't there any more. I didn't feel him in the car. I reasoned that he must have left when he recognised the area we were driving through. Perhaps I had even passed his house and had never known it. Once the terror subsided and when I got home and into bed, the sadness took over me. How long had he been waiting there, in whatever form it was he'd been able to exist in, waiting for his parents to come and find him? Waiting for someone to come and help. Waiting just to go home.

And my god, I realised – I was the first person, outside of Mrs. Huggin in the place where it all happened, to tell anyone that there was a little boy trapped in the boiler room, unable to get out, waiting for someone to come and release him.

That's why he'd gotten into my car. He knew what I'd done, somehow.

Jess came back from holiday. She asked me how it was all going. 'Fine', my answer was. We cycled through my clients in review. We got to Mrs. Huggin. I reported that she hadn't made our appointment the day before. It took a week or two for the news of Mrs. Huggin's death to reach us, when I could finally speak to Jess about it. And even then, I was dying to tell her more. To tell her about the phone calls, and finding her in the staff bathroom, and that last awful half an hour in the boiler room.

But of course, I didn't. I couldn't. I never did. I never shall. Never to Jess...Maybe even not to anyone I really know. I wrote this entire story because I've been aching to tell it, for years now.

How Mrs. Huggin managed fifty whole years is quite beyond me.

# BITTERSWEET KEEPSAKES

I shan't pretend to anyone that I expect what I speak of to be believed. I'm sure there are some that might give it credence, but many more that would not. This is why I have not yet spoken of any of what I here confess to another living soul before this moment, not even to save my life. But as things come to light, and stand they way they do, with it still looking bad for me, I would tell the truth and I have no other medium left to me than this, for I dare not tell the priest who takes confession, and I've no friend left to tell it to, but tell it I must, according to my conscience, to confess the truth.

My name is Julia Biersley. Always has been – I never married. I never wanted to, much. I saw when young how my father treated my mother like he had no more use for her than a dishcloth that was past cleaning, yet she set her sight by him, worshipping him like he was our Lord and Saviour Jesus Christ reincarnated. Well, I decided fairly young that this would not do, and it was early that I put aside all thought of marrying, unless of course someone very different from my father were to ask me.

I was greatly fortunate when I was quite young to have a member of the gentry in our community that was fixing on doing good works, including putting some handful of the poor through schooling and giving them an education. Well, he says, I am well presented and a polite child and I ended up with a place. I made good of my school career, though it sounds as if I congratulate myself. My mother, God rest her soul, was never able to work a day in her life, and my father, God rest his as much as he can, earned enough for our survival, but nothing more. So when I was offered to teach at that same school not long after my leaving, working with the youngsters, which was my real joy, you'd have found no woman the length and breadth of the county as proud and content as myself.

Now before I go much further, there is something else that anyone who wishes to fully understand how I came to be here, must know. My family on my mother's side has a history that is heavily connected – I shame to confess it – to some scandals with witches of old. A great grandmother of mine, skipping back a few generations, she was hanged for a witch. I don't know the particulars of that ancestor, and I can't therefore say as she deserved it, but there is a very popular belief among the superstitious - and my father was one of them - that if one has a witch in one's direct line, especially through the mother, there is every likelihood that the women of that family shall be, like it or not, a Natural Witch. It may sound as if I am trying to excuse myself from some contract with the Devil, but I never met him, and would shun him if I did, and as I see it, there's only so much blame I can take. She was a fair enough mother, but I never chose her before birth, so how can I be held responsible for something from my mother, something in my blood, something in our history, from long before I was even born? Anyhow, I do not wish to dwell on this too long: it has some bearing, I suppose, but some may judge it does not.

There had been a number of comings and goings of the masters, teachers and a few of the sisters over the years while I had a place there. But I will always remember the day that Mr. Saltworth arrived.

I supposed he must have moved out of London for his health, for he was a well-spoken sort of gentleman, with the kind of speech as you hear with people of breeding and education: not really the prime candidate for working in a small school such as ours, even with its good reputation. He was young enough, only maybe ten years older than me. I readily admit that the first time I laid eyes upon him, I would be telling a falsehood if I did not report that I found him good-looking and becoming indeed. I blush to say that I blushed then.

I was introduced along with all the rest of the masters and teachers in the schoolyard as he arrived early one afternoon no more than a year before now. *Mr. Saltworth, this is Miss Biersley who is in charge of the youngest;*

*Miss Biersley, this is Mr. Saltworth, who shall be teaching* \_\_\_\_\_ and all the subjects with which he was acquainted. He smiled straight at me with a sparkle in his eye. I held out my hand for him, but rather than shake, as he had done with the masters, he cupped my hand and held me by my fingers, as if I were a lady. I turned the brightest shade of red I must have done since I had a tipple of sherry the Christmas before. I opened my mouth to say something, likely: "How glad I am to meet you, Mr. Saltworth. Was your journey long?" But instead, something happened which had never happened to me before, which knocked all words from my mouth and mind.

As I stared into Mr. Saltworth's face, it seemed to me that a thing like a picture – I suppose you might call it a vision of sorts - came between he and I. Instead of standing tall and smiling at me in the open air, I suddenly beheld Mr. Saltworth, lying on a wooden floor, his eyes rolled back so that the whites of his eyes were more visible than anything else, blood flung across him and the floor all about him, and he was so still and motionless that I realised in the same moment that he must have been quite dead.

This happened in a moment, then was over, but it was so unexpected, so sudden and so very vivid, that I took a sharp breath in, as one does when startled, and Mr. Saltworth lifts his head, as if I am to make some great declaration. But of course, I had none to make, except to tell him that I had seen a vision of his own death, and that is not the sort of thing you tell people who you have just met. So I stood there like a stupid person, saying absolutely nothing. With some clumsiness that was my fault, Mr. Saltworth asked me some questions, I seem to recall – how many were my charges and how long I myself had been at the school, and I answered what I answered, but barely was conscious to be able to listen to myself. I did not in the moment remember the whispered tales I had heard from my family members, about our witch ancestor.

Mr. Saltworth, to all reports, settled in well to his place at the school and was instantly well-liked by the children, who were very impressed that they were now being taught by someone from London. They continually asked him questions of it: What was the place really like? Was it true the roads were paved in real gold? Had he met the Lord Mayor, Dick Whittington? Yes, Mr. Saltworth made a fine addition to the school, and from all accounts, even now, he was a good teacher indeed. Yet it became apparent a short time after his arrival, that he had his mind on more than teaching.

Mr. Saltworth had been at the school perhaps three months, when rumours started. One of the boys had been in his rooms to get some books one evening, when he had spied a picture the master was drawing, hardly paying attention to anything else besides this task. On a moment's closer inspection, the boy realises it is a picture of me.

As is the way with schools, it was soon the main subject of chatter that Mr. Saltworth was desperately in love with me; had been seen kissing this same picture of me; was on the verge of asking me to be his wife. I believed very little of this much, it should be said, but when Mr. Saltworth asked me into his rooms one day, I was very careful to leave the door open behind me.

In I go to Mr. Saltworth's rooms which though it was fairly small, he had decked out nicely. He had a small hearth and mantelpiece, two very comfortable chairs before it, and a desk beyond – a fine, old specimen that was likely older than I myself. He had across his fireplace a rod like a spit, on which he was brewing some tea as I stepped through the door with a soft knock.

"You asked if I could step inside to see you, Mr. Saltworth," I said.

"Indeed, Miss Biersley," he replied, and indicated I should take one of those comfortable chairs by the fire, while he slipped into its brother. "Will you take some tea?" Without waiting for my answer, he reached across and poured a cup for me. "I am sorry to take up some of your time, but… You have no doubt heard that some of the children have created some… stories."

"As children are wont to do," I reminded him, sitting in the chair.

"Quite. I thought it only right to make you aware of them in case you heard them and were offended by any insinuations."

"Oh no, not at all, sir," says I. Good grief, how nice and polite he spoke – me be offended? "Stories of the kind have always flown about the school. Why, some year or so ago, they suggested that Sister Winifred was not really a nun at all, but a hardened criminal in disguise, but has found he rather likes being Sister Winifred, better than his life before."

Mr. Saltworth frowned deliberately, but the corners of his mouth turned up. "How very disrespectful. I hope the children who started such rumours were punished accordingly."

"Oh Mr. Saltworth," says I, "such stories are rarely able to be traced to their original source. I don't even know who it was that I overheard, talking about you having a picture of me, but I know he was not the first to tell of it."

At this, I thought he might offer some explanation as to how such a thing might have been mistaken, but something far more unsettling happened. He smiled, and as he did so, I saw again that same picture in my mind's eye – the vision of him lying on the floor at my feet, with blood all about him, dead. I moved my head a little, to shake it off far quicker, but realised, as I averted my gaze from him to the floor that the wooden floorboards of this very room, right upon which my eyes rested was the same place where, in the image my mind had given me, I had seen Mr. Saltworth's corpse. The shade of the wood, and even some of the knots and particulars of the beams underfoot were unmistakable.

"Are you cold, Miss Biersley?" he asks me here. "You seem to shiver. Here, draw closer by the fire if you have need," and he fetched from behind his desk a thin blanket of sorts for me.

"You're very good," I said, "but there's no need."

Nevertheless he draped the blanket over my shoulders and tossed the sides up to cover my legs and knees as well. I had never been treated so by a gentleman before, nor any man. As I tried my best to put that last horrible impression from my mind, I replaced it, instead, with wondering. Wondering if it would indeed be such an inconceivable thing that Mr. Saltworth's fondness had grown into admiration for me, and what I might say if he were to suddenly, unexpectedly, declare himself.

My hands fell on top of the blanket. Even in its coarseness, it preserved a wonderful amount of heat. As my hands truly took hold of the material stretched over me, I had the strangest sensation. It was as if someone were underneath the blanket trying to wrest it back again from me. How odd it was. The blanket never moved, but still I held my grip on the material, as I was sure that if I let go, it should be snatched away from me by a force I could not see! Mr. Saltworth had, for this second or two his back to me and just as he seated himself comfortably again -

I heard a voice, such as I have never heard a voice before. I could not tell if it were that of a boy child, or a girl child, but it seemed to come from the blanket Not beneath it, as if someone hid, but, in a way I could make no one understand, as if the voice were woven into the very material itself. It was the only way that I knew that the voice could not be real. Yet such a pitiful cry as I never heard.

I deliberately dropped the blanket onto the floor. The cry instantly ceased. "Thank you for your kindness, Mr. Saltworth," I said, doing my best to remain composed. "But I feel I might not be well. I should be aggrieved if you should catch something to further damage your health, from something that was a kindness from you."

He smiled easily and picked up the blanket and folded it across his own lap. It was quite obvious that nothing of the same effect overcame him when he had hold of it. No one trying to grab it from him, and no trying to call out to him from it. "I'm sorry for your illness, Miss Biersley. Do you believe you have the strength for this interview or shall we speak another time?"

I barely had the strength, considering these awful shocks with this man, to hold his gaze, but I assured him: "I will leave if I am overcome, sir. Pray continue."

At this he put the blanket down, stood, and began to pace about the room. Presently, he shut the door. His bearing was too humble for me to fear. Then he goes to his desk and takes out a sheet of paper or parchment, upon which something had been sketched in pencil or lead – I can see it through.

"Miss Biersley," he says presently, "I must confess that I have indeed taken a great liberty, and the hearsay is entirely my fault, for which I beg your forgiveness."

He put the sketch down upon his desk and turned it so I may see. Now I have caught my look in a mirror a good few times, but if that picture was of me, it flattered me greatly. All the same, even I could tell that it was a really rather good rendering of myself.

"You see, I have an amateur's passion for art and one evening while you sat at table, I committed your profile to memory and made it the subject of a sketch. I hope you are not offended, nor displeased with the outcome."

"My profile, sir?" I repeated. "Why on earth should you choose me as a subject? I can think of any number of far more interesting faces that you might choose."

"I cannot deny that," he said with a flare of his eyes. "I'm afraid that one evening, a boy came into my room without knocking and I had not time to put it away before he had seen it and identified you as the sitter."

"The unknowing sitter," I pointed out. "If it gives you peace, sir, I do not believe that it is thought among the children, or anyone else that anything inappropriate has taken place. Surely we would have had far more uncomfortable conversations than this before now, with our betters."

"Of course, of course," he said. "For which I am well pleased, and would be much dishonoured otherwise. But I would be a fool, now that the moment is upon me…"

I did not know at first why he still seemed so apprehensive and slowly it began to dawn upon me.

"If I were not to make you at least aware that… In my short time here, I have found your face to be the one that delights me the most, and so it was my privilege to sketch it."

I must have turned as red as a beetroot, but I tried my best to hide it. "You flatter me greatly, sir," I informed him. "I'm sure I don't deserve such attention."

"On the contrary," he said. "Now I have something to put to you, Miss Biersley, considering that it has been some little time that we have known and passed conversation with one another, and now you know my… sentiments…"

I did not speak. I had read enough books and heard enough stories to be able to suppose what was coming next, but could scarcely believe it.

"Miss Biersley," he says, and he draws himself up a little taller, "I put to you a very simple proposal. You seem to appreciate my portrait of you. If you like, you may have it as a keepsake."

I slowed my breathing. What a fool I was in those few moments. What had possessed me? What did I think that this London scholar would see in a country schoolmistress such as I myself?

"…It is yours, if you so wish. Yet, if you prefer, you may have me instead." He swallowed. "Just as you please."

I stared at him, my heart swelling. I had misheard him. I must have misunderstood him. "Have… you, Mr. Saltworth?" I repeated.

"Sadly, I doubt I shall look as well as the portrait still will in ten or twenty years time, but I have much to offer beside looks. As a… husband," he finally said.

Heaven knows how I looked, sitting there, my heart flushing fresh blood into my cheeks with every beat. "You wish an answer immediately."

"If possible," he said meekly. "Though of course, I can well understand that you may need pause to reflect…"

Now any woman or girl, I have no doubt, had she not had the experiences I just had a moment before, might fairly have bitten the hand off the man, to get a ring from his finger and onto hers. A girl who had not seen the ominous pictures before her, or the strange voice from an inanimate object, such as myself would have stood to her feet and declared she'd wish nothing more. Yet I did pause.

"I am indebted to you, Mr. Saltworth," I presently rejoined. "I daresay you cannot know how flattered I am at your proposal. But I shall indeed need a little time. That would be sensible. Also, it will give you further time to think of everything that might come along with a marriage to a young woman such as I… I do have one request, however. You may, of course, refuse, but I beg you let me have the portrait tonight… Along with one other thing."

"Of course," he says, fighting his own bewilderment, I don't wonder. "You may name it."

Here I leant forward and I picked up the blanket. Just now, it was silent, but I kept hold of it. "Merely this."

"The blanket?" he said, and he seemed greatly amused, then in the next moment, pleased as punch. "Well, of course, should you wish it! Is there a chill in yours and Sister Winifreds' rooms? But of course! Take it, please! I admit I was keeping it as something of a bittersweet keepsake, but if you want it, why then - it is yours."

"You are most good sir," I said. "I shall sleep under it tonight, with your beautiful picture of me at my bedside, and give you my reply in the morning. Does that meet with your approval, Mr. Saltworth?"

"Naturally! I am glad you have not turned me down outright, or else I shall have been such a bundle of heartbreak and shame, I should have to have left immediately. But I eagerly await your decision in the morning."

"Indeed," I said, and with some minor pleasantries, I quit the room.

I took the blanket back to my chamber, a small room within a small building which Sister Winifred and I shared, a standing wooden screen between our beds for some privacy. When the day's labours were at an end, and I returned to my room, the blanket folded once and spread along the bottom of my small bed, sleep seemed an unnecessary and faraway prospect. What use had I for sleep, other than to waste away the time between this night and the morning?

To never have to sleep in that place again, I thought as I readied for bed. Perhaps Mr. Saltworth and I might even have a place of our own. A little house, not too far from the school, with a pretty fireplace and my very own chair, kitchen and garden. Perhaps we could eventually leave the school and go to live in London someday, where we'd have a servant or two and I'd never know how to talk to them or what to give them to do. Or perhaps even our own children would come to this very school, and roll their eyes when we couldn't see, to be taught by their own flesh and blood, until they were older and grew proud of us instead. The endless possibilities that a married life, as I'd never considered it before ran through my giddy head and I was delighted at each and all of them.

Yet, whenever they got too intense and I, too happy for words, I reminded myself of that terrible vision. Surely it was not a portent of the future. Must be that it was some kind of warning that I had been delivered in order to keep Mr. Saltworth safe from harm. But how?

There was a single window in our room, and I opened the shutters, for the romantic in me wanted to be able to look at the same moon, high and nearly full as it hung in the black night sky, and hope that Mr. Saltworth was watching the same moon, which shone down on my little rickety bedside table and showed me the beautiful sketching of me he had made, and so how he saw me. I stood at the window for a little time after Sister Winifred was in bed and snoring quietly. Then I went to bed myself.

I slipped beneath the blanket, and cared not a jot for its coarseness. It smelled of his room and his tea and something else which I could not tell, but it all reminded me of him.

As I settled beneath the blanket, almost having forgotten my experiences that very day, I suddenly became conscious of something. My bed was small, and if anyone had tried to to get into it, you can be sure I would see and know of it: candlelight, moonlight or near pitch darkness. Nevertheless, as I pulled the blanket up to my chin, I had the most curious sensation that someone were under the blanket here with me.

Though I knew it was impossible, I said: "Sister Winifred?" She may have heard me in her sleep, for she snored a little louder momentarily, but she had not mistook – she was clearly in her own bed, and I clearly in mine. I dared not speak again for fear of waking her, and she thinking I'd gone mad, so I did not ask who it was that was clearly in a bed that was not their own. Instead, I looked down to the edge of the blanket, and how I managed not to scream or die of fright then and there, I shall never know, but I saw a tiny white face peering out at me from under the blanket.

The face looked at me and I looked back, daring never to move, for I knew that, indeed I was alone in bed, apart from this thing that I could plainly see, its eyes reflecting the moonlight as it stared at me. Then I felt two arms, bone and flesh alone, go about me, and just as I feared the creature was sure to drag me off to whatever hell from whence it had come, I heard a voice, and it was the one from the blanket before.

"Where is Papa?" she asked, pitiful and weak. "I feel so sick…"

As this was said, I instantly lost any and all fear I had of the creature. Why, it was a child and whoever and whatever she was, she was a child in fear, not to be feared.

"Oh Little'un," I whispered, a common pet name I used for some of my own flesh-and-blood children in the school. Do not ask me how, but my own arms managed to get about the child, as if giving comfort. I felt, as with some of my charges, that I ought to say something to soothe her, and I managed: "There, there, Little'un. Don't you fret."

"Where is Papa?" she asked again, as if these were all the words she knew. "I feel so sick…"

I swear, I could have cried for the little lamb. I knew who she must mean, though I knew not how, or how I knew it beyond that it was obvious. "Your Papa will be here soon," I cooed to her, "and your sickness will pass. No, you don't you fret, Little'un. I'm here. I'm here until your Papa gets here."

The little face was turned towards me as she made a tiny sound, like a happy little sigh, and I suddenly felt the child no more. The blanket was once again a coarse cover to keep out the cold, and I was once again completely alone in my tiny bed, with nothing but the sound of sister Winifred gently snoring nearby.

I did not sleep much that night at all, but it was not merely from the shock. It was from agonising over what it must mean. Papa, she had asked for. And Mr. Saltworth had said that he was keeping the blanket as a – what was the phrase he used? Bittersweet Keepsake? How terrible. But then it begged the question – who was this child's mother?

Next morning, which was a Saturday, I rose early, dressed and took myself straight to Mr. Saltworth's rooms, forgetting to take with me either blanket or portrait. He answered the door confused, for he was barely finished dressing, but before either of us had said a fair greeting, I had bustled my way into his room.

"I have thought, Mr. Saltworth. I thought all afternoon after we spoke, even as I taught, and as I readied for bed and looked again over that picture you made of me. I have thought all this time, and I'm sure you know I'd be glad to be your wife." He was about to smile, and he looked mightily pleased, but I went on immediately, because I had to. "I must know, though. You know that I am a maid, and know nothing of marriage or even men, save what I've seen of my own folks', but that wasn't the best education. If I am to be married to one who's been married before, I say I must know it now."

His expression reverted to one of puzzlement. "Forgive me, Miss Biersley, but I cannot follow you."

"Sir…" I tried, as I had the day before in a different temperament, to keep my head, "I ask you something I must have you answer honestly. I will not judge you nor pry too deeply, but I must know if you've been married before."

His face lit up with an easy grin. "Me, married?" he responded, the grin in his voice as well. "No, my dear Miss Biersley. I am, I fear, up to this moment, a lifelong bachelor."

I was greatly surprised at this. "You never married, sir?"

"No, indeed. I've never so much as courted before, hence my nervousness yesterday."

If he had not answered, I should know. If he had anything other than that easy, pleasant, honest grin on his face, I should surely know he was being dishonest. But I read not a drop of falsehood on his face. I was ineloquent about it, and indelicate too, but I forced my way forwards. "Did you ever then have a brother or sister, then, sir?" My quick-thinking saved me. "I think a little on child-rearing, if you are disposed to that kind of thing. Have you had a hand in raising a child before this?"

His face again, while maintaining fondness, showed I quite befuddled him. "Why, no, I fear, Miss Biersley. I was my parents' only child. You and I, if we are to be so blessed, shall face new, undiscovered countries such as that as novices together." His eyes searched my face. "Forgive me, these seem pointed questions and... Did you sleep at all last night? You do not look your usual, buoyant self."

I had been ready to confess all and had, indeed, looked forward to it. To disclosing the horror, together with the good news of safe passage onwards, from the night before, but I was thwarted. He knew nothing of it. If I were to tell him now that there had been a dead child in his blanket, why, I'd not only never be able to work again, but would sure lose the man. And then I reminded myself of my purpose. What had kept me at the window last night and what I had come here to settle.

"I did not sleep well," I said carefully. "But it is my own fault. I had much to think of, for it would be a great change in my life. And I must ask you if you, having reflected yourself... believe the sketch you made of me good enough for a frame, that we may hang it in any home we come to share?"

He blinked several times and his smile teetered on his lips, as if unsure. "I do, if you'll have me."

I needed no other persuasion. Sure I could not understand half of what I had experienced, but I knew that I wished it, and I agreed. The blanket, in that moment and all the rest of that morning was no concern of mine, and Mr. Saltworth – Charles, as he bade me call him in private from then – seemed beside himself, but having no point of reference what newly engaged couples do, he poured me a cup of tea to have, and himself had a small amount of brandy to steady his nerves before we left to see the vicar and find what could be arranged. I found I did not fear the looks of others as we walked side by side down the lane, the tips of my gloved hand in his gentle grip, but I did fear, even as we approached the church and spoke at length to the vicar, that surely I did not deserve so much happiness.

And well might my feelings have tended that way.

We made our way back to the school and he drew close, speaking softly in my ear. "I know that you shall make a fine wife, Julia. And hopefully I, a decent husband to you. Someday, even," and he stole a kiss from my cheek, right in the street, "we shall both make happy, good parents."

I had quite forgotten the little child all day until then, but I thought of her now, and her pitiful cry for her Papa. I gazed at my fiancé, my Charles.

"I knew I should say Yes to you the moment I awoke this morning," I said. "I had several dreams, and you were in many of them. Apart from the one at the end, but I suppose I was glad of that, for it was a very sad dream."

"Oh dear," said he. "Very sad? Or like a nightmare of sorts?"

"Oh it was nothing," I pretended to sweep away. "It was silly. I dreamt that I had a little girl, a child in the bed with me under the blanket, sick and chilled to the bone, crying so pitifully for her Papa that it broke my heart. I only just remembered now, because all the other dreams I had were of you."

Mr. Saltworth's pace slowed ever so slightly. Had I not been holding his hand, I might not have noticed. "Well, sad indeed. But as you say, a silly dream." Yet his pace slowed a little further and he was rather quiet for perhaps a minute or two. "This dream you had... Is why you asked this morning if I were ever married? And asked about children?"

I feigned all strain of my memory, as if I had put it all quite from my mind. "It may well have been a touch of that. There are superstitions in these parts that say it is bad luck to marry a dead woman's husband inside of seven years, and that's not minding what the church says on it."

He seemed to ease. "Well, I can reassure you – no wife, no children, nothing of the kind before. Simply you, I, and whatever children may come."

"Is there something the matter?" I asked just as we got back to the school, for he had fallen into silence again for some time.

"Your... sad dream. What do you suppose it means?" he asked.

"I don't know," I said. "I half expected you to confess something and as I have said, I would not have judged you for it. Aside from that...?"

"Hmm," he said. "It is strange that you should have such a dream. I have not deliberately kept it from you, however there is something you may wish to know now. Or perhaps not, once it is told. The blanket that you took from me yesterday... It was my mother's, God rest her soul. She was a very charitable woman. Towards the end of her life she ran a very small home for poor, sick children, whose parents had nowhere else to take them.

I fear that you may have had something of a visitation from one of those children."

"Good God," said I in earnest, crossing myself. "Do you mean to say a child died with that very blanket about them?"

"Not just the one, I fear," he replied.

"But... surely," I said, testing him more than I had so far done, "such a thing as a 'visitation', as you call it…You think it that, and not a coincidental dream? You cannot believe in such things."

"Not as a rule," he admitted, "but then there are so many things that we cannot understand. May never understand. And I suppose I must ask your forgiveness if whatever has happened in the past has burdened you somehow. Perhaps you are sensitive to such things. Have you ever had anything similar happen to you? At all?"

Of course, I remembered his body on the floor of his own room, looking very similar to how he looked now. Not much changed that I could remember. And so how many days was I assured with my beloved? But of course, I did not wish to burden him with such inexplicable and maybe false news. "No," I answered. "I can't think of anything like."

We talked by the fireside in Mr. Saltworth's room through the afternoon and into the early evening, seeming never to be exhausted of things to say. Mr. Saltworth made us up some more tea to warm ourselves beside the fire in his room. As I sat and sipped, he blew ripples over the surface of his own to cool it, all the while gazing like a puppy at me.

"You shall blow your tea away, it must have cooled by now," I jested.

He seemed to be contemplating something, then without a word he put his tea aside and stood, went to his desk, and brought out a little object from a drawer. He returned and placed it with care and reverence in my lap.

"This is another keepsake," he explained. "I helped my mother with her work at times. I wished to be a doctor when I was rather young. I grew rather attached to some of those children. My mother had some of the better ones make things from old pieces she had lying around to distract them. It's something one of them made me. Sentimental, I know, but I'd never part with it."

It was a tiny little cross, fashioned, from what I could tell, from tissue-like paper, glue and petals, made hard. It was crudely made, as if by a child not yet ten and half an idea only of what they did, but very nice to the eye all the same – the more so for his sad story.

"In truth, I am thinking quite seriously now that after we are married, I might well set up a similar home here," he said to me. "Carrying on my mother's work. Would you be willing to help me with it? I have noticed how good you are with children… It was one of the things that drew me to you after your charming face, I must confess."

I stared at the cross and touched it gently with my finger. I was waiting for something. Maybe a voice. Maybe a vision. But nothing happened. I turned to Mr. Saltworth and it seemed from his expression that he had been waiting too, to see if there was any effect it had on me, but was as quietly contented as I to see it had not.

"I should be glad and honoured to help you in such a thing," I said. "How good you are, my sweet Charles." My hand touched his face affectionately and I saw he was happy.

"Perhaps this is why God enabled us, having been born so far apart, to meet despite all the odds against such a thing." And returned my gesture.

I shifted in the chair. I had begun to feel a little queasy a few minutes before, but hoped it was the effect of a bad night of sleep, or perhaps I had miscounted my months. Now, however, I felt light-headed after that terrible vision the day before, but thankfully, there was no vision now.

"I feel very responsible that you have suffered some horrible impression because of that old blanket," he said, oblivious to my silent suffering. "If you return it to me, I'll buy you a new one as soon as I am next in town." When he said this, his eyes settled and he watched me, as if he expected me to jump up and run and fetch it straight away. It was, even with what we had both had between us, the first truly awkward moment that we had.

"You're too good and kind," I said at last. "I shall indeed return it."

"Shall I come back with you and fetch it? I feel uneasy about the possibility of another dream, another uneasy night, and it really would be all my fault."

"Oh do not worry," I said. "I shall not be under that blanket tonight!" I felt I would throw up. "In fact… If you'll excuse me, I may well catch up on some sleep now." I got unsteadily to my feet.

There was concern in his face as he stood as well. He pressed the back of his hand to my forehead. When it came away, it felt almost wet. "Julia,

I do not think you are very well, my dear."

"No," I agreed. "Perhaps… But I'll be fine. I hope I've given nothing to you."

"What about the blanket?" he said as I tried to turn.

"What of it?"

He looked steadily at me for some moments. "Some of the children died of things… That others might catch. I never thought of it until this moment. I was among them, I was used to them, but you…" He put his hand to his mouth and chin.

The thought was sobering indeed. "You think a doctor should be called?"

"Let me tend to you," he offered. "We can send someone in the morning if you're no better, but I know the signs and may be able to help."

Without warning, something more horrible and unexpected than anything so far happened to me. A girl appeared. A poor girl, standing by the fireside behind Mr. Saltworth, maybe in her early teen years. But she was angry. Oh, so angry. The look on her face alone was enough to make anyone quake, but to know she did not really stand there, that she was nothing but air and anger, made me quake on the spot. I suddenly realised that I still held the little cross keepsake in my hand. Fearing it was hers, and she so angered that I was to take it without thinking from whom it belonged, I threw it across the room at her. "No!" I shrieked. "No, no, for God's sake! Go! Stay away!" Then even as weak as I was, I ran from poor, unknowing Mr. Saltworth's room as fast as I could, he calling my name after, and some of the children boarding with us even poking their heads from their rooms to see what the fuss was. There would be new rumours in the morning, but what care had I for that? I raced into the open air and was violently sick.

Sister Winifred promised Mr. Saltworth, hovering in the doorway for a little time like a moth trying to get at a flame, that she would look after me, and let him know I was well in the morning. However, since being sick, I was beginning to feel better. As the moon rose and Sister Winifred, assured I would not die in the night, went to bed, I could think of nothing but that young woman by the fireside, with all her rage. I almost talked myself out of doing so, but as night came, I leant out of bed and picked up the blanket, throwing it once again over my prostrate form.

Would the child come again? I wondered. I worried I should fall asleep too soon. Yet not even a minute had passed when I was aware once again that there was some other form, some other thing with me in the bed beneath the blanket. I lifted its corner, but was surprised to see this time I face I knew not at all. Another face. A different face. This was of a boy, maybe eight years old at most, looking pitifully sorry for himself. I felt his little arms go about me, and I returned the gesture.

"Don't be afeared, Little'un," I told him. "The pain will soon pass."

"How long?" his hollow voice asks.

"Soon," I promised him. "Soon, my dear."

"I wish I'd never come," he said sadly. "I wish I'd never pretended to be sick."

I looked sharply at the boy, not catching his meaning. But he too had gone.

I slept about as much as I had the night before, for I had to be awake for morning prayer with all the boarding children, and Mr. Saltworth and I could do little but smile cordially in the chapel. Yet my mind was not on church lessons, or the hymns. Something caught me in a strange feeling, and having caught me, like an insect in a web, it refused to let me go. Refused to let me think of other things. After chapel, I caught the sleeve of a young one who only some years before had been a charge of my own.

"Horace," I said to him, in confidence. "I have something I wish you to do for me. There's a penny in it for you."

His eyes went wide as saucers. "Really, Miss? What is it?"

I steeled myself. "I want you to go out among the boys and find out who it was who went into Mr. Saltworth's room and first saw that picture of me. Make sure you find the right boy - don't let them tell you any tales. Whether he's here or not back 'til tomorrow, when you are sure you've found him, tell him he can have a penny too, if he comes to speak to me about it."

I must, in hindsight, congratulate young Horace, for I expected a day or two to elapse before I had the boy before me, but barely twenty minutes had passed before Horace, with an older, pale boy in tow, returned. I duly gave Horace his penny and sent him on his way.

The older boy, Patrick, I knew, for he had been in the first class that I had ever taken in the school. It was near his time for leaving, by my reckoning, but he seemed more like the small boy that I had once had charge of as he stood in front of me than ever before. "Please, Miss," he says before I can say a word, "I didn't mean to cause trouble for you. I didn't realise when I first talked of it how far it would get. I didn't mean to embarrass you, Miss Biersley, or Mr. Saltworth, really I didn't."

"Never mind that, Patrick," I said. "Here's something I want to know, and I want you to be as truthful as you can be. I am not cross, do you understand? Good. Now. Think back, and think hard. When you went into Mr. Saltworth's room that evening, and you saw my picture that he had drawn, is it true that you didn't knock upon the door?"

He squinted a little. "Oh, no, Miss," he says with assurance. "I always know to knock. I wouldn't ever forget, not on a teacher's door."

"You're sure, Patrick? We all forget things sometimes. Think hard."

"Oh no, Miss. I'm certain I did. After all, I remember him calling through 'Come in' and so I do, and he is sitting there with your picture before him."

"Did he try to hide it away, my picture? Or make it so you couldn't see?"

Patrick thought for a moment. "No, Miss. Well, I couldn't miss it. He had his back to me, on the wrong side of his desk, and he was holding it up, then he just puts it down. Maybe he thought I wouldn't recognise you, Miss, but I did! Straight away. It was a very good picture, after all."

"So would you say, Patrick," I spoke carefully, "that Mr. Saltworth might even have been hoping that you would see it?"

Patrick shrugged. "I can't say, Miss. I just know that I saw it was you, and he must've seen that I could see it was you, and did nothing to hide it. But as I said, it was a very good picture."

I thought upon this, and gave Patrick his penny, thanked him for his time and that I would be obliged if he did not discuss what I had said with anyone. If someone asked, he might even say that I'd had harsh words with him. Now, I was sure that Mr. Saltworth had wanted someone to see his picture of me. It had been niggling away at me all this time, but I still didn't know what it might mean. Nothing with Mr. Saltworth or that damned blanket made much sense.

Drat, I thought. The blanket! Mr. Saltworth would definitely suspect something if I put off returning it to him again, or avoided him. So I returned to my room and picked up that blanket, hugging it to me as if promising when we were married, I would take the time to listen to them all. All the poor little souls tied up in that coarse, harsh material that had been their last, unfortunate comfort.

But the further I got from my room and the closer to Mr. Saltworth's, the more I felt I heard something. Pitiful, tiny voices. I had thought they belonged to one child before then, but now I knew there were many voices, and could tell them apart, even. I knew I could not tell Mr. Saltworth any more than I already had. The voices increased, and seemed to grow louder.

Did I love Mr. Saltworth? It had been with his coming and seemingly everything to do with him that, whatever it was, the curse of being a Natural Witch, had flared. Why with him did I have such power? Was it because I loved him? For I felt I must. Even as the voices grew and pleaded, saying things I could not understand or make out, I knew I must love him, or be as close to it as I had any desire to be. For something told me I had to break it off with him. What I would say, I did not know. That we had moved too fast over these past few days. That I was terrified of my ability to love. That there were things, terrible things happening to me that I had no control over and my god, I'd do anything to keep from being a wife to cause him shame. I had been a fool to let my heart run away with my good sense. And now I had to break his, and I might never get another chance for anything half so good.

I clamoured at Mr. Saltworth's door, trying to drown out the voices that I couldn't make head nor tail from. I knocked as if to tell of fire, but he did not answer. I didn't like to leave the blanket outside, to be taken by one of the children, or trodden upon, so lifted the latch and took the liberty of going inside.

I half expected for an awful moment to see him on the floor, as I had seen him in my mind, but he truly was not there. The voices, as if crying out, were so loud in my ear, I could barely hear my own thoughts. I was tempted to burn it in the fireplace and claim an accident, but I could not in good conscience do that. I was light-headed and as I thumped the blanket down on top of his desk, and the voices instantly stopped, my parched lips begged I must have something to drink.

Mr. Saltworth's kettle was hung over the cinders and while it would not be fresh and warm, it was something. So I went to get a quick mug of tea.

And then, several horrible things happened at once.

The first was that the tea cup which I had taken in my hand, came loose from my fingers and crashed down onto the floor, shattering into pieces, as if someone had ripped it from my grip. I was horribly shaken, but as I looked up, I saw that there were children in his room.

They were not speaking now, not like when I held the blanket to me. Far worse, in fact. They stood about the room, lining the walls, sitting in the chairs, perched on his bed. One even sat cross-legged atop his desk. So many young children: some only just able to stand, some just on the lip of adulthood. I saw the little girl that I'd seen the first night, and the angry girl, and the boy from last, and I thought I couldn't bear it. I wished for their clamour now, loud as they pleased, but not this terrible silence. Not the stillness with all these eyes turned upon me. I put my hands over my ears and shut my eyes as tight as they might go, but instead of peace, I saw the same first vision of poor Mr. Saltworth on the ground, dead and bloodied. I grabbed the first thing that came to my hand, which was the blanket itself and threw it, I knew not where or at what, and shrieked for it all to stop, stop it at once, for God's sake, STOP!

But as if my thoughts had been whispered as a command unto death for the blanket, the corner of it fell over the side of the grate and caught alight in the fire's embers. I snatched it out, quick as I could, and stamped the very end of it into ash. My word, I thought, how am I to ever explain this to Mr. Saltworth? It is quite one thing to tell a man you must put off marrying him, but that you have burned a keepsake, something that belonged to his mother as well?

I looked over my shoulder again. The children had gone and their voices were still.

I bent down by the fire to check the damage. It was not so severe, but it would not go unnoticed. Perhaps Mr. Saltworth had something in his desk that might help. My God, I would pray with Sister Winifred over this blanket. Say The Lord's Prayer and a few Hail Marys, and perhaps even read from the Good Book. Yes. This I would do. And when I'd saved the blanket from some of this damage, and the prayers were said, and the children released, I would tell Mr. Saltworth all. I opened the drawer in Mr. Saltworth's desk, the one I fancied the keepsake must have come from, to see if he had needle and thread – anything!.

But a life can change depending on what you do and what you do not. A strange, confusing little scene lay before. That same drawer was near filled with tiny, similar little keepsakes. Some looking like a cross, for I suppose that was easiest, but some like horses or the shape of a crescent moon, of the sun, a cat or dog or tree or star. All were arranged in neat little rows along the bottom of the drawer. Some appalled part of me rejoiced, for now I had many things I could pray over and with, and how loved Mr. Saltworth must've been. I saw that beneath each of these keepsakes was a tiny label, the writing so small, I could barely read it. I peered closer. This first one I looked at said: 'Phillidda Morris. April, 1843. Fourteen days.'

This was a curious way to keep keepsakes, I thought. And so strange a way of keeping a record. I read others, my eyes darting about the drawer. 'Benjamin Stone. May-June 1845. Eight days.' 'Marabella Crossthrop, December 1850. One week.' 'Gabrielle Shepherd, September 1852. Thirteen days.' 'William Kosminski, January 1853. Six days.'

Keepsakes, these were. The child's name writ. When they were admitted to the establishment, I supposed. And that last account, why, that must be how long it was before they -

My hands, with a life of their own, began trembling. This was not right, what I was seeing. It felt as wrong as it had to stand in this room and be surrounded by children who were not there.

I was nearly quite sick all over again like yesterday, when I glanced over at the tea and stopped my retching. The cold tea was splashed about the floor, among the remnants of the tea cup. And a horrible, horrible thought came to me. I would not have given myself credit of it, had I not seen all that I had seen, but I had been queasy, on and off, for the past few days.

And each day, had Mr. Saltworth not offered me tea? Had I not gladly taken it?

The door opened and in surprise, and some quiet confusion, Mr. Saltworth came in. He paused in the doorway, then shut it firmly behind him.

"Julia, my dear," he said, then stopped. He saw the blanket and its burn, or smelled it. Saw the smashed teacup, and the look in my face. Saw the drawer that I had opened.

*Bittersweet keepsakes,* I thought.

"What are you doing at my desk, my love?" he asks me outright.

I grabbed at an effigy from the drawer and offered it up for him to see. "Bittersweet keepsakes, you said. How many bittersweet keepsakes should a man have, and why are they labelled so?"

He laughed in his throat, as if I were being quite ridiculous. "I flatter myself that I've been a popular teacher over the years. I've been given many keepsakes by the children I've taught, and whom I have helped in my mother's establishment, as you can see."

"And the days?" I demanded, though my voice was weaker than I had known it could be. "Was that how long they lasted... after you started giving them whatever it is that is in that tea?"

A change came over Mr. Saltworth's face. His eyes seemed to narrow now. I barely recognised him, standing in front of me. "What can you mean?"

"You know precisely what I mean," I insisted quietly. "You gave people – children – swaddled in that same blanket that you gave to me - something. Some of them, I dread to think - some of them may even have guessed towards the end what it was that you were doing to them, and there was nothing they could do about it." A helplessness had come to my body, and I thought I should die in it, like that, standing there. I felt the children surge as if they were all about me, each laying a hand upon me.

He made a move, as if to counter me, and then seemed to think better of it. He reached back to the door and flipped the latch over, so it was now locked. "I'm not sure what has brought you to these conclusions," he said, and he began to remove his gloves. "Then again, unless you were truly unworthy, I knew at some stage, you would know."

I felt my hands begin to shake once more, and I put them on the desk to steady myself. For a moment like a lightning flash, I fancied I saw each and every child again, to whom a voice from the blanket belonged, standing with ashen faces and sad expressions all about the room. But they stared now at Mr. Saltworth, one and all. I could not bear it. One that I could not see reached out behind me and put their hand on top of mine, as if to steady and gird me, but there was something cold too, under my fingers, I thought...

"'Twas not I that started it," he said, in a voice that sounded, strangely, more like his own voice than anything I had thus far heard. "My mother took broth to the poorhouses in my youth, before she started her 'poor hospital'. *'They cannot help themselves, Charles, they all are like children, and you must do your best to help them.'*

"You poisoned them," I said, my own voice strange and unknown to me. "You killed those children, those poor innocent things."

"Innocent?" he flung back, as if dishonoured. "What has innocence to do with any of it, Julia? It's quite simple – there are far more of them than there should be. I cannot expect you to understand, for you have never been yet to London, but you will know it all too well when we first visit there. My mother entrusted her work to continue with me afterwards. It was her dying wish."

"But they were not all dying," I said. I thought I should scream again. "You caused their deaths.... And you have been trying to do the same to me!"

"Nonsense! God, no!" He came forward, close to me, his tone genuinely soft and doting. "I just needed to be sure. To be sure you were strong enough. I assure you, it pained me to think some evil might befall you, but I could not have a weak wife, and I had to be sure of you. You have survived, and I am glad of it: truly I am, and you should be proud. You were not chosen arbitrarily. You also are so loved and admired by those in our care. You may be more entrusted than I, as we continue with our great work."

"Your great work," I scoffed in a whisper.. "Was it your great work that had you scurrying away from London like a rat?"

"Our Great Work," he corrected me. "And yes, it was. My mother died, and questions had been asked, by those who knew nothing about it. We have a duty, Julia, you and I. As my wife, you will be part of my work now."

"How dare you." Cold as metal pulsed beneath my fingers. "How dare you bring me into this horror and expect me to keep my mouth shut, when you deserve the noose, not me for a wife. If you think for a mere moment that I would turn against these poor creatures - "

"You have no choice, Julia," he continued, standing close still, and his voice was calm and still and full of a soft cooing, like I could imagine were the last things those poor children had heard. "A wife cannot speak against her husband, it is simply not done. Besides, should you say anything, a single word from me can ruin your reputation. You'd be out of school and home with nowhere to go in a moment. And if you grow tired of the very good life I offer you as your husband, I can have you put in the asylum for the rest of your life. And wouldn't you rather be the wife of a respected and loved man? A man who can look after you, and all the children that we may have?"

I screamed in the moment, for the vision was come again, more powerful and horrible and pressing than it had ever been before, and I was powerless, in its mercy, unable to do anything but shriek and scream and make the most unholy noises I never heard man or beast make. I screamed and heard them running up and down the corridor outside, trying their best to get in at the door. And my breath was deep and heavy and I feared I should faint as I screamed to be rid of it all. I didn't even know that I was holding his letter opener until the door had been broken down, and the thing wrest, quite easily, from my hand. I didn't even manage to count how many marks I had made on the man, so suddenly and unexpectedly for him, that they covered his torso, his hands for defence, his chest to get at that wicked heart of his, even one in his neck. All I knew was standing over him, looking down at those familiar wooden beams that made up his floor, and his eyes rolled back in his head as his blood decorated all in my field of vision, was that this was never to be a vision again.

I am told by my counsel that I stand a good chance of being let off, or at least not hanged, with all that has since come to light about Mr Saltworth, and all that happened in London before he came to us. He is confident than no jury in the land could find me guilty of murder, but I am not as assured. Who knows who else may be on that jury. May find themselves squirming in their seats, worrying over people like me, who find out things that can be held over their heads, as threatening as a noose. No, I do not believe I stand as great a chance as my counsel says. Besides, it is already being said that I was a jealous woman, who suspected my future husband of carrying on with another, and the story may well go that I am a danger, not in control of myself at all. And for a few moments, those that mattered, I was not. Yet I can tell you this: As God is my judge and my witness, I do not grieve over it. I fear greatly they will ask me if I feel I could ever commit such a crime again, for I should have to tell them the truth.

There is only one keepsake, as far as I know, that still speaks as to all that happened. The rest, I suppose, to be in the hands of the law. But here in my little cell, I was permitted to have a sheet of paper upon which an evil man once drew my likeness. I don't know why I keep it, but I do. Perhaps, I wonder in my darker moments, for the same reason he kept all of those precious little things in his drawer. For a macabre reminder of what I had done. Also, because, of course, he asked me once to choose between him and that picture. I do not think considering, that I am so very sorry that I see that picture every day.

# The Problem With Ghosts

4<sup>th</sup> November, 1996

Dear Auntie Ida,

    Mummy has told me that I must apologise on all our behalves for how long we've left it since our last letters. Also, that you have to put up with my handwriting. Mrs. Baxter says it is improving, but is still somewhat scrawly now and again.

 I'm writing, because Mummy really isn't up to anything just now. She's alright really, but she's had a few days in bed and the doctors have given her something for her nerves. It's strange, isn't it, that it's only when a shock has happened and then has passed that you see people get ill because of being shocked or horrified or, in our case, have had a really rather nasty turn of events. Mummy has suffered the worst, but we were all there. Daddy is being as strong as possible about it all, but he's very much affected too. As for me, Jamie and Marie? We're dealing with it best, I think.

 So here's what happened and why you've not heard from us in a while. We're only just beginning to come to terms with it all and carry on now, and the whole thing came to a head nearly a week ago.

 You know that we had moved house in September, ready for school. Marie and I didn't want to change schools, but we finally had rooms of our own, especially as Jamie has gotten even more annoying. Mummy was pleased because of the kitchen and the place under the stairs to both store and use as a snug, and Daddy had the garden. He's been wanting to grow a vegetable patch and 'get back to nature and making our own food' since Marie and I were little. So on the first day, we were a little bit tired and worried, but mostly excited.

Then Malcolm ran away.

He was in his cage while we drove here and Mummy told all of us that we had to keep him indoors until he got used to the place. But the day after, first thing in the morning, I went to feed him. That's my job at the moment. I went to open his cage – we put him in there overnight so we knew where he was, but the cage door was open and I couldn't find Malcolm anywhere. I called for him and clinked his bowls, but he'd just gone. Everyone made sure that all the doors and windows were closed. "Who opened the cage door?" Daddy demanded. "That's what I want to know."

No one said anything. So while Mummy and Daddy sorted the furniture and the places for things, Jamie, Marie and I all started making Lost Posters, and put them up on the local lampposts, and in the post office at the bottom of the road.

I don't think anyone thought that someone had done it deliberately, but now, it all makes much more sense.

Three days after we moved in, I was reading, when I heard Jamie and Marie start playing Hide and Seek. There were still boxes everywhere, because we had to sort out our own rooms, which meant we hadn't done a thing. I heard one of the boxes outside my door bang, as if someone bashed into it or was trying to get round it, and then I heard a voice right outside: "Come find me!"

I got up and opened it. There was Jamie, crouching behind a stack of boxes.

"Caught!" I declared as I grabbed at his arm. "You need to hide better than that."

He looked at me as if I had two heads. "It's Marie who's hiding," he informed me. "I'm seeking."

"But I just heard you shout 'Come find me!'" I told him.

"No, I didn't," he answered. He's not always the ideal brother, but he's not a liar, I don't think. Not even when he's in trouble. And his and

Marie's voices are very different - as you know, he's just turned eight, but she's twelve in a month.

There was a crash at the bottom of the stairs. We jumped and peered over the bannisters. On the floor, a large box was on its side, the remains of Mummy's best dishes, which she'd been saving for the ormolu, in little pieces all over the floor nearby. Marie flew out from her hiding place and we all stood gazing at the fallen box, looking guilty, though we knew that none of us had done it.

Mummy still blamed us. She thought it must have been Jamie, and Marie and I were covering up for him, and so none of us had dessert that night.

That same night, just as I was getting ready for bed, there was a noise on the landing. It sounded, again, like the boxes, which me and my siblings still had not seen to. I ignored it, but after a minute or two, I could still hear it, as if someone were continually moving the boxes. Just as I peeled back my covers to get into bed, my bedroom door thumped, and the slit of light under the door was suddenly covered , making my room all the darker.

I went and opened the door. There was a box right in front of me, stacked on top of other boxes, in a big, wide pillar in my doorway. I was just able to see round them and down the hall. Everything was still, apart from the distant sound of telly Mummy and Daddy were watching. But on the landing, there was nothing but three equally tall piles of boxes right outside each of our doors.

As I looked down the hall, Jamie's pile of boxes being the furthest, I saw the flap of one of the box lids suddenly fall. I don't mean it dropped. I mean it looked, when I first saw it, as if it were hanging at an odd angle and then someone had let go of it… as if someone had seen that I was watching them… then let go and hid. I saw it. I saw it as it happened. My imagination tried to tell me that Jamie must have ducked out of sight so quick, I didn't see him. But then Jamie came and opened his door, and Marie hers. We all stood looking out around these boxes into the hall, then towards each other.

We pushed the boxes back I told them what I had seen. Marie didn't look very convinced, but then Jamie said: "So why did you say 'Come find me'?"

I squinted at him. "I didn't."

We looked at Marie. "Well it wasn't me," she said. "You were probably starting to dream, Jamie."

But Jamie was trembling. We followed his line of sight. At the end of the hall, where the rail met the landing, the light didn't quite reach. And when we looked, we saw a shape. It was so indistinct, I couldn't tell you how big or small it was, but it was there, where nothing had been a few moments ago. Then two small portions disappeared and reappeared again and we realised that the thing had eyes and it was staring at us.

We fought each other to get into my room – the room furthest from the top of the stairs – and shut the door with a great slam behind us.

"Go to sleep! Stop slamming doors!" came a cry from downstairs.

I propped a chair against the door. I didn't know if that would do anything, but it made all of us feel a little better. The three of us, like mice in a nest, huddled under my covers and went to sleep, in the one bed as we hadn't done for many years.

Mummy was the first down to breakfast in the morning. We told her why we had all been in my room. She was, of course, convinced we were scaring ourselves, or maybe we didn't actually like this house as much as we had the old one, and were looking for excuses to go back. Mummy started talking about the change with us. Everything, according to Mummy, can be rectified with some honest talk.

That is unless your spoon has just left your breakfast, is now hovering several inches into the air, and then the sugar bowl launches itself from the middle of the table straight into the wall.

There was a horrid, loud smash. We all jumped, Mummy most of all.

"Did you do that?" she asked aloud in bewilderment, looking at each of us in turn.

We none of us moved.

"It's the ghost," Jamie said.

This was the first any of us had put a name to it, and as soon as it was said, we all looked a little more horrified. "It stacked those boxes up outside our doors last night. It was at the top of the stairs, with eyes in the dark, Mummy. It made that box fall over yesterday and you blamed us. It's nothing to do with us. It's a ghost!"

## The Problem With Ghosts

Mummy was about to reprimand or correct us somehow when several feet away from any of us, the box of cereal we had not yet poured into our bowls flipped over on the counter and spilled its contents out all over the edge, and onto the floor. Mummy jumped up, a hand to her face. We'd never seen her frightened.

Daddy ambled into the room in his dressing gown and slippers, looking tired and in want of a shave. "What's all the noise?" he asked grumpily. He slipped on some sugar from the broken bowl, landed in the cereal, gave a cry: half of surprise, half of pain and then one after another, every single drawer, cupboard and box in the room came open of its own accord. We could do nothing at all. We just watched until it stopped.

"What the hell's going on?" Daddy asked.

Mummy was on the phone before Daddy had managed to stand up again. While Marie, Daddy and I all tried to put the kitchen back together – Jamie was clinging to Daddy's legs and not much help – Mummy called the estate agent. Then she called our new, local church. She called several other people as well. I've no doubt, Auntie Ida, that she might have called you had you not still been in India. But every time that the rest of us had the kitchen almost tidy again, something else would happen, or we'd hear a noise somewhere else in the house and have to go and investigate. The refrigerator rattled, and on opening it, we found things open or scattered about inside. All the drawers in the kitchen opened a second time. The mirror in the hall that my mother had hung only the day before fell with a crash to the floor, inches from my now-near hysterical mother. "There must be *someone* who can help!" she insisted to whoever she was on the telephone to at that point.

We spent the remainder of the morning either tidying up, or looking into each others' faces in disbelief. I'd always liked a good ghost story if we ever had a sleep-over, but I never thought any of them were real. Not in the middle of the day, in a nice area in a new house, with church bells from the local chapel clanging down the road, and the odd murmur from local gossips drifting through the windows as they went past. It didn't seem the right setting for a ghost story yet, suddenly, we had found ourselves in the very middle of what my father diagnosed as Paranormal Episode. Specifically, as he put it, we were being haunted by 'An Unquiet Spirit'.

"They're called poltergeists," Marie informed us, with not quite so much effort to show off her intelligence as she might have under other circumstances. "It's German. I read about it. It means a Noisy Ghost, I think."

"This is not noisy," I pointed out as the refrigerator door banged open, startling us again. I shut it. "This is chaotic."

"It's horrendous, is what it is," Daddy said. I don't think he really had grasped what was going on still, or if he did, he was being really brave about it.

There was a suspicious quiet after my mother's last phone call. We were all shell-shocked and silent in the front room, when the front door banged open. We rushed into the hall to see what had happened now, but instead of another mess, we saw a lady standing there. Short and stocky, with rather bizarre clothes, she took off her hat as she looked at my mother and held up Malcolm. Malcolm mewed in annoyance, jumped down from the woman's grasp, and bounded out of the house again, standing with a swooshing tail at the end of the path. The lady stood up straight and said in introduction:

"Word has reached me that you are having a problem with ghosts!"

\*

"The real problem with ghosts," Lavender said, smiling in something lost between serenity and sleepiness, "is that so few of them realise that they're dead."

It seemed to me a rather ridiculous thing to say. Of course ghosts didn't realise they were dead, surely. That was why they were ghosts. As Lavender had hypothesised, ghosts simply thought they were still alive and either didn't know we were there, or couldn't figure out who we, the apparent interlopers, were. They carried on living, despite their death, because they were none the wiser.

But then, such a ridiculous thing might come out of the mouth of a woman who I thought was rather ridiculous. Who has a first name like 'Lavender' anyway? And what's more, she had a slight whiff about her that led me to believe that her odd mismatching clothes may not have been as thoroughly washed as one might hope since they were first tailored.

"What's more," she carried on, as if giving a great a speech or holding court, "is that there is so little intelligence behind their manifestations. That isn't to say that in life they weren't clever people, but ghosts themselves don't realise the trouble they are causing the living. They are condemned to be mere echoes of themselves, you see, the very walls in which they are enshrined acting like a mirror and you must agree, there is no intelligence in your reflection in the mirror, is there?"

My mother nodded. None of the rest of us argued.

"But if one is to rid oneself of these things," my mother said with a heavy breath, "how is one to begin?"

"Well you certainly don't need priests," Lavender said quickly. "Exorcism and all that nonsense. These aren't minions of the devil. They can't see a white light to walk towards," she carried on, getting rather heated about the subject. "I've heard the most outlandish things about what can be done. Usually, all that is needed, in my experience, is to let the minion know that they have passed on. This in itself is enough to frighten the thing into reality. If someone told you that you were really a ghost," she said, focusing on me for one awful moment, "you'd be frightened out of your wits and never go near whom had said it again, would you?"

I considered how I would feel if someone tried to tell me I was a ghost, and I nodded in agreement, though perhaps not for the reasons Lavender thought.

"However," she went on, "I think we ought to try something a little different for this one. This particular ghost, or poltergeist, I should say, is obviously desperate for some kind of attention. Why do we not try, in the beginning, simply... ignoring it?"

"Ignoring it?" my mother repeated, aghast.

"Yes," Lavender confirmed. "Let us try treating it as a child demanding attention. When this ghost misbehaves or causes a nuisance, don't react. Take your time before cleaning up after it. Don't give it any more attention than necessary. That may well be the answer. So, instead of reacting with shock and horror at the opening of a door with no one beyond, or starting at something else implausible, simply carry on. It may well get bored."

"Right," Daddy said with an air of finality. He clearly didn't take much of what Lavender said too seriously. "I'm off to ignore it in the garden then, I've got a veg. patch to find. This poltergeist is not going to rob me of my gardening, I can tell you that."

We took Lavender's word and went around the next few days trying to ignore the poltergeist in our house. When my sister's plate, full of food, flew off the table and hit me as I came down to dinner, Mummy sighed and picked up the bits while Daddy went at me with a damp cloth advising me to put my clothes in the linen basket once dinner was over. When all the pictures, carefully lining the stairwell fell down in unison in the middle of the night, Mummy and I stood at the top of the stairs and huffed, quietly declaring we would see to it tomorrow. That Saturday, when literally everything in the front room had been moved at least a little – the T.V. to the other side of the room, lying face down on the ground, with three of my Nanna's doilies adorning its back – we smiled and either put things back where they should be, or just left them.

Malcolm, having returned, became an outdoor cat. We put his meals, at sunrise and sunset, on the path. He did not come into the house. He would not even come to the bottom step, and if you picked him up to bring him towards the house, he would screech terribly and scratch as he desperately tried to get away.

We were very careful not to draw any unnecessary attention to it. No one screamed. No one even spoke the words 'poltergeist' or 'ghost' the entire time. We just got on with it. We tried, for over a week, even with us beginning school. But then, as if the thing had realised that we were specifically ignoring it, went on what Daddy might have called 'A Bender'. On Sunday, every pipe in the house seemed to be groaning. A leak sprung in the bathroom. The fridge door opened and shut itself for about half an hour, and the toaster nearly set the kitchen on fire.

It was clear that while we'd had a valiant try, this method was not working.

"How's it going with the garden?" Mummy asked, trying to make small talk and ignore the madness.

"Not bad," Daddy replied. He wasn't fooled. "But that veg patch might take a while – there's piping under the garden. Thought it was an Anderson shelter at first, so I've had to move - "

She'd stopped listening. Every sound, every movement, every slight flicker out the corner of her eye had her in high alert. The sound she had heard was the reappearance of Lavender.

She'd returned to see what progress we had made, but did not ask any questions when she saw our tired and pale faces.

"Well," she said, refusing to be beaten, "we simply move on to the next idea."

"What is next?" Mummy asked with a worried tone.

"Next is finding out What and Why."

We didn't understand.

"There is something or someone causing inconveniences in this house. If we find out whom or what, then perhaps we will find out why, and then we may be able to get them to stop."

"Do you mean," I tried to clarify, "we're investigating? Finding out if maybe something happened here?"

She beamed at me. "Exactly."

That gave us all something to do. Daddy got in touch with the estate agent again, and asked for any information they might have about who had owned the house before. That was a dead end. The house had been rented out for years to an older couple, and there had never been talk of any supernatural happenings. Mummy looked into the parish records, but all we got was a list of names and dates that meant very little.

"I don't care what Lavender says," Daddy said to Mummy as he picked up the phone receiver. "I'm going to call to get an exorcism done."

"Mummy, Daddy," Jamie said.

"I suppose we ought. I mean, we've tried it her way," Mummy reasoned.

"Look what I found," said Jamie.

He was standing in the doorway to the front room with a bag of marbles in his hand.

"Those are yours, dummy," Marie said. "You forgot you had them, but we've had them for years."

"They're not mine," Jamie said indignantly. "They were in my room."

"Probably because Mummy and Daddy put them there," Marie reasoned. And Jamie went off to play with his old treasure.

## The Problem With Ghosts

The house was quiet that evening. Daddy thought that maybe the loud and pressing threat of an exorcist had been enough, but we all knew that if that were the case, it would only be for the meantime. Jamie was late for dinner, and Marie and I went to fetch him. We found him in his room, playing with the marbles, set out in a pattern.

"Dinner time, dummy," Marie told him.

"Watch this," Jamie said excitedly. He bashed one marble into another, sending the second careening across the floor and under his bed.

"Well done, dummy," Marie continued. "Now what are you - "

The second marble suddenly reappeared from under the bed. It rolled gently across the wooden floor, towards Jamie. With less than a centimetre to spare the marble suddenly ground to a halt in front of Jamie's marble.

"Do that again," I told him, and he did. It happened just as before, as if someone were grabbing the marble at the last moment before it hit the one Jamie was holding to the floor.

"Is that because the floorboards aren't very even?" Marie said hopefully.

Mummy shouted up again that dinner was ready. I didn't want to call her. She was trying to be brave, but this whole thing had her very shaken. So, I swallowed quite hard and bent down. When the others realised I was going to look under the bed, the whites of their eyes grew larger and Marie, with a hand around our brother's arm, took a small step back.

I breathed as normally as I could as I bent my head down next to the underside of the bed. I took another last breath, steeled myself and willed myself not to cry....then turned my head.

Complete silence. Nothing. Everything was still under there. I breathed a sigh of relief. And two little portions of the darkness, a foot from my face, shifted and blinked at me.

I scrabbled back with a great gasp and the other two sprawled in other directions, eager to get away. We sat deaf to Mummy's calls and shouts until she walked in. We hadn't dared move until the light fell across the space under the bed, and even though it showed completely empty now, we crowded and barged past Mummy to get out of the room.

We ate dinner in miserable silence.

"I think it's time we thought about moving," Daddy announced. Mummy's eyes filled with tears. So did Marie's. Jamie's hand found mine and I gave his a squeeze. He was worried some of it was his fault somehow.

After dinner, I thought about what we had seen. The game under the bed with Jamie was different. It'd been playful. Not chaotic and causing mischief. So what had been different?

"Jamie? Show me that bag of marbles." He dutifully handed them over.

Holding them in my hand now, I realised Jamie had been right in the first place: they weren't our marbles at all. This bag was older, dirtier, made of rougher cloth than our marble bag. The embroidery on it was small enough that I hadn't seen it before.

"Where did you find this?" I asked him.

"It was in my room," Jamie replied hotly. "And I can prove it's not ours. Look, there's a name on the inside, and it's none of us."

Delicately sewn into one corner, again, so small I had previously missed it, was a little name. Elspeth Drummond.

At about half past seven, I opened the telephone directory.

There were a few Drummonds in there, local to our town. Not as many as you might have thought, but that was a help in itself. I picked up the phone in the hall as Daddy, Mummy and the other two were watching TV. With a hushed voice, I dialled the first number for a Drummond. No one answered. I called the second. They were very angry when I tried to explain, and pleaded all ignorance to our house and plight. The third didn't seem to be a real number, or otherwise had been disconnected. Then I called the fourth:

"Elspeth Drummond?" a male voice repeated back to me.

"Yes! Do you know her?"

"Well, yes," he said with a bit of a chuckle. "That is, well, she's not Elspeth Drummond any more though, not for decades. She's a cousin of mine."

"You wouldn't happen to have a 'phone number for wherever she lives now, would you?"

"Well, Elsie's an old lady now, I don't want you to go troubling her."

"Oh please," I begged. "I wouldn't ask if it weren't important. Look, you wouldn't happen to know if she ever lived at this house, would you?" I gave the address.

## The Problem With Ghosts

There was a pause. "Yes, I think that might have been where she lived when she was younger."

A few more pleads, and Mr. Drummond gave in, and supplied the number I needed, threatening that if I made mischief for his ageing cousin, he knew where we lived!

I called the number possibly a little later than I should have liked, but I didn't feel it could be helped. The phone rang for a long time and I was just getting despondent when the receiver picked up and I could hear a voice, old and almost familiar.

"Hello?" the lady said.

"Hello! Is that Elspeth Drummond?" I asked.

"No," said the voice, but then: "This is Mrs. Elsie Roberts. Who is this?"

I gave my name and started the odd story from the only place I knew: "Your cousin, Mr. Dummond, gave me your telephone number. I think that my family and I are living in a house you used to live in." I gave the address again.

"Yes," she answered with a degree of caution. "I lived there, but many many years ago. Who is it who's calling?"

I gave my name. "I am sorry," I apologised, "for getting in touch so late. I was looking for someone called Elspeth Drummond, you see, and I was hoping you'd be able to tell me something about the house. We've been having problems here, you see."

"Are you trying to be funny?" the aged voice said at the end of the line. "If you are, I shall put this phone down."

"No, no," I begged. "Honestly. We've been having trouble with…"

I stopped myself before I said 'ghost' or 'poltergeist', predicting she probably would hang up on me. So I finished with:

"The history of the house. We found an object that we thought might be of sentimental value to a previous owner. It has your name in it, you see."

The voice paused for a moment. "What is the object?" she asked.

"Just a little bag," I supplied. "A hessian-type bag, with some marbles in it."

There was an intake of breath, and then she didn't speak for so long, I worried she had gone. "Yes," she said slowly. "I know the marble bag you mean. Those marbles were mine, many years ago. There's sadly no point in returning them to me," she went on. "I don't think my grandchildren would be interested."

"Oh," I said. Perhaps it had all been coincidence after all. "You're sure you don't want them returned to you? We wouldn't mind."

"That's kind of you, but I'm afraid I don't want them. They don't hold particularly happy memories for me, you see."

"I see," I said. "My brother found them and then I saw the name."

"Yes, boys like marbles a little better than girls, I find," she said. "They were my younger brother's for a short time."

"Oh. Well, would you like us to try and get the marbles to him? Perhaps he might like them instead?"

Again, an intake of breath. "No, I'm afraid not."

"I'm so sorry," I said, realising. "Is he…" What was the phrase Mummy had used once to describe Great Auntie Edith? "Is he no longer with us?"

"I'm afraid I couldn't tell you," she said. "Arthur disappeared when I was 11."

For some reason, the word disappeared struck me as singular and important. "Oh my gosh… What happened?!"

"Arthur ran away one day while we were playing hide and seek. My mother caught a fever and died partly from that, partly from grief, a few years later. My father then sent me off to live with aunts and cousins for a few years."

It was a good job he did, I thought, otherwise that cousin Drummond might never have known what I was talking about when I'd called.

"I have very few happy memories attached to the object you describe, or indeed, the house itself," she reiterated.

"I'm so sorry," I said, desperate to keep her on the line. "There's none of it in the history of the house you see, or I'd have been more careful about calling. Did you… ever find out?"

"No," she said shortly. I've stopped wondering about it, because I think it's what did for my mother, you see. She went slightly… off, over the next few years before she died. I'd rather not talk about it any more."

My heart beat like a dull drum in my chest. "That's awful," I caught myself saying. "I'm so sorry, Mrs. Robert."

"Yes, well, you'll have to excuse me," she said, rather clipped all of a sudden. "I have things to do. Please feel free to do with the marbles what you want. They're rather old now and perhaps they'll be worth something to a museum, someday?" And without saying goodbye, she put the phone down.

The next morning, I told my family everything that I had heard from Elsie. She hadn't seemed at all like a nonsense-case and didn't have any reason to lie to us. But at last, we had the name of our spirit –

"Arthur," my father said. "How old was he?"

"Must have been quite young," my mother said sadly, doing the calculations in her head. "If he was younger than Elsie, and she was last living here aged eleven, well he can't have been older than nine or ten at most."

The door slamming announced Lavender's presence. We filed out into the hall, the low level of excitement apparently written on our faces.

"You've had a breakthrough," she predicted. "Tell me what has happened?"

"A little boy got lost here years ago," I supplied as the person who had known it first. "He and his sister were playing hide-and-seek and he just disappeared. They thought he might have run away, but he was never found."

"Of course!" she said, punching the air in her eccentric way. "So – now we know what we're looking for."

"What are we looking for?" Marie asked warily.

"We're looking, my dear, for that little boy."

Mummy was horrified. "But he disappeared." She argued. "He's quite clearly not here anymore."

"He quite clearly is!" Lavender corrected her with a wagging finger. "He must think this is still his home. He possibly even thinks you're members of his family, and can't understand why he's not getting any attention. It all makes perfect sense!"

"But where would we look?" I asked. "His mother searched for ages. The police looked. They couldn't find anything."

"They searched what they knew of the house, more than likely," Lavender chimed merrily. "We need to think bigger. Where would a small child go, maybe even nearby? Where would a small child fit, that might be difficult for him to be found?"

"There's nothing in the children's rooms," Mummy sighed. "Harry cleaned out the basement and the garage and the attic – nothing there. I haven't found - "

"Oh God," Daddy spoke, though it sounded like a stranger's voice. "There's… there's a...a pipe," he uttered, an odd colour creeping over his face. "In the back garden, where I tried to put the veg. patch at first. It's huge – thought it was an air raid shelter at first. It's all rusted, but there's a gap in it, like a hole from years ago. I mean – it's filled with earth, but it's a sizable gap. You don't suppose…"

Mummy called the police while we stood about the kitchen, excited and in dread at the same time. If there was a body to be found, one way or another, we would have to tell them. They were a little confused by the story, but two large, burly chaps came around about midday.

The pipe was in thick undergrowth where Daddy had been trying to clear the earth. I looked from it to the house. It was a long way from the back door to the pipe, and if you didn't know the pipe was there, or that there was a hole in said pipe… But your little boy, or your little brother had found it and thought of it as a great hiding place…Earth shifts as you climb into it. If no one at all knew, sixty or how ever many years ago it had been...

"Found something, Frank," one policeman said to the other, his serious face appearing over the top of the mound of freshly dug earth.

"Back inside, folks," Frank said to us. "We'll need to use your phone in a bit."

Lavender arrived again not long after the small army of police officers had come, collected their cargo, and gone again, asking us not to go into the garden at all. After they'd all gone, the house felt eerily still; almost empty, even though my entire five-strong family and Lavender were with me.

I broke the silence at long last just as the sun had set and we'd fed Malcolm, who was now feeding from the bottom step for the first time since we'd come.

"I wonder if we should call Elsie," I said. "She ought to know that we found her brother at long last."

"Oh, I don't suppose she'd care," Lavender said with a wave of her hand. "It's no good telling a child she's terrible at hide-and-seek sixty years too late, is it?" she almost laughed.

I was going to laugh with her, just to get some jollity back into me, but - "How did you know that, Lavender?"

There was an odd noise from the kitchen, like a small clank.

"Mummy…" Jamie's slightly nervous voice trilled.

Mummy went into the kitchen. There was a muffled shriek and we all jumped up and followed hot on her heels.

Jamie was sitting cross-legged on the flag floor on one side of the kitchen. On the other, dressed in short trousers with long socks under small black boots and a shirt with a huge, great collar, was a little boy who I'd never seen before. But there was something about the way he seemed so interested in what Jamie was doing and yet with such a faraway look, that made me realise that he wasn't really there at all.

He wasn't a very old little boy either. I felt ever so sad when I realised he couldn't have been more than five or six, younger even than Jamie. He sat with his back to the cupboard, opposite my brother, playing marbles. Then he looked up at us and gave a very odd kind of laugh. The kind of giggle I had heard from Jamie when he was little, worried he was in trouble, to try and make light of it for Mummy or Daddy. I don't know if I was the first, or even the only one to realise that when he laughed, he was looking at Lavender. I looked at her too and the strange smell of leaf mould started to make sense, and Elsie Roberts' strangely familiar voice….

"I wholeheartedly apologise for the trouble," she said with a quiet sigh. "There haven't been children in this house for many years. Finally, someone he could play with. But I still couldn't find him. I've chased him around and around this house, suspecting that nothing could stop him playing or me tearing the place apart looking, except what you've finally helped me with today."

She was addressing my mother, but my mother could not speak. She stood dumbly with her hand over her mouth, shaking her head.

Lavender sighed loudly. "Well, there it is." She patted Mummy on the shoulder. "Don't you worry, dear, I can take him along with me now."

At that, she turned towards the little boy and in a voice that sounded as if it didn't come from her lips, she said: "Arthur! That's enough playtime. We're going home now."

And then it happened. The little boy gave a slightly doleful nod and walked right up to Lavender, taking her hand. The two of them turned towards us with an appreciative smile.

And then, Auntie Ida, they disappeared.

## THE SILENT GIRL

I didn't give a statement at the time because I didn't know what to say. Just because we were... 'friends', doesn't mean I have a right to say anything, to change how other people saw them. Any more than anyone has a right to how I feel, or felt, or thought, and think, and have processed things. It's not that I'm secretive – I'm entitled to my privacy. I'm entitled to stay quiet if I just bloody well want to. And I don't care what you want to know, but it won't be my version of events.

No – never. Not with my first love in the flush of youthful hormonal rampages. Not as I went from person to person looking for something lost between romantic and impossible. Not even when my thirties crept up on me unexpectedly – or rather, I was unprepared for them - and I wondered if it would be possible to settle for someone I was not truly in love with (the answer, for good or bad, was No). No. I never loved anyone as much as I loved them. You can ask me in ten years time - the answer will be the same. You can ask me in fifty, if any of us are still around. I could never love anyone as I loved them.

    They were a Leo. That will be their name for this story, though they are not themselves the main subject of it.

    They were in love with a Gemini, so her name will be Gem.

    I was there, as much as I was allowed to be, and for this purpose, I will be Aries.

## The Silent Girl

I remember what day and date it was, of course, but it doesn't matter on the whole. It had been raining all day and I had been trying to get some work done with very little success. Shortly after six, I gave in and switched on the TV to distract or inspire myself: happy, at that point, to let either happen.

The knock was so faint, with my TV on at a certain volume, that the first time, I thought it my imagination, or something off-screen. But then I heard it again. Seven quick, quiet knocks. It's strange how you remember and recognise things of people that you never thought you'd retain. The exact pitch and pace of their voice. How their veins look in their wrists, or the difference between their going into a genuine smile, or a faked one. Even, it seemed, their own personal knock.

It was the first time I'd realised that the sun had long set and it must be late. Between the living room and the front door, I told myself it was coincidence, and someone obviously knocked like Leo. Yet when the door opened, it was them standing there, drenched in rain, blinking every second, straining an inappropriate-for-the-moment smile. This was one of their fake ones.

"Hello Aries, old man," they said. "Don't, er… don't expect I could come in?"

That summer had been the last time we'd spent anything like a full day together. There was a cafe not far from their flat in London: small, kitschy and very fashionable in its off-the-beaten-track style. We'd sat and eaten vegan food, which I surprisingly didn't mind, and then they'd said, with a strange look: "You're interested in… Other Realm stuff, aren't you, Aries?"

"Other Realm stuff? What do you mean, what kind of thing?"

"You know. Things that you see that you know aren't there." They thought long and hard before speaking again, and glanced at me several times. "The closest thing I can think of, is to call it a sort of…. Ghost."

"A ghost?"

"Not strictly a ghost, but like one."

"Okay. Interested, not an expert. Give me an example."

The next word they used was so specific, and I hadn't heard it spoken in such a long time, I knew this was more than a frustrated Google search:

"Doppelgängers. Doubles. Of People."

"Doppelgängers?" I clarified. "What, you've got a stalker who looks exactly like you?".

"Not – me," they corrected. "And not a stalker…"

And in horror, I realised I knew exactly what they were talking about. I had been hoping against hope that up to this point, it had just been me. Hence, I hadn't said a thing.

"Sorry, old man," they said, coming in through the door. "I had to get out of London and I suddenly thought of your place."

My heart leapt, but only minutely. It was one thing that they had thought of me in my little flat in Kent near the sea, but another that there was a reason why they 'had to get out of London'.

"Well, you know you can stay as… long as you need."

"This isn't inconvenient, is it? I'm not in the way?"

"Of course not." I didn't tell them that I could have been moving house or dealing with bereavement, and my answer would've been the same. "It's absolutely fine."

I gave them my embarrassingly long, woolly dressing gown after they'd peeled themselves out of the thin shirt they were wearing. I'd looked away. Partially because I was trying to be polite. Partially because I couldn't stand to be there with their flesh, cold, clammy and riddled with goosebumps, but just inches away from me.

I'd loved Leo before they achieved their success. I loved them fairly straight away, and never stopped loving them. They suffered in their younger days and somehow still were able to laugh and joke and be happy for others. We were the opposite of Fair-weather friends. We were there for each other when it was all awful, and that was fine. That they'd had some success wouldn't have meant anything to me, so long as I'd met them. I knew, almost as soon as I knew I loved them, that they were lost to me. They were never going to be mine. I was just Me.

However, I still loved them.

She'd just shown up one day, with her almost unnerving perfection, and blown on through everything, including my own private dreams. Gem's shadow was long and cast shade across the rest of her sex. They had met

Gem at what had thus far been the peak of their renown. I had tried my best not to resent her, and perhaps because I was aware of it, I'd been able to conceal it. Though she didn't seem overly materialistic, some part of me wondered if she loved Leo because they too were famous. I didn't like that thought and so tried not to wonder – the more I thought of it, the less I liked her. And she had been annoyingly perfect. Perfect weight. Perfect height. Perfect teeth. Perfect complexion. Perfect voice oscillating between husky and serious. And rather tellingly, something that I'd never expected of someone to take Leo's fancy...

Almost perfectly silent.

I knew writers and creators could be a funny lot, some very introverted or shy, even. However, Gem wasn't shy. I imagined she was one of these types who saved all her words for her writing, which was how she had thus far found her own modicum of fame, apart from modelling, acting and anything else that everyone kept insisting she was perfect at. She hadn't won any awards, but she had been something of a minor hit with the critics. It took me a good few months to bring myself to read her work, as I didn't really like the idea of torturing myself with yet more of her perfection. I have to say, I was quite surprised. She obviously knew what she was doing. She knew a good turn of phrase, and I couldn't fault how she plotted her stories. They were, on the whole, very readable, but there was something still missing. It might have taken me until the third work of hers that I read to identify what it was:

I couldn't find her voice anywhere in her work. I couldn't find Her. I would not have been able to pick her words, characters or phrasing out amongst others'. Had I not known the woman, I might never have seen it. Throughout her work, however, it was all but impossible to find her singular, unmistakable voice anywhere.

Even in her writing, it seemed, she herself was oddly silent.

"Where's Gem?" I asked.

The question was meant innocently enough, but they didn't answer me, just bundled into the gown, wrapped and knotted the belt around their annoyingly slim waist, and sat on my couch. They were shivering something chronic. There was still enough damp in their hair that it started dripping on my cushions. I went and fetched another towel without a word.

"Leo, how did you get here?" I asked, laying said towel behind them. I knew the trains weren't running as regularly as before Lockdown. "What are you doing here? You should've called me, I'd have gotten things ready."

Their eyes were half-closed as they smiled quite genuinely up at me. I hated that smile almost as much as I loved it.

"You're in trouble?"

They took a moment before they nodded. "Something happened to Gem."

I was in my best clothes: ones that flattered me the most. I'd had no choice but to wear them; doing so was the only thing that made me feel even slightly confident enough to meet Leo's new girlfriend. At least there would be a few of us. I wouldn't have come had it just been me.

As it turned out, there were more of us than anyone planned. The Gathering swiftly became an unofficial party. Leo told me that sometimes happened in their work – people just called others to come over, they'd turn up with armfuls of drinks and the night would carry on. I wished I'd not worn my best clothes. It was obvious I was trying to make an impression. And I knew Gem saw through it from the beginning.

"Gem, this is Aries!" Leo said. They rattled off a couple of things I was into, things I had done, then did exactly the same with Gem. I brought my best smile. The one that said 'I love this person. Please look after them. Make them happy, and I'll be happy for you.'

Her smile said nothing. It was perfect and symmetrical and on the surface, very friendly. But her eyes were not connected to the smile. They were probing me, sizing me up. I'd never have seen myself as any kind of threat, but those eyes of hers made me wonder…

I hardly ever drink, but I may have had one or two that night. I was in Leo's bathroom. I hadn't locked the door, maybe because I was only supposed to be in there, giving myself a pep talk to just stay another twenty minutes or half an hour, and didn't expect to take long. However, I forgot and the door opened, Gem appearing in the mirror.

"Oh! I'm sorry," she said quickly.

"I'm sorry," I almost echoed. "Rather hot. Be right out"

She folded her arms across her waist and looked at me, shaking her head and I felt about an inch tall. She was laughing at me. She was amused, because she'd figured out why I'd come in my best clothes, and now here I was in the bathroom trying to keep it together.

I turned to say something – I don't remember what – but the door was closed. Gem had ducked back outside no sooner than I'd said I was sorry.

I looked back at the mirror. And there she still was, laughing at me in the glass.

So I left, because I'd been spiked.

My first impulse was to turn on the news, but worry kept me in the seat. Leo stared ahead at nothing. I flipped on a lamp, so the light was low, though that had not been my intention – I don't normally go for the kill when someone turns up traumatised on my doorstep. Others have done that to me, and I've never forgiven them.

"What time is it?" they asked.

"Nine-fifteen."

They nodded. "I had to come see you. I'm sorry I haven't come before."

I touched their hand very gently. "It's alright. Do you need me to get you something?"

I stood, the kettle on my mind, but they reached out and grabbed at me. "No!" they insisted. "Just… stay where you are, please."

I did so. When they finally spoke again, I hadn't been expecting what they would say at all.

"Aries… I got the impression from you that you…" They tucked their head in that way people do when they are hoping you will read their minds. "There were…feelings."

I found myself nodding, but it was too much to confirm in spoken word.

"I thought you did. I didn't want to say anything. I didn't want to embarrass you."

"Thank you."

"I suppose I've come because I want your forgiveness," they said.

"Forgiveness? For what?"

"Everything. For not seeing you. I've been thinking of you a lot recently. And I thought you… felt that way."

Each time they alluded to it, it was a little like they turned and accidentally knocked a steel spike a little further through my skin, a little more blood flowing from a wound that I alone knew was there.

Everyone's moral compass is different. Mine has a point in it that says - 'Even if you don't like the person the love of your life has ended up with, you stay quiet. Unless you're worried about them being abused, you stay silent. It's not your life and they're not your feelings, and they are not yours.'

Gem arranged a picnic, and I don't know how they convinced her to invite me. I knew that the type of relationship the two were developing was the kind that will make friends drift from one another, so I couldn't say no.

We set up the large blanket across the grass. Two other people, mutual friends, were with us, but it was Gem and I that offered to go back to their car to pick up the rest of the necessaries.

"You love them, don't you?" she said when we were out of earshot.

I wish I had my best clothes on then, not slightly unkempt hair and standing shorter than she. I left it too long to answer for her to think she was wrong. "Why do you bring it up?"

"I just wondered."

It seemed an almost vicious thing to bring up and then not talk about. "I can control it," I assured her. "You don't need to worry about me making a move or anything."

"Alright." Her tone was so placid, so unworried, it felt like an insult. She wasn't worried in the slightest. We got to the car and started unloading the last bits and pieces.

"I just want their happiness. Literally it."

"Then we're on the same side."

"... I wasn't aware there were sides."

"There's always two sides."

"That quote's about stories," I noted.

"But it's true of everything," she said and shut the boot of the car.

In the shaded glass of the back windscreen, I saw her suddenly lunge at me, teeth bared, and her hands were around my throat, tight and strong. I staggered back, dropping everything I was holding, falling onto the gravel of the little car park.

Yet her hands, though I had felt them, were not about my throat. She stood looking bewildered, a metre or more away, staring at me with a bag hanging from each gripped palm.

Neither of us said a thing. I picked myself and the necessaries up and we walked in that oppressive, unstable, now-terrifying silence back to the others, and I pretended the rest of the day that I was fine, even to myself.

"Have you ever had a moment where you've suddenly realised something right in front of your eyes is just not real?"

The question wanted an answer, but I refused to give one, verbal or otherwise.

"Remember our talk at the cafe?"

That, I nodded at.

"I'm sorry I got angry," they said in a low tone.

"The mistake was mine," I was quick to admit. "We were talking at cross purposes."

"You didn't make sense to me then."

"I should have known you were talking about a play or work or something.... I didn't mean to make you upset."

"...I was upset because I realised you'd seen it before I had."

Again, I refused to give anything away.

"I shouldn't have reacted like I did. I was… I was scared…"

"What did you see?"

"You know what I saw."

"And what's that?"

"Don't be obtuse, Aries, old man, not a good look."

"So you did believe me?"

They nodded. "But I didn't want to believe It. I wanted you to give me a rational explanation. And I am very… very sorry that I took it out on you when you didn't have one." They leaned their head back against the towel I'd spread across the couch. I hadn't noticed they'd stopped dripping. "That's another thing to forgive me for."

Leo had first noticed it coming in unexpectedly one day. The two of them were sitting, like mirror images, at the kitchen table – Gem and...Gem. Then there was just Gem, less than a second later, and Leo took themselves to bed early. They'd call for her, and follow her into a room only to find she wasn't there, or had been in that room a while, too long for her to have just come in. She started acting distant, and they feared they were losing her. At an anniversary date, out of the corner of their eye, they kept seeing faces that were not hers, expressions too cruel to belong to that perfect face. They noticed, for the first time, that they did most of the talking. She ate and drank and nodded and smiled and said the odd thing, but they'd never realised before then how little she spoke. Leo started taking anxiety pills not long after.

When they weren't reading scripts, they were reading her words, going over her work, as if trying to remind themselves why they'd fallen in love with her. Then they found what I did – her lack of voice in her work. At this, they went a step further. Perhaps I might have done, had I read more of it. But that wasn't my fate. It was Leo's alone.

"Get the news up," they instructed with an upward look towards the TV.

I fiddled with the control. The Ten o'clock news was just starting. An overview, the usual political scandals, something from America, and a body found. Floating facedown in the water, there was a distant shot of it being hoisted out. A preliminary identification.

It was Gem.

"I'm sorry, old man," Leo uttered. "I had to get the truth from her and she just wouldn't tell me. I saw the two of them at once. They couldn't hide it any more."

"Leo, what did you do?"

"Turn it off again."

I reached out and touched their hair. "You can tell me," I promised.

"I really wish I could."

They took my hand from their head and held it between theirs. Despite my growing sense of dread, I was tingling. "Do you think you can forgive me?"

"Why do you want forgiveness for now?" I asked.

"Because," Leo started, "...because I think, if I'd known. If I'd seen. If – maybe a number of things - I think you and I might have been happy."

I'd never known it to do so spontaneously, but that was the moment at which I actually felt my heart break. As if a large thin-shelled effigy, like an egg, had cracked asunder inside me and let out a myriad of unwanted emotions into my system, all of them heavy and fast and crashing about inside me. I tried not to let it show on my face. I don't know how successful I was.

"I like to think so too." Then my mouth opened and I started talking and I barely heard myself. "I'd have done a lot for you. Probably too much. I'd have spoiled it somehow by loving too much, if that gives you any comfort. But yes, I'd have made sure that you were very happy indeed. As happy as I could have made you."

They blinked slowly, pushed their lips together and smiled at me.

"You need me to hide you," I realised.

"No," they said. "Let's be honest. If I'd come here to ask you to hide me, you couldn't believe a word I said. I just wanted a bit more time… And I thought of you."

"…Leo, you need to tell me what happened." Every fibre of my being was protective. If we'd had to drive to Dover then and there; if I'd had to tear across the motorway to the airport; if I could think of a single place on earth that I knew that they would never think to look, I'd have jumped on it with never a second thought.

When Gem had come in, she'd been alone. Leo sat in the living room and almost startled her.

"What do you know about Doppelgängers, Gem?" they'd asked.

Gem stopped dead.

"Doppelgängers. Doubles. Evil Twins, that kind of thing. What's your take?"

She said nothing.

"They're never a good thing, are they?"

Still nothing.

"How do you get rid of one?"

She shook her head.

"You can't?"

She kept shaking.

"So what do we do?"

"Nothing."

"Nothing? You expect me to carry on like I did before, and just ignore it?"

She shrugged.

"How come you speak so little?"

She shrugged again, a tiny smile working up her face.

"What's the smirk for?"

It was indeed, now a smirk.

"You've got to give me something. I want to help, don't you get it? Give me something I can do."

She laughed quietly.

"You don't think I can help?"

She shook her head.

"Just give me something!" they urged. "Why did this happen to you?"

"It didn't," she responded. "I chose this."

Leo moved their head now, waiting for more.

"People who are perfect can be loved. And if you have parts that aren't perfect, you just put them elsewhere."

They looked at her, and both were quiet for a very long time. "Is that what it is? It's where you put all your imperfections?"

She didn't move, except for her eyebrows, ever so slightly.

"How did you do it?"

It was a scoffing laugh now.

"I can't live like this any more, Gem. I'll help you, I swear. But you need to help yourself."

She laughed with even more abandon, but there was little voice, little sound to it now.

"Summon it," Leo said, standing. "Bring it here."

She laughed and laughed. Leo was holding back tears. "Stop that. I'm trying to help you. Why are you being so cruel?"

"I'm already summoned," she said. Her voice, however, was slightly different. A different pitch, a different rhythm to her words.

Leo didn't realise their body was reacting to the stress at all. It was simply background noise. "Which is which?" they asked.

"Why do you think there are two of us?" this new voice asked. "Why don't you accept that there is one. In two?" She held up her hand, but Leo almost reacted like they were being touched by a snake. "Don't worry," said a more familiar, husky voice. "You'll forget by the morning. You always do."

Leo stepped back. "We've never talked about this before."

"Not you," she said. "I mean You. All of you."

Leo glimpsed what she meant and then they weren't terribly sure what had happened next. It was as if everything went dark.

I looked several times up at the clock without taking in what the time was. I paced about the room without even realising it, the intelligible pictures and phrases from the television providing some noise that meant we wouldn't go mad, even if we couldn't, in our current state, understand anything beyond our own tiny bubble.

"What do you want to do?"

Leo's blink was long. "I want to sleep."

"I can say I didn't know anything. I can say you just turned up, I thought you'd broken up and needed - "

"You don't need to worry about any of that."

I hadn't yawned all night. I was surprisingly wakeful, though I suppose that's what happens when the person you love kills their demonic lover and then seeks refuge with you.

"You're not going to get caught up in any of this," Leo said. They extended their arm out to me and their grip was gentle but firm. "And I'm so sorry that you have to even see me like this… I couldn't risk… I couldn't risk being asked if that was what I wanted. I didn't want to turn into her. And I almost did too…"

"What the hell do you mean?"

"Well it could be like an infection, couldn't it? Like this Coronavirus thing now. I just feel as if… If I'd been actually asked, I might have made the wrong choice."

"Leo, I'm sorry, darling," I said, trying not to focus on the pet name that had just slipped out. "But I haven't got a clue what you mean."

"You know why I came here really, don't you?"

My own evil twin, deep in my mind, was hopeful, but I didn't suggest it. "No."

They brought me to sit down. I hated and loved that I'd have done anything they asked. "Because...you and me… We have… Oh I don't know how to put it, not without using a phrase I'll absolutely hate… We have… Unfinished business?"

They smiled at me in the way I had always wanted them to. And the TV made no sense. The picture was blurry and the words weren't real ones. I'd looked at the clock, but the face of it was all wrong – no wonder I couldn't read it. My living room was as it had always been, but I recognised nothing.

"You're not really here."

The smile remained. They gently shook their head.

"This is a dream," I spoke as my heart broke afresh.

"Something like that," they said. "You know the rule is that you'll 'wake up' in the next few moments."

Moments? Oh God. That was no time. This was just a dream. But it wasn't – couldn't be a dream, not like a normal dream. They were here, with me somehow, closer than I'd ever thought they'd be.

"I don't want to wake up."

"I know." Their hand against my face, as I'd always wanted it to be – I could feel it. "I didn't want to either. And I was asleep for a while."

"Can't we just stay here, asleep?" I asked, but even as I asked the world was fading. They were all that was left at all.

"No," they cooed. "I'm afraid I have to wake up too."

I didn't know when the night before I'd fallen asleep in front of the TV. There were no towels on the couch and the time said 7 a.m. I realised that the news reports on the bodies found must have been circulating a while, because I knew exactly what they were going to say, word for word. I'd heard them before. They'd found her first, then...

I turned the TV off. I didn't want to hear their name. I wanted to preserve how it had been, mere moments ago, yet it felt like last night, and yet was never, and yet was real. I couldn't get distracted, not yet. Just in case I started to forget. You do, with dreams. Not this one though. I was going to keep it and hold on to it, if my every other significant memory vanished around it, and it was all I was left with.

From somewhere nearby, my phone started vibrating, and the unending pleas for statements began.

## THE PHONOGRAPH

I wish these people would just go away. Police officers, newspaper reporters, friends who I never thought of as real friends before, but they like to pop up and let you know they're there for you if you need anything. I'm too old to believe 'em. They might mean well enough, but I reckon those people are only here to make themselves feel better, somehow. It's almost as if you can't get enough people in my house just now. It's her mother you want to be watching out for – she doesn't know what I know, and she wouldn't believe me. As for the boyfriend... I'd let him go. I don't think he's done anything. Same for Mr. Toby Stone. It just doesn't fit. I don't think either of them knows much about it at all. You may just think I'm being old and foolish, but if you want to know what I think, I'll happily tell you. And I don't mean to boast; it's just that I've had time to think and reflect these past few weeks and I think - if you were able to see so much of it, like I can, given how long we've all been a part of it without even knowing - you'd come to the same conclusion...

It might sound sentimental, but to make you understand properly, everything what's happened, I've got to go way back. It starts, but sort of doesn't start – it had already started, you see - with my grandmother. A while before my mother was born - turn of that century, that kind of thing, we'll say no more - my grandmother, Doris, she gets herself a job under the housekeeper up at the Stone house. When Doris talked about it years later, she thought it was the best thing that could have happened to her at the time. Here she is, young local village girl, sense but hardly any reading,

# The Phonograph

that kind of thing, and she's got a nice job making beds and straightening curtains, the odd spot of ironing - as far as she and her family were concerned, she'd landed right on her feet. And that's how me and my family first had direct dealings with the Stones and the house. We're connected to that house, as much as the Stones are.

If you don't know Stone House, well, anybody will be able to tell you're not local. You've seen the house? The one beyond the church? The huge, old one, gates and gardens and things, leading up to it? That's Stone House. I'm sure it had a better name once, but the Stones have lived there as long as there has been a family of the name of Stone in this region. Used to be big landowners after William the Conqueror, then fell out with Oliver Cromwell, that kind of thing. Hardly a mansion or a castle, but one of the biggest in the district that's so old. Anyway, that house, with its lovely old gables and its ivy climbing everywhere, and the gravel drive and the coach house – it's all still there, if you ever need to visit to verify - that house, or one very like it, has been on the same spot for centuries. And naturally, just like you'd imagine a house as old as that, with that much history and so many things it's seen within its walls, what do they say of the place? That it's haunted. Of course, they would. I believed that, once. I suppose it is, if you believe me, but…

Now there were stories about Stone House being haunted even when my grandmother was a girl, so that just goes to show. These were the usual – white ladies who foretell deaths or misfortune; noise of a crying child when the children of the house are all grown-up; Henry VIII having a right old moan in the best bedroom about his most recent wife, you know, you've heard 'em all, I'm sure. But even them what talked about such stories, they wouldn't talk too much about the attic…

Superstition can be very powerful, even and sometimes especially for God-fearing Christian folk. When Doris first started there, under the 'Original Family', as I thinks of 'em, it was a different story. But a couple of years after, ooh, you couldn't have gotten a single member of their staff up into that attic, not if you paid them their entire annual salary for one day's work. And I suppose it was only because he was such a young, adventurous thing once, and because he was desperate to have some little space for himself, that Master Thomas Stone had his room entering up into the attic when he was young.

# The Phonograph

Now, I might be starting this wrong, because now you'll want to know who Thomas Stone is.

Doris told me that in his day, he was quite a handsome lad, and I know she had good eyes, because years later, I would come into possession of a couple of photographs of the family, when my mother decided in her dotage to try and set up a local tourist museum, help for a bit of local income when the season was right. There was one picture that for some reason I had a great fondness for, probably because it was so different to how I came to know him when I was young. I don't have it any more – I'll tell you why soon enough - but it's one of those pictures that was candid, before candid photographs were really a thing at all and you didn't have to stand for hours and hours being still. I suppose he must have stood sort of still, but he's this great, tall young lad, maybe over six foot. He was certainly handsome too. Rather slender, but such an innocent, sweet face. I don't mind telling you that if I'd worked in the same house as a young man my own age who looked like that, just as my grandmother did, I can't say I'd have me mind on me work all the time, and that's just the truth.

Eighteen-seventy-five, or thereabouts, there's the first child of Mr. Everard Stone born. Now Mr. Everard, at that time, owned pretty much everything you can see around this village, and more beyond. When we were mining and ploughing and all that back then, it was all going into Mr. Everard's pocket. I don't think he was a particularly soft man, shall we say. I remember my grandmother referring to him rather than 'Everard Stone', as ''Ard As Stone'. Years after his death, our little museum comes into possession of his diaries, doesn't it, generously donated by Mr Toby Stone, the current Stone there. Now if you read between the lines, whenever he's writing about his firstborn son - young Thomas Stone, he does not seem that impressed with his offspring. Doesn't sound like the lad could do anything right, at least not according to his father. For some reason, right from the beginning, this old man just takes a plain dislike to the boy.

Well, as the son, Master Thomas Stone, grows up, he decides, quite understandably, that he's not that disposed to his old man either. So he takes off for university, far from home, but diligently writes back to his mother every single week. She, according to the diaries, was always a bit delicate, so I suppose he didn't think too much of it if he didn't get a letter

## The Phonograph

for a few weeks or even a few months.

But when he comes to visit after five months without hearing from her, he's in for a real shock. My grandmother had just been taken on, but she recalled that first day he came back. The lad turns up unexpected and finds a young lady he's never met in his mother's room. He demands answers – loudly. It's up to the staff themselves to tell poor Master Thomas that four months previously, his mother had suddenly died. Caught a fever and was dead inside of a week. Mr. Everard didn't even send him a letter to tell him about it, or the funeral. Instead, he pops off to London, isn't at the house for two months and when he comes back, he's got a new bride on his arm, not much older than Thomas himself and most staggeringly of all, she's only just these past few days found that she's with child. Well, of course this causes a big ruckus, but there was not a thing young Thomas could do about it, except try to embrace his poor little new half-brother and the woman who, if you believed everything my grandmother said, didn't even know Mr. Everard had ever been married before, let alone had a grown up son. Thomas, well, he's got nowhere else to go, so what does he do? Beside himself with grief, he bundles himself up into that attic so he doesn't have to look at his father all the time. And this is all just the beginning, you see.

The new Mrs. Stone is from a good family and on finding she has a step-son, tries her best to make good between them, buying him presents and things to furnish his little attic home with. To all accounts, they bonded fairly tightly, as not long after the baby was born, Mr. Everard started treating his wife almost as bad as he treated his eldest son. Starts acting suspicious of them both. Though Doris even told it like she shouldn't be saying anything at all, Mr. Everard seems to have got it into his head that his pretty young wife and his rather strapping son are getting on a little too well. One day, Everard is upstairs in his study when he hears his son and wife speaking intimately with one another in the attic above. Incensed, he dashes up the stairs to catch the two of 'em in flagrante, but when he gets there, his wife's not there. Just his son. Few days later, he hears the same thing - words of love whispered above his head, but this time, as he dashes out, his wife's in the hall, coming towards his study to speak with him. He doesn't know how they're doing it, and simultaneously trying to make out he's mad, but he accuses them both. There seems to have been a horrible time where priests and justices were called upon to try and make account of it, but they can't.

Then one night, Mr. Everard hears it again – Thomas speaking and his wife responding in the attic above - except at this moment, Mrs. Stone happens to be lying in the bed asleep next to him. Old and paranoid, and certain his son's trying to send him mad so he can inherit his fortune, 'Ard as Stone gets out of his bed, grabs a pistol, and goes to confront his son up in the attic. Now nobody knows exactly what happened, but the outcome was the rest of the sleeping household were awoken by the sound of Mr. Everard shouting something like "Devil's work!" and accusing Thomas with screams and calls. Then there is a horrible bang of a gunshot, then a piercing woman's scream, enough to wake the dead. As they come out of their beds, they see the most appalling sight - a woman in white passing through the rooms like a flash, shimmering and terrifying, Thomas following as if trying to catch her. He follows this apparition out of the house and vanishes into the night behind. Piling into the attic, there is Mr. Everard Stone, the most awful look and colour on his face, and he is very much dead.

Thomas returns the next day and has to face a lot of questioning. But you see, Mr. Everard, so the doctor says, has not a mark on him. He's not been shot, strangled nor poisoned from what he can tell. He says that Mr. Everard was frightened to death, in his professional opinion. All the staff start to say that it was the former Mrs. Stone who had passed through the house last night, come to get her revenge for her, her boy and even the new wife being treated so ill. Yet here's the strange thing – Thomas confirms he was there, and saw his father die, but he pleads all ignorance as to this woman that everyone else saw. He couldn't see a thing, he says. He's been ghost-hunting up in that attic for years, he says, and even with his father newly dead, he's very put out that everyone else saw something and he didn't.

Now that is the main ghost story that everyone always tells these days about Stone House. It always comes back to Mrs. Stone. 'Dare you seek Mrs. Stone's ghost?' That's written on some of the leaflets I've got for the museum. She ain't properly been seen since that night – the odd thing here and there, but never by more than one person, and never conclusively. Then again, like I say, if you knew what I knew already, you'd suspect that

## The Phonograph

she never will again. So, apart from Mr. Everard... and I don't think anyone shed many tears... But that old If-You'll-Pardon-My-Implied-French Everard cheated poor Thomas, even in death. Turned out, his most recent will left all of the estate to the younger son, who's not yet ten when the old geezer pops his clogs. But, by the grace of the same young Master Richard, of course Master Thomas stays.

Here is where it all gets very confusing. By this time, as we're going into the 1900s, two very different pictures of Master Thomas seem to emerge. Doris stayed working at the house til she got married, and promptly had my mother, but she could remember that just as she found out she was going to have Mabel, she finds out Master Thomas is getting married. She's delighted to be invited along to a little party, a kind of reception, and it's only a small affair, with a few staff and some relatives, but Doris said it was a very strange thing. She's certain that at some point, she's introduced to bride, the new Mrs. Thomas Stone, who is very pleased to meet her, but she can't remember nothing else. The party, she said, was lovely, and everyone seemed very happy, especially Master Thomas, but she can't even remember what the bride looked like. Said she was somewhat familiar, like they'd met before, but couldn't remember what the lady's name was, or anything else she was told outside of the lady herself being so pleased to meet her. Another maid was there also and when they caught up, years later, as friends who've worked together will do, she said fairly much the same. She could remember there was a party, and Master Thomas was there, and his step-mother, Mrs. Stone, she's there and kisses the bride Welcome to The Family, and even young Master Richard is allowed to stay past his bedtime, but... was it for a wedding? Well, who was the bride? And neither of 'em could remember rightly.

It doesn't get any clearer as time goes on, I fear, and this is the real mystery that plagued me for many years. Course, I understand it all now, or at least think I do. I could be wrong.

From that time, people from the village, when they do catch sight of Thomas, they sometimes see him arm in arm with a lady, who he seems positively to dote on, but none of them seem to know who she is. Doris saw them coming through the gates one day with my mother, who was rather small at the time. She lifts her hand to wave, and calls to them, politely, with a bow of her head. My mother Mabel asked who she was

## The Phonograph

waving to. 'Why, that's Master Thomas, and er... his wife, Mrs. Stone, of course.' My mother was confused. "But Mum, there's only a gentleman there, no missus." Doris hushes her. Doesn't want 'em to think she brought up her daughter bad and disrespectful. "But Mum, there's only a man there!" Mabel kept insisting, and Doris turned pink and hurried on.

And here's the even stranger thing. I went looking in the local parish records once, to try and find out what I could about this wife of Mr. Stone's. And as God is my witness, the first time I went looking, I found it! 'Mister Thomas William Stone Esq., born 1875, of Stone House' - so you know it's him ' and Miss ___ ' and then her name; her age, given as a few years older than Thomas; and her address - she too is a resident of Stone House at the time of their wedding. There's the date, and even the vicar that married them. Well, there it is, I says to myself - he was married! And I go to make a note of it, more for people asking and to settle some quiet arguments than for the Stone display at the museum by this point. But then it happened. I looked away for what must've been a second or two - no more. And when I looked back, the same record that I'd seen with my own eyes had vanished. What's more, I couldn't remember much about it. I remember what I've just told you, but not the lady's name, nor her actual age, nor what the date had been, nor even the vicar's name, and the vicars round here tend to stay in situ for decades. Now you may reckon it's because I'm old, or because I typed the wrong thing on a computer. Well, you'd be wrong. I saw that marriage record, plain as day with my own two eyes, in a book written in front of me in ink, like in the old days. And I didn't do this a few years ago. Oh no. I wanted answers when I was looking into it when I was helping my mum at the museum. This was a couple of decades ago now. And I remember my surprise, looking for hours to find what had taken me but a few minutes to locate at first, but it just wasn't there. This thing, in black and white that I'd seen and read right before had simply vanished.

It's almost as if Thomas Stone was living two lives. Strange stories started to surface. That Master Thomas is, actually, married, but no one sees the wife because she's shut up in that attic, and he won't let her out. Of course, a few people, my grandmother included, said this was complete rot. Anyone only had to look at the couple to see he set his eyes by her and she seemed very in love with him. But that was the problem. It was almost like some people could see her, and some people couldn't. Like she was there, but she wasn't there. Thomas had taken over the local family business, or was sort of running it with his brother and step-mother, I suppose, but for saying that, he didn't really socialise in the village that much. Doris said she could count on the fingers of one hand how many people outside of the staff had met her, and of them, they never seemed to know much about her. What her Christian name was. Where she was from. When they'd first met her. If we weren't all such busybodies in this part of the world, I suppose none of us would ever have noticed. But I did. Listening to Doris talk about it all, and my mum telling me not to listen, because there never had been a Mrs. Thomas Stone... She knew because she herself went to work under the housekeeper there for a while, not long after the First World War – they had a lot of fondness for Doris. But she didn't last long, did my mother Mabel. The ghost saw to that.

She thought she was tired at first, overworking. But she keeps seeing things out the corner of her eye. Keeps hearing a voice, a woman's voice. And she was so terrified because it could happen at any time, in any place. Didn't need to be night. Middle of the day. First thing after she got there of a morning. Near the attic, in the living room, in the gardens. A face that seemed to appear then in a blink disappear in a family portrait on the wall. A face going past a window, none of the other staff and she'd wait for someone to emerge, but no one did.

The last straw, so she confessed to me like she never would have Doris, was when she was right in the middle of her work. She hears footsteps, she looks up, and there is a lady. Middle-aged, she reckoned, with a look of astonishment on her face. She knew straight away it was a ghost. Not just because she didn't know the face, but because there was something about her - like she was made of something other than flesh and bone, my mother said. 'Like she was there, but she wasn't really there'. The woman walks towards her, saying words but Mabel can't hear a thing. The only thing she heard that she needed to hear was as the ghost stood right before her, and said her name: 'Mabel Chalmers', as clear as you please and then 'where is Mary?' And then the thing vanishes. My young mother is so shook up, she gives her notice there and then to the housekeeper as, white-faced, she grabs at her coat and without another word or explanation, she leaves and never has set foot even within striking distance of the gate of Stone House

## The Phonograph

since. Nope! Never would even come along that road that leads to the gate.

I sort of knew what she meant, but I suppose when I met the lady, and Mr. Stone, I was too young to know anything about it, really, but they wasn't mad or scary. Nothing like it.

You see, when I was going to school – this is during the war, you see – the schoolhouse wasn't where it is now, it was on the clear opposite side of the village, but a nice shortcut I found was through the back end of the Stone Gardens, where some of the wall had fallen away, and I could climb over the other side because there was a tree with low branches. A bit precarious, I suppose, but it took me all of two minutes, and shaved off near twenty!

Well, one afternoon, I'm making my way home and have not long jumped down into the gardens, when I suddenly come face to face with an elderly couple, sitting on a spread blanket like they're having a picnic. The gentleman, who must be nearly seventy, with some difficulty gets to his feet and shakes his fist at me. "Go on, child, you know you're not supposed to cut through – didn't your parents tell you?!" I wasn't frightened, and he wasn't trying to make me so, just to get me to move sharpish and not do it again, but as I bend my head, I hear a sort of gasp, and this is the first time that I get a proper look at the lady sitting with him.

Now if ever there was a person I met who was a fairy, a ghost, a shade of some kind, or just something from another world, it was that lady, who stood up from the blanket. She took a step or two towards me and this older lady, who might've even been older than the man, was perfectly beautiful. She looked the age she was, I mean, but her face. Her entire form, in fact, seemed to glimmer with something that reminded me of light bouncing off water and hitting a wall or a dark surface, so that she seemed completely real and yet somehow, she was something else as well.

"Oh Thomas," she breathes quietly as she looks at me. "Oh Thomas, look, it's…" She bites her lip, as if there is too much emotion flowing through her, then she shakes her head a little and smiles. "It's a lovely little girl."

I stay right where I am and let her come up to me and put her hand on top of my head. She felt real enough, but close to her, like this, it seemed even more obvious, the way she was there but not there, like an image from

## The Phonograph

a classical painting cut away and put on top of a drawing in a magazine or newspaper. She almost didn't make sense in the world.

"Is your name Mary Chalmers?"

I started a bit at her knowing who I was, but then Mr. Stone said quickly - "Your mother worked for us for a while. And your grandmother too, when I was quite young. You look very like both of them."

"Oh look at her," this lady says, stroking my hair and rubbing my cheek, looking like she's about to cry any minute. She turns to Mr. Stone suddenly and says: "Thomas! Thomas, you must fetch the camera."

"I don't know that that's a particularly good idea," he says quietly, as if he wished I couldn't hear him.

"Oh please," she implores him. "Just one. Just one picture, that's all. It's not as if…" And here she is struggling to hold back some strange kind of sorrow.

"Alright, alright," Mr. Stone says, and he takes off for the house, leaving me with this glimmering, beautiful lady. At last, I find my voice and ask:

"Are you Mrs. Stone, Miss?"

She smiles widely. She's got perfect teeth. "Yes, I am. I'm Mr. Stone's wife."

"Are you the lady up in the attic, Miss?" I blunder on.

"…Yes, Mary, I suppose that was me."

"Are you a… ghost Miss?" I ask a little more hesitantly.

Her eyes half-close, but she still smiles. "No, Mary, I'm not a ghost."

"How comes you know my name, Miss? Did my mother tell it you?"

She might've said more, and she probably did and I've forgot it, but it seemed no time at all before Mr. Stone was back with us with his camera. It was the first one I'd ever seen, but Mr and Mrs. Stone posed me, and Mrs. Stone was on one side and Mr. Stone at first said he couldn't figure out how to be in it himself, but then Mrs. Stone, obviously a very smart woman, she showed him how, if we didn't need the rest of our bodies in and we just wanted our faces. So we crowded towards the camera and Mr. Stone clicked the shutter, but he did it a few times, at Mrs. Stone's insistence. At one point, Mrs. Stone's cheek was right up against mine and Mr Stone had to blow at some of my hair so it wasn't in his face.

I took a piece of cake that Mrs. Stone gave me and went on my way, polite as I could be. As I left them – I suppose they both thought they were talking quietly enough that I shouldn't hear them - I heard Mr. Thomas Stone say:

"Isn't it a shame we couldn't have our own?" and when I looked over my shoulder, they were embracing and Mrs. Stone was definitely crying now. And yet, she looks after me, and she's smiling through her tears.

So you see, I've never believed these half-stories and nonsense things they come up with – wife shut up in the attic. Never let her out. Or even that she was a ghost. I saw her, whatever she was, and she was real and if I know anything else that was merely the evidence of my own eyes, Mr. and Mrs. Thomas Stone were a more devoted pair than I have ever otherwise met.

After that day, I cut through the back of the gardens both to and from school, just hoping that I'd see them both again, but I never did. There's little to say between then and quite recently, I suppose - I don't know any more than anyone else what happened at the Stone house between my being a young schoolgirl, and the 60s when I was a little older, and Mr. Thomas Stone died. He lived to a ripe old age, he must have been around 90 or so. But by that time, he was more a legend around here than personality. His younger brother Richard had married and had children, and not long after, that eldest son had a son, and I think it happened again - that would be the current Stone, if you see what I mean - Toby Stone. Very generous, Mr. Toby Stone. He donated most of what you see in our humble museum I kept going after my mother was gone. The little dollhouse of the Stone House. Lots of the photographs, including the one I used to have of Mr. Thomas. Family tree, bits and bobs - most of it is from Mr. Toby. Loves his history, and we've had many a chin-wag in here when he's not in London. I'm pleased he's stayed in his family home, for it looked during the recession recently he'd have to sell-up. But instead, he hit upon the idea of doing what other homes of that size have done, and living in one part - and other parts of it, being surplus to requirement, he rents out. But I think I'm getting ahead of myself.

Struck me the other day that it's been the best part of sixty years since my grandmother died, God rest her soul, and over twenty since my mother, and she lived far longer than even she thought she might. I wonder what the world, now as it is, would be made of by either of them. I wonder what either of them would have made of these turns of events, anyway.

As for me, I married in 1960. My Benjamin was a good sort, but no longer with us, and I miss him. He and I had Dawn in '61. I hoped she'd stay local, but she didn't. Seems that a love for history is in the blood. I never got the chance to go to university, but my girl gets a position in a London school to go and teach history. I was very proud. She came to visit us around Christmas time and maybe for a few days in the summer holidays, but she's ambitious, my Dawn. To a fault, I might add. She takes up with a fella in the eighties, talking, when she will, to me about how nice he is and how handsome and how he's promised to look after her, and he seems a bit wealthy. All loved up for a year or more. But Dawn was hankering, by this time, to settle down and be a mum already. Didn't go down very well, however, when she tells him she's having his baby, so they might want to think about getting married. Turns out, somehow, he's been stringing her along all this time – he's already married. Three kids. And no, no chance of his getting divorced. Cheeky git gives her a load of money to get rid of the baby. Instead, she uses it to get a house. Nothing he can do. My Benjamin told Dawn that she was being almost as dishonest as this fella was. And I told him to keep out of it. "You wouldn't do the same, would you, Mary?" he says to me. "Not when I actually was that age, no I wouldn't. But given what he's done, and if I were that age now, I bloody well would." And there was an end to it.

Anyway, that's how our little Amelia comes into the world. Brought Dawn home a little more as well, as she starts to realise London's not as good a place to bring up children as it might be fun to be in when you're young. And Amelia's a bright little spark, older than her years. Lit up me and Benjamin's otherwise very dull lives when she came. I tell you now, I doted on that girl, and the two of us was never happier together than when we'd be in the museum. I called her My Little Helper, and she makes herself a badge and everything. She used to love coming in with me, and always had questions. 'Tell me about Stone House again, Nanna'. 'Tell me about poor old Mr. Stone and his wife, Nanna.' 'Tell me all the stories you know.' And I fair enough told her everything over the years. Told myself that if Dawn weren't up to it, well, maybe Amelia'd take over from me at the museum someday. You know, as something to keep ticking over, make sure we don't lose our history - it's important, after all! Though as

## The Phonograph

she grew up, she had better things to do. You do when you're young, and she always put on a good show of coming round the museum whenever she visited. I remember her eighteenth like it was yesterday. Not like any other eighteen-year-old I thought. We all asked her what she wanted and we didn't believe her at first. Her answer was always:

"I want to spend a night at Stone House, so I can see if I can find the ghost."

She said it for ages in the lead up. And then, the cheeky little mare, you'll never guess...

She's met Toby Stone before, of course, so one day when he's dropping one or two things off his then-living parents didn't really want, bold as brass, she asks if it would be possible for her eighteenth, coming up, if she can spend the night at the house, in the attic. I went to tell her off, but Mr. Toby was fairly tickled and said if she wished to, bring an adult and a couple of friends, and by all means, you can have a couple of rooms to yourselves, so long as you don't make a mess of 'em. And just like that, it was happening. Dawn's rolling her eyes, and Amelia and her friends think it's a great bit of fun.

But I remember that night. I remember the phone ringing from downstairs and Benjamin telling me not to answer it, but I did.

"Mum," I hear Dawn say, "I can't find Amelia. I just went in to check on them all, but..."

Her friends had all been in one room, but readily said Amelia had been very wakeful when they'd finally dropped to sleep. Well, I was ready to call the police but a thought occurred to me:

"You've checked the attic, haven't you?"

Low and behold, there's Amelia, no idea that everyone in the world below is looking for her. Dawn gives her a talking to, I suppose, but she can't get in the museum fast enough the day after.

"Nanna," she whispers to me, all conspiratorial-like. "Guess what you've got wrong?"

"What? What've I got wrong?"

"The ghost," she says, with the straightest face. "The ghost up in the attic at Stone House."

"Don't you tell me any fibs and try and make me think you've seen something," I warned her.

## The Phonograph

She seemed rather hurt at that didn't want to talk for a while. Of course, I gave in in the end. "Alright. What about this ghost then at Stone House?"

"It's not a woman, Nanna," she said. "It's a man."

"What did you see, then?"

"I didn't see anything, Nanna. I heard it."

"Heard – what?"

But here she grins, like she's holding back a secret. "I heard Thomas Stone."

She wouldn't say anything else beside, and when you're that age, I suppose everything feels like it could be a secret. She did spend a lot of time, that particular day, around the Stone display, but it wasn't until a few days after that I realised one of the pictures was missing, though at the time, even though you may guess which, I wasn't sure. I meant to ask her about it, but you forget these things in the grand scheme of things. We didn't have much time to talk about it at length anyway, because she went off to university that same year. She'd ring every now and again, but we only really saw her at Christmas. And I've no idea how – the internet or something - she starts up a friendship with Toby Stone. She talks about him like they're friends and know each other well. I was a bit concerned, because after all, he's more than ten years older than her, but it seemed all innocent enough. Toby got married anyway. But he still let Amelia come and have a night over at the house with a friend or two. Though I did notice as well that as time went on, one night turned into a few, and then there was one friend and then there was none. I only wanted to make sure she was alright, but I did worry about it.

The years go by, like you can't stop 'em doing. After she left university, Amelia really had a struggle. She was always working, but never seemed happy. She gets herself a boyfriend on one of them dating things, but I thought from the beginning it was a bit off. He just seemed so… I dunno. A nice enough lad, but not much to him. For Amelia, rather boring, I'd have thought, and that's coming from me at my age. She starts on these pills. The boyfriend thinks it might be the living in London what's doing it, so he offers to rent a place, closer to here, seeing as she loves it so much. Now Toby Stone, is by now looking for people to rent within the house. Well, Amelia practically bites his hand off trying to get a couple of rooms. I was worried then. I thought it was dangerous, Toby being so fond of Amelia and Amelia obviously having taken a shine to him, but they've both got other people. God, this could be really nasty, I worried.

Benjamin would've said she was just growing up, but she was changing so much. No optimism, no contentment… I missed that sweet little girl that used to come into the museum and please herself helping me set up the stands. She'd still do so when she was over here, but I'd catch her pausing in whatever she was doing, distracted. Staring at the doll's house or looking through bits and pieces, all deflated.

"Tell me what's wrong, love," I asked her a while back.

"Nothing, Nanna," she said. "It's just… I didn't mean to, but I've fallen in love. With someone I can't have."

"It's, er, not my business, of course, but might I be right in thinking that it's maybe a certain mutual friend of ours, up at Stone House?" Mr. Toby had been married by this point for a few years, but there were whisperings not all was happy.

She grinned at me. "I know I can't have him, but… Nanna, when I talk to him… He's been the truest friend I think I've ever had, all this time. And I'll never have him."

"Oh love," I said.

"Do you think I should at least tell him how I feel?"

"But darling, how'll you do so and not let his wife find it out, or cause upset?"

"I've never actually talked to the wife," she admitted. "Or even talked about her to him. I guess I didn't want to know."

She put her hand on top of the doll's house, caressing it like it was a living thing and she caring for it. "I fell in love with the stories, and the house first and then of course…I know already how he feels for me. He's told me."

"What? He's told you he loves you?"

She smiled in that way ladies do when a man they love loves them.

"Amelia, you're in very dangerous territory, you know. You can't go stealing husbands. Your mum'll tell you that."

"I won't," she promised. "Nanna… Do you remember much about the ghost, up at Stone House?"

"I never saw one," I said.

## The Phonograph

"But the lady. The one outside."

"That can't have been a ghost," I said. "She was as real as anything. Maybe incredibly different, in a way I can't understand, but I don't think she was a ghost." Amelia was casting her gaze through some of the Stone pictures. "Besides, you said you heard a man. Specifically, I remember you saying you reckon you'd heard Thomas Stone."

She looked a little shocked at me for a minute. "I did tell you that, didn't I?"

"Well? You never did say what happened that night you heard him, or whatever it was..."

She looked at me with this wistful look. Don't reckon I'll ever forget it. "I didn't just hear him, Nanna. I talked to him."

"You talked to him?" I responded in horror. "You talked to Thomas Stone who's been dead for more than fifty years?"

"And he talked back," she confirmed.

"And... and... what did he say? What did you say?"

"We told each other a story," she said after a moment. "We both had stories about... lonely people. People whose fathers didn't love them. People who'd always felt different, somehow, without really knowing why."

"Amelia..."

"You know I wasn't scared at all. Strange, isn't it?"

"...Have you told any of this to Toby?"

"No, Nanna. You're the first person I've ever told... Nanna, if I ever took an opportunity, away from here, and I might not be able to make it back again. You know, while you're..."

"Oh love," I said. "Sounds like you're weighing up a sin against an uncertainty, as my own Nanna Doris used to say. I don't want everything to be horrid for you here. Maybe you should think about taking it, going away. But you can't worry about me. You gotta do what's best for you, while you can."

And she smiled the happiest I'd seen her do so in ever such a long time.

A few days later, Toby, perplexed, turns up at the museum, a large box in his arms. "Amelia wanted me to give this to you," he said, a little divorced from the statement. "She wrote a note with it – don't know why," he said.

## The Phonograph

But I did. And I was fearful then. I tore the note open:

'*Dear Nanna. This is for you. I don't think anyone else will appreciate it. Or understand. But look after it. It's very, very precious. If you want to know any more, ask Toby if you can go up in the attic at the House. I owe you more than you'll ever know, and I'll miss you. All my love, Amelia*'

Toby didn't know what it meant. So I open the box and inside is what I think, on first glance, is a gramophone. But it's not the same – not like back in my day. There's no room for a record, and the horn's smaller and instead of a flat circle in the middle of the contraption, there looks to be a cylindrical piston-looking thing, made of metal with a handle. Inside the larger box is a smaller one, and in that, some delicately-placed tubes. Both were discernibly old - original, I didn't wonder, though they had obviously been well looked-after.

"It's a phonograph," I tell Toby. "They used it to record themselves in the late Victorian times. And, I suppose, to listen back to themselves."

"How did she get this?" he asks with a nervous chuckle.

"I'm not sure it's hers," I tell him. "In fact, I'm fairly certain it's yours. Technically, at least. Give it to me straight now, Toby Stone – what's going on between you and Amelia?"

You should've seen his face. "What? Nothing! Nothing at all." He clears his throat. "Why, what has she said?"

"That she's fallen for you," I informed him.

"Me?" Darkly, he looked away. "I… find that rather unlikely. She's never said or shown it to me."

"Well, do you know where she was going?"

"Going? Where? She said nothing to me." And I saw from that man's look that he was truly worried.

Well, I had to call Dawn, who called the boyfriend, who called the police and thus started the big search. No tickets bought, no bank cards used, no passport use… Just a Missing Person. My Amelia. Gone.

It was only me that started to glimpse the truth. Before too much of the ruckus really started, I took advantage of Mr. Toby's concern, I'm ashamed to say. I got him to say he'd lend me the phonograph for a while. And that night, I sat down with those wax cylinders and that phonograph and as delicately as I could, I started on them. Listening back to them.

## The Phonograph

And first, crackling and trying to clear itself up, a thin, unsure voice. A young man, maybe in his early twenties. This is from the period, I realised.

*"Can... can you hear me? Are you still there? Please do answer if so."*

And then another voice, answering, shaky but still intelligible. Familiar and soft, and playful and happy, just like I remembered her being once upon a time.

"Yes, yes! Can you hear me clearly enough?"

*"There you are! I was worried I'd not be able to find you again... Hello Amelia."*

"Hello again, Thomas."

There was more, of course, than that, but I suppose it's private. Like listening in on a phone call between lovers, which I suppose it was. But strangely, I seem to be the only one who can hear her voice. Everyone just hears Thomas wittering away to himself. That makes me sad, that I can't share with others what their love grew to be.

I don't know how it was done any clearer, and I don't really care to know. I just know the most important part – that there are answers, even if they're only partial ones, and that my Amelia, while everyone's busy fretting over her, she's off being happy, and loved very dearly. And who knows? If it works one way, it must work another. She may yet visit me, in my last few years.

My two last words on the matter, especially for those who think I've gone soft in my old age – you'll not hear much argument – start with this one. I wonder if Mrs. Thomas Stone wasn't so difficult for people to see, remember, get their heads around, or even to understand, for folk like me mum, because well – it hadn't happened yet, had it? Her going back, I mean. I suppose if you believe in some kind of Power, they'd be trying to protect us and our fragile minds from that kind of thing, don't you think? Perhaps that's why Mrs. Stone was always the way she was. There but not there. I wonder if it changed at all, or if that's impossible. More impossible, I mean.

And lastly, I bet you think you've guessed what was up in the attic, haven't you? Hundreds and hundreds more cylinders? Well, you're right, but only half-right. Something else far more precious to me was up there.

## The Phonograph

Another box. Smaller. No cylinders in this one. Just a few old photographs. Some I've been able to use in the displays at the museum. And at the bottom, there it was – the very picture. My squashed up, childish face in between. I've kept it precious in a frame out the sun by my bed since. Not even bothered trying to show anyone. But on the back, in a nice, light hand, it reads:

'1945, Stone House. Thomas, Nanna and I.'

# ABOUT THE AUTHOR

Lexi Wolfe is originally from Sheffield. After a childhood between Sheffield and Pakistan, she studied Creative and Performing Arts at Liverpool, going on to achieve a Masters in Acting at the Liverpool Institute of Performing Arts. After moving to London to act, she started writing and producing her own work, initially under the title of Wild Wolfe Productions, then more formally under Slade Wolfe Enterprises Ltd. in a company she set up with her best friend, Andrew Slade. She has won multiple awards for acting, writing and as a female filmmaker.

She lives in Folkestone with best friend and business partner Andrew, and their dog, Mark the Greyhound.

You can support Lexi and have access to exclusive content by following her Patreon page at:
https://www.patreon.com/lexiwolfe

Printed in Great Britain
by Amazon